SO MUCH MORE

a novel

Kim Holden

Published by Do Epic, LLC

So Much More Copyright © 2016

ISBN (paperback): 978-0-9911402-8-2

Cover photography by Andi Hando

Cover design by Brandon Hando

Editing by Amy Donnelly at Alchemy and Words and Monica Stockbridge

Interior design by Amy Donnelly at Alchemy and Words

Early praise for So Much More

"The story has interwoven layers of emotion that you can't help but feel deep in your heart as you read, and complex character development that can make you go from hating a character to hoping for their redemption in the breadth of just a few chapters. You'll feel everything: love, hate, joy, anger, pain, healing... This book is intricately crafted and rich in detail; an emotionally intelligent story." –Aestas Book Blog

"I felt like I was inside Seamus and Miranda's heads, hearing the things we never say out loud to a spouse." –Renée Carlino, *USA Today* bestselling author

"Kim intricately entwines words to create beautifully fragile, yet resilient, souls...each needing to be loved. And I love them all." –Rebecca Donovan, *USA Today* bestselling author of The Breathing Series

Everyone loves sheep

Miranda

past

"I bet you were the kid growing up who always had his name butchered by the teacher when they called role the first day of school?" I ask.

He nods emphatically. "It still gets butchered, but yeah, let's just say the 'pronunciation of Seamus' YouTube clip would've been helpful back then."

I eye him suspiciously. "You're lying. There's a YouTube clip?"

He chuckles at my accusation. "Swear to God, search it. There's a clip."

I make a mental note to do an internet search when I get home. "Seamus McIntyre is an Irish name." I'm probing for history, lineage, with that statement.

He smiles that smile of his. The one that's effortlessly good-natured in intent. "It is." The way he says it, I know he's gone down this road of ancestral interrogation before, not unjustified because he's a walking contradiction.

"Shouldn't you have red hair, green eyes, and pale skin? Instead of all of this." My outstretched hand motions wildly, showcasing him to illustrate my point. "Your name is false advertising." He's the opposite of red hair, green eyes, and pale skin.

He laughs before he says, "My dad's family was from Ireland, a few generations back. My name was an attempt to reconnect to that, I guess. My mom was Hawaiian, born and raised. I look more like her, obviously." The malice I hear in his voice when he speaks of his father flips upside down to reverence when he speaks of his mother. He's opened up a bit to me about his

8

past. His father was an asshole and has been out of the picture, by his choice, since Seamus turned eighteen. His mother, on the other hand, from Seamus's stories, would've given Mother Teresa a run for her money. She died when he was a senior in high school.

"Obviously," I agree.

He nods. "My middle name is Hawaiian, though. Aouli, it means blue sky." Sentimentality, something I'm unfamiliar with, oozes from him. It's fascinating, he's an ongoing experiment. Questions and answers like this only add to the pro column. Yes, I'm mentally keeping track of pros and cons. I have plans for an extraordinary life. Seamus is unique in almost all areas, a priceless piece of beauty, and that fits well amongst the extraordinary I'm building. He's a 'look what I have and you don't' kind of specimen.

We've been dating for months now. He's the only man I've ever met who can hold my attention. And vice-versa, I'm clearly holding his. I usually get bored. They usually get intimidated. Blah. Blah. But with him, there's an odd pull that I can't walk away from. It's as if the universe has administered a biting, backhanded slap to my face, warning me to open my eyes, while screaming, *'It doesn't get any better than the man in front of you! Don't be a goddamn idiot!'* My life has been orchestrated in my mind for years. A strict timeline, complete with deadlines for success in all areas: career, most importantly, and the picture perfect façade that surrounds it.

I've decided that Seamus needs to be a permanent fixture in my life. I need him to chase away the bad mojo I'm no doubt going to create. It's not my conscience I'm worried about. I, like my grandmother before me, am not equipped with one; it's my future façade. An enviable husband and a few spawn look good for well-rounded appearance's sake, a wolf surrounded by cute, likable, soft little sheep. Everyone loves sheep.

So, I've stopped taking my birth control pills.

9

Seamus doesn't know.

We've talked about marriage. And children. I break out in hives while he looks so contented with the idea I would swear he was put on earth solely for the purpose of procreation and his loins carry only angelic seed.

Cue the commencement of shuddering.

If I get pregnant, he'll marry me. And even when I can't pretend to be the Miranda he wants me to be, and the real me shines through eventually, he'll never leave us. A baby is my guarantee.

The world I'm creating for me

Miranda

"I love you." His words are haunting in the dark. Spoken as his lips make repeated contact with my shoulder, my neck; painting promises and devotion. I'm greedy and love hearing it. It's affirmation he's mine. All mine. Compliant to me in matters of the heart. Willing, emotional servitude is like a drug, heady and boosting. I don't love the idea of mutual love, but I damn sure love the idea of *being* loved. It's powerful, because those who love are easily coerced.

Seamus is lying behind me. We're naked, coiled in the midst of intimacy. He excels at it. I tolerate it. I do what I need to do physically to keep the emotional free flow on his end perpetual.

Kissing, touching, penetration, he's skilled at translating what he feels into action.

I'm skilled at faking it. "That's it, Seamus. Like that," I sigh as he enters me. The sigh was a token for him. *I should enjoy this*, I think, as he eases in and out. He's a massive, potent man, who always handles me with care and affection. His arms are wrapped around me, one hand masterfully stimulating from the front while the other pays close attention to the rest of my torso. His lips worship every inch of skin within reach.

This will go on for a while. We'll exchange words. We'll probably change positions. Orgasms will be achieved, mine included.

But here's the thing.

I don't enjoy sex.

Never have.

It feels submissive.

The physicality of it seems unnecessary, when my vibrator can achieve the exact same goal and in a fraction of the time. I'm too selfish to dole out pleasure to others. Which given the man I'm with would be nothing short of sacrilege in most women's minds. Seamus is endowed beyond belief, passionate, attentive, romantic, and gorgeous. I'm fully aware that I'm wasting his resources with my lack of appreciation. I've seen the way women prowl him with their eyes, fantasies of role-playing the goddamn Kama Sutra written all over their horny, needy expressions.

My lust is for power. And that's where sex comes in. Fucking is merely a means to an end for me. A power play. I've always taken this approach: my vagina is a weapon in my arsenal, and any stiff cock can be defeated by it. Weakened. Vanquished. It's a tool to conquer.

And speaking of conquering. *I win!* Though my uterus objects vehemently to that statement.

I'm pregnant!

And I have a ring on my left hand!

And though I'd love to gloat and celebrate my victory in raucous fashion, I'm biding my time, quietly letting Seamus bask in the world I'm creating for me.

Yes, *me*.

There's no we.

He can have the kid.

I just need the façade.

Third time's a charm

Seamus

Divorce.
A severing of sacred ties.
The end of a dream.
The death of a family.
This word defines me.

The first time she asked me for a divorce was at the end of our first date. She was joking and followed it up with our first kiss.

The second time she asked me for a divorce was when she was in labor with our second child, a labor that due to its rapid emergence disallowed the administration of pain dulling drugs. She also told me she hated me, cursed my penis's existence, and said my sperm were the devil's work. I think it was the pain talking.

The third time she asked me for a divorce she meant it.

Third time's a charm.

This divorce is all I think about. I dwell on it. It rules my thoughts, especially on a day like today. The kids and I are moving into our apartment, minus Miranda.

Because.

Divorce.

How can a word so benign become uglier every time I turn it over in my head? It's just a word, seven little letters. Letters that should be harmless. But those seven letters have ganged up on me and every time I think about them, it feels like an attack. An attack on my heart. An attack on my children. An attack on my pride. An attack that's muddied my soul.

13

Thank God for my kids. They're my life. They're my purpose. They're my everything.

"Daddy, hurry up. I gotta pee." It's the pained, 'I'm not lying' whine of a little girl in dire need of a bathroom. My five-year-old, Kira, is standing at the top of the flight of stairs with her legs crossed, holding her brother's hand. She looks so much like her mother: curly caramel colored hair, almond shaped eyes the color of the sky on a stormy day, and lips that form the shape of a heart when they're resting one atop the other.

"I'm coming, darlin'." The walk up the stairs is slow. My legs don't work like they should, especially when I'm carrying a heavy box.

"Throw me the keys, Dad. I'll get her inside." Kai to the rescue. Again. He's always been incredibly mature, but his mother leaving has aged him. A boy of eleven shouldn't be expected to fill the parental void. He does though. And never complains about it. Maybe he saw our marriage falling apart before we did. Certainly before I did.

We were never perfect, but I didn't suspect the affair.

I was in shock when the papers were served.

I was in denial during the entire court proceeding.

And I still half expected her to be there when I came home. Weeks after she moved to Seattle to be with him.

Him.

My downfall. The man who not only stole my wife, but who stole my kids' mom.

Did that sound bitter?

Yes?

Good, because I am. I serve up my bitter with a heaping side of bitter.

I set the box down on the fourth or fifth step and dig in my pocket for the apartment key and toss it up to him. Apartment three, our new home. The throw is too

14

hard, and it hits the door behind him with a tink and falls to the ground next to his feet. As he picks it up, I hear him whisper to his sister, "Come on, Kira, race you inside."

She giggles and her feet start bouncing off the pavement as if she's warming up for a sprint. I can't help but smile at these two.

As I pick up the box again, I look at the front windows of the apartments just below ours—apartment one and apartment two. The curtains are drawn on both. For a moment, I wonder who's inside. Families? Maybe there are kids for my kids to play with living there? The thought disappears as my toe catches the front edge of the stair three from the top. It's not a violent, painful fall because the box I'm carrying breaks it for the most part. I'm embarrassed more than anything. The fact that my legs don't always cooperate is embarrassing.

I glance behind me, down the stairs to the sidewalk and parking spaces below. No witnesses. The realization brings with it relief I didn't know I needed. My heartbeat begins to slow, and I let out the breath I was holding; a strained breath that attempts to grasp at straws, better known as dignity. Maybe I should've looked for a first-floor apartment, but my stubborn side wouldn't allow me to consider it.

As I stand, righting the box with both hands, Kai comes out. "You need some help with that box, Dad? Or should I just grab the other one from the car?"

"I've got this one. Why don't you grab the other one, buddy? And see if you can coax Rory out of the car," I ask Kai, brushing off my current exasperation.

Rory is my nine-year-old. He's not happy about our move. Or with his mom and he's not shy about letting her know. He scornfully addresses her as Miranda.

Kai lopes down the stairs, taking them two at a time. He's tall for his age at five feet five inches, and athletic. He's pretty much a mirror image of me when I was eleven. A carbon, genetic copy with dark hair and

15

eyes, golden brown skin, wide-set shoulders, and long, gangly limbs.

When I walk into the apartment, Kira is perched on the arm of the couch. Her stuffed cat, Pickles, is in one hand, and the TV remote is in the other. She's flipping through channels at breakneck speed.

"Can I help you with anything, Kira?"

She responds without taking her eyes off of the screen of flashing images, "No, Daddy. I've got it all under control."

I smile and shake my head realizing she's heard me say that one too many times if she's worked it into her vernacular. When I say it, it's mental coaching to prompt self-assurance; when she says it, it's confidence. I love her confidence.

"Knock knock," a singsong voice calls from the landing outside the open door.

I set the box I'm carrying on the couch next to Kira and turn to see our landlady, Mrs. Lipokowski, standing on the worn, faded welcome mat. All of the letters are worn away except the W and E that bookend the word. The mat, like everything else in the furnished apartment, is old and worn. I'm not complaining, there's character and an almost identifiable charming essence encapsulated in this time capsule my family will call home for the next year.

Mrs. Lipokowski and her husband have owned this small brick building since it was built in 1972. It houses a deli that they run, two tiny apartments on the first floor and two larger apartments on the second floor, one of which the Lipokowski's live in. It's three blocks from the beach, and two blocks from John F. Kennedy High School, where I'm a counselor. The location is ideal.

"Hey, Mrs. L. It's good to see you. Come on in."

She walks in and immediately takes my hand in both of hers. It's a motherly, friendly gesture. She does it every time I see her, which is most every day since I

16

survive on her deli sandwiches during the week for lunch. "I see you're getting settled in, Seamus. Anything you need?"

I glance around absently, not really looking for anything in particular. "No, I think we're good. Thank you."

She pats the top of my hand with hers which draws my attention back and my eyes land on her Janis Joplin tie-dye t-shirt. She wears tie-dye every day in some fashion or another: shirts, pants, skirts, shorts, scarves. You name it, she owns it in tie-dye. She's a hardcore hippie. I don't think she's changed her wardrobe, or her lifestyle, since the sixties. Some would call her dated, I call her authentic. She is who she is and she owns it. And I love that about her. Authenticity is rare. Either people don't know who they are, or they're afraid to share themselves with the world—I myself fall into both of those categories: I don't know, and I'm afraid. I wasn't this way before. And I'm not happy about it. Life has beat me down. I fought for a long time, but after the divorce I woke up one day and couldn't remember the man I used to be, only that time and circumstances have changed me. I need to find me again.

"Stop by our apartment tonight and I'll brew you a cup of my herbal tea. It helps calm the nerves." She winks and smiles warmly, and I wonder for a moment what type of herbs are in her tea.

"Okay," I answer.

"Just pop in the deli if you have any questions about the move-in or your apartment." She looks at my daughter and says, "And you come down later and I'll give you some pickles, Kira."

Kira's ears perk up at the mention of her name and pickles in the same sentence. Pickles are her favorite thing, followed closely by television and cats. "Five slices?" she asks excitedly.

Mrs. L nods. "Five pickle slices for the five-year-old."

Kira stands on the couch and throws her hands up in the air over her head in an act of jubilant celebration, the remote and Pickles the cat still clutched in her hands. "Yay!"

"Well hello, boys." Mrs. L's greeting pulls me back to the front door where Kai walks in carrying a box with Rory trailing closely behind.

"Hello, Mrs. Lipokowski," Kai says politely.

"Hiya, Mrs. Lipokowski," Rory says in a flawless British accent. He discovered Harry Potter movies and Dr. Who a month ago. His obsession with all things British was instantaneous. The accent was adopted immediately, and he hasn't deviated from it for weeks. It's gone from a quasi-Australian/British confused hybrid to sounding like a Sherlock Holmes doppelganger in an impressively short amount of time. I find myself forgetting my little boy is indeed not Benedict Cumberbatch when I listen to him.

Mrs. L smiles at me approvingly. "You've done well with this lot, Seamus. Strong personalities each and every one." She doesn't have children, but the way she looks at them makes me feel like that was a choice made by the fickle hand of fate, not by her and her husband.

"Thank you." I smile inwardly at the compliment. I can't get much right lately, but my kids are my pride and joy, and I love and encourage their individuality. That's something their mom and I have differing views on. She's cookie-cutter. I'm not.

"Bye, everyone. See you at lunchtime. Sandwiches are on me today, Seamus."

Normally I would fight her, turning down the kind gesture because my pride wouldn't let me accept the charity. But I don't have any food in the house with the exception of a half empty can of sour cream and onion Pringles and a warm bottle of Sunny D, and I need to save the sandwich money for our trip to the grocery store later this afternoon. Money doesn't go as far as it once did. Instead, I swallow my pride; it goes down uncomfortably and rebelliously like a golf ball-sized lump of bull-headedness, as I say, "Thank you. We'll see you around noon." And just as she steps out onto the W...E mat my thoughts drift back to the image of apartments one and two, their drawn curtains, and I'm speaking before I formulate the questions fully in my mind. I usually think everything through before it escapes my mouth. I choose my words with care because years of counseling teenagers has taught me it's best not to always say the first thing that comes to mind. "Who lives in the apartments downstairs? Families? Kids? Married? Single?" My cheeks warm at the last word I uttered, and I immediately lock down the flow, because that probably sounded desperate and needy. I'm not desperate and needy. Truth be told, I don't know if I'll ever date again. The divorce crushed me. My heart may never know trust, the type of trust required to allow love in a second time in my lifetime. Remember what I said before about bitterness? Bitter is practically my middle name. In fact, I may just start going by Bitter instead of Seamus, kind of like Prince or Beyonce. A single, purposeful name. I'll just be Bitter.

Her smile is markedly presumptuous; she read single as a match-making plea, instead of an innocent question based solely on my children's social life, not mine. "Two *single* women. Faith in two is a free spirited, young lady. She's energetic and such a kind soul. And Hope in one is a...a..." she's struggling for the right word, "bit reclusive. Older than you and she doesn't come out much. She's quiet as a church mouse, though, you'll never know she's there."

I'm still stuck on their names, Faith and Hope, which are no longer names. Instead, they're concepts that have been foreign to me in past months. Concepts that tucked their tails between their legs and beat feet when

19

bitterness swept in like a hurricane leveling everything in its path.

When I don't acknowledge her assessment, Mrs. L waves politely and heads down the stairs. "Bye, Seamus," she calls back.

"Bye," I answer dumbly, roused from my unintentional rudeness.

There are exactly two beats of silence before Kai shuts the front door and announces, "Let's unpack."

I nod in agreement with the mini responsible adult standing before me. "Let's unpack."

That evening after dinner, I leave Kai in charge for two minutes and walk next door to Mrs. L's for the tea she offered earlier. She opens the door a crack and peeks out before she sees me and swings the door open. The scent drifting out is unmistakable.

"Hey, Mrs. L, I was wondering if I could take you up on that cup of tea? Maybe just put it in a mug and I'll brew it at home. I don't want to leave the kids." I'm standing outside on her doormat so I can still see my front door and window.

"Certainly," she says. "Hold this and I'll grab you a cup."

Before I know it, she's handed me the joint in her hand and is walking away toward the kitchen. "Shit," I mutter, trying to figure out where to hide the contraband. I step inside, so I'm not in plain sight of a passerby. Mr. Lipokowski is stretched out on their couch watching the local news. He looks very relaxed; I guess this is how they unwind. *To each their own*, I think to myself.

She returns less than a minute later and trades me the joint for a cup of tea.

"Thanks, Mrs. L."

"Anytime, Seamus. Have a good one." She flashes me a peace sign before she shuts the door.

20

The housewarming mango

Seamus

"Bloody hell, who's eaten all the Lucky Charms?"

"Language, Rory," I remind him. In my head, I'm repeating, *Don't laugh. Don't laugh.*

He's shaking an empty box of cereal into a bowl, and all that's drifting out are the powdery remnants of grain and sugar dust that's left behind to illustrate his point while he looks at me in utter disbelief.

"Sorry, buddy. I think your sister killed what was left this morning while she watched TV." Cereal is on the short list of foods Kira will eat, along with mac and cheese, pickles, bananas, hot dogs, and bologna sandwiches.

He mumbles something under his breath, something I'm glad I didn't hear, and walks to the trashcan and dramatically deposits it. Then he turns to me and says, "It's *rubbish.*"

I don't know if he's referring literally to the box being trash or to the situation in general, but I humor him and nod.

He nods in return, apparently pleased with my act of solidarity, and walks with new resolve to the loaf of bread, from which he takes two slices and goes about making toast for breakfast.

There's a knock at the door. And it's not your average knuckle rap. It's a succession of raps that vary in length and intensity. The knock is odd, to the point that my hesitation to answer the door is exaggerated, I'm questioning if it was actually a gesture asking for entry or something else entirely, like Morse code. When I come to my senses and shake the early morning fog from my brain, I walk to the front door and answer.

The stranger standing at my front door is wearing a white, strapless top with a big, red heart on it and frayed denim shorts. She has long dreadlocks in different hues of blues, greens and purples so vivid that rainbow doesn't seem a sufficient description. My first reaction is one hundred percent male, instant initial appreciation. She's eye catching. I'm not a perv, but no one would argue she has the face of an angel set atop a strikingly, well-proportioned body. Her hand is extended across the threshold in what I assume is greeting, like she's offering to shake my hand, but then I notice she's holding a mango in it. "Good morning, neighbor."

I look from the mango to her glittering blue eyes and shake off the momentary shock of being unexpectedly greeted by a Technicolor goddess. "Good morning." She smiles, and it makes her look younger. Innocent. Friendly. I take off my *male admiring female* hat and put back on my *neighbor greeting neighbor* hat.

"This is for you." She shakes the mango like a maraca. Her hips follow the silent rhythm that only she's hearing. "Little housewarming gift."

I take it reluctantly. "A mango?" I question. I hope my surprise doesn't sound inconsiderate.

She shrugs and when she does my eyes are drawn to the words tattooed below her collarbone, *Life blooms in second chances*. "Sorry, I know it's a little unconventional, but it's all I have."

My hand reflexively tries to hand the mango back at her admission. "You should keep it then. If it's all you have." That sounded stupid. She wasn't making a literal statement. Think before you speak, Seamus.

She smiles at my response and gently places both hands on top of the fruit in my right hand and slowly pushes it back until it's touching my chest. "It's a gift. Keep it. There's this store a few miles down the street."

She raises her eyebrows as if she's letting me in on a secret. "It's called a supermarket. They sell replacements." Her smile softens her teasing, and I find myself chuckling a little with her.

"Okay. Well, thank you...for the housewarming mango..." I pause and lift my eyebrows and chin, silently requesting her name.

"Faith," she says as she turns and walks to descend the stairs. There's a bounce in her step that reminds me of Kira when she's playing. It's carefree. She glances back over her shoulder and waves. "Nice to meet you..."

When she pauses on my name I fill in the blank, "Seamus."

"Nice to meet you, Seamus." When she says it, it sounds like she means it. That it really was nice to meet me. Nice. Genuine nice is such a rarity.

"Nice to meet you, too, Faith." I look down at the mango in my hand and repeat the next word only for me, "Nice." It feels at odds with the bitterness; the bitterness resents even the fleeting consideration and stomps it into oblivion.

I shut the door and take the mango to the kitchen where Rory asks, "What's that?"

I tuck it away in the refrigerator while I answer him, "Housewarming gift from the neighbor."

"Looks like fruit," he responds dryly.

"It is."

He's looking at me for further explanation while he crunches through his slice of toast.

"A mango," I offer.

"That's right weird." Rory sounds so proper with the accent.

"It's a bit odd, yeah," and I quickly add, "but it was nice too," because I don't want my kids putting the *weirdo* label on the neighbor on day two.

Hope your day is as awesome as you are

Seamus

present

"Kira, darlin', you need to wear real clothes today. It's your first day of kindergarten."

She tilts her head to the right. She always does this when she's contemplating a comeback. She negotiates everything. "I want to wear this."

"It's a nightgown, not acceptable for school." I counter while making three bologna sandwiches for their lunches.

"It's a dress," she challenges sweetly, complete with batting eyelashes.

"Nice try. It's a nightgown with a cat wearing a tiara on it that says *I'm feline like a princess*. Nope. Not wearing it to school." It's not that their school is strict on dress code, but I know a nightgown would earn me a call from the office as soon as she walked in the door.

She slips down from her chair at the kitchen table. It's one fluid movement, sulking down out of the chair, rather than standing from it. She grabs Pickles the cat from the table and looks determined as she heads to her room. That determination will translate in the nightgown being replaced with something equally as obscure, I'm sure of it. Kira is agreeable but she has a rebellious streak. Problems are rectified quickly, but always with a twist. And always with a sweet smile I can't say no to.

"You want some help picking something out?" I call after her. Getting her dressed is always a production. She takes forever.

"Nope. I've got this, Daddy."

I put extra pickles on Kira's sandwich, wrap them all in baggies, and put them in their insulated lunch sacks along with a banana and a juice box. And then I grab the pizza flyer that's lying on top of a pile of junk mail on the counter, tear it into thirds and I write the following note on each of them, along with tons of hearts because it embarrasses the boys, and put them in their lunch sacks along with the food:

Hope your day is as awesome as you are.
Love,
Dad

When I walk into the living room, Rory is sitting on the couch with his backpack in his lap. He's fiddling with the straps, needlessly adjusting them. He's always been fidgety. "It would be ace if they had a quidditch team at my new school."

"Yes, it would. But alas, Montgomery Academy is not for wizards. Sorry, mate." I play along because I can tell he's nervous about the first day at his new school. He likes it when I call him mate, the little prideful smirk on his face every time I say it tells me so.

"You think there's a chance I could be a wizard, though? Maybe I just haven't discovered my powers yet?" he says with a straight, hopeful face.

"No such luck. You're a Muggle. No powers. Except your sense of humor." I wink and walk out of the room to check on Kira and Kai.

"I'd rather turn someone into a toad than make them laugh," he yells as I walk down the hall.

"Ribbit," I yell back.

He laughs. I love to hear that laugh. It's hard earned, and I feel triumphant when I can coax it out of him.

Kira is standing in the kids' bedroom wearing a pink skirt with yellow polka dots, a blue plaid shirt, lime green flip-flops, and a sparkly tiara. I'd likely be a bit disappointed if her outfit matched. "You look beautiful, princess. Your chariot awaits. Grab your backpack. We're off." I smile as I hang my hand low, palm exposed.

She giggles and picks up her backpack from the floor near the closet and high fives me as she walks through the door into the hallway.

I knock on the closed bathroom door. "You ready, Kai?"

He's brushing his teeth when he answers the door, but gives me a thumbs up.

We're all loaded up in the car by seven-thirty and on our way to the schools — two of them. Theirs and mine. Their school, Montgomery Academy, is the neighborhood charter school, kindergarten through eighth.

Before the divorce, we lived twenty miles from here, which meant the kids had to change schools when we moved. I feel guilty about that, but it made sense to be closer to my job. And the apartment is affordable. Our old neighborhood wasn't. But I still feel guilty. And guilt is heavy, like an anchor holding me in place and hindering any and all advancement.

Disturbingly human

Seamus

present

"Isn't that our neighbor?" Kira asks.

"She looks knackered," Rory adds.

It takes me a few seconds to scan the people gathered on the beach and to translate knackered into American English. And when I see Faith standing on a milk crate on the boardwalk a few feet from the sand, both make sense. "Yes, that's Faith. And she does look tired." The kids like Faith. They've all met her in passing and think she's nice and funny.

She's holding a sign that reads *Free Hugs*. Everything about her looks exhausted, from her mildly slouched posture, to her half-lidded eyes, to the sallowness of the skin on her face, but her smile shines true and pure through the fog. It's the beacon that lures people in. As I stand here with my children, we watch person after person approach her. And each time she steps off her milk crate, puts her poster board sign on the sand, and she hugs them. Sometimes the recipient is enthusiastic. Sometimes the recipient is shy and guarded. Sometimes the hugs are quick and sometimes they linger on for five to ten seconds. That doesn't sound like a long time, but when you're trading physical contact with a complete stranger, five to ten seconds is an eternity. My emotions sway from complete and utter awe, to cringe-worthy apprehension, to cautious alarm for her safety within the span of the few minutes we look on. But, what's most astounding to me is that no matter what Faith receives from the huggee, she as the hugger consistently delivers a sound, loving, strong, heartfelt embrace. She's consciously transmitting kindness

27

to each person through touch. It's the most disturbingly human thing I've seen in a very long time.

I wish I could say it was the most beautifully human thing I've seen in a very long time, but my knee-jerk reaction to the display is fear. Because what I'm seeing, when it's distilled down to its most basic element...is love.

And love equals fear to me.

And divorce.

Damn.

Told you I was bitter.

Kira is antsy as hell to run to Faith for a hug. She's a hugger herself and, even at five, she knows she's discovered one of her own. "Daddy, can I give Faith a hug?"

My mouth is saying, "No," while my head is nodding yes.

I don't even realize the contradictory denial and permission I've just given until she wrinkles up her forehead in confusion and asks again, "Can I give Faith a hug?"

This time, I don't let my mouth answer and my head nods.

She runs across the sand as her brothers and I wait a few dozen feet away. Kira stands in line behind an elderly woman and a twenty-something guy. When it's Kira's turn, Faith recognizes her immediately and drops to her knees before bundling Kira into an embrace. Kira blooms into the hug. She nuzzles her head into Faith's shoulder and she wiggles slightly with every second or two that passes. The wiggles are the excitement she can't contain bursting to the surface and breaking free. But after ten seconds she settles into a still, contented, gentle squeeze. It's the hug she gives me every night. It's the hug that says I trust you, I feel safe around you, and I love you. It melts my heart to be on the receiving end, but to watch her give it to someone she barely knows is startling. Kids are excellent judges of character. Instincts are sharp before the cynicism of time decays them to the point they're null and void, useless to most adults. Or maybe we're just good at ignoring them the older we get.

When Kira returns to us post-hug, she's beaming like her heart is burning so bright it's lighting her up from the inside out. I silently thank Faith for giving my daughter this moment. This experience that reaffirmed to her how magical kindness feels when it fills up your being.

Kira wants us to do it too. She tells us we should all give Faith a hug. Kai, Rory, and I decline, a united front of manliness. Though for a split second I wish my boys would go get a hug and feel what their sister was gifted. Their mother has been gone for a month now, and she was never a hugger. Then the split second wish evaporates as I watch my boys continue our walk back to apartment three.

And my bitterness feels like sadness.

It hurt like hell and we named him Kai

Miranda

past

I never realized how much I craved Seamus's full attention until it was gone. It's not that he smothers me with it, but he's always present. Always adoring and takes his end of our relationship and marriage seriously. He nurtures it: with thoughtful comments, encouragement, praise, compliments, open conversation, support, touch, sex, kindness, and care. And I feel the love in each of them. Not over-the-top, put on love, but genuine it's-who-I-am-in-my bones love. He doesn't have to try; it's effortless.

I greedily take everything he gives me; it feeds my insatiable ego, and I piecemeal it in return. Just enough to keep him on the hook.

But when the baby was born I felt the tide turn, an instantaneous shift in attention. I don't want to share his attention. It's mine.

The very moment the doctor pulled that gelatinous laden, squawking life form from my body and said, "It's a boy," Seamus's face ignited with a look of love like I've never seen. It was so intense I wouldn't have believed it if I hadn't witnessed it myself, firsthand.

It felt like my lungs deflated with each swell of Seamus's. They laid the baby on my chest, but all I could do was watch Seamus fall in love. Not with me, but with the tiny human I'd just harbored for nine months and given life to. He should be looking at me with adoration for the sacrifice I'd just made. But he couldn't because he was never going to see anything but the baby.

Seamus's hand moved, and I could sense that he was stroking the baby's head with a loving gentleness I'm sure had never been bestowed upon another in all of human history. It should have been heartwarming.

But instead, it hurt like hell.

"I think we should name him Kai, after my grandfather. It means ocean or sea." He said it softly, reverently, with tears glistening in his eyes.

My lungs still vacant, all of the air drawn out by the betrayal I felt, left me unable to speak, so I nodded. And we named him Kai.

Stretch marks are for life

Miranda

"I'm going back to work tomorrow." I know they're words he doesn't want to hear. Seamus wants me to take advantage of the six weeks maternity leave that Marshall Industries offers their employees.

"It's only been three weeks, Miranda. Give yourself some more time." He's holding a sleeping Kai in his arms; contented baby, contented daddy, the picture of familial perfection.

"I don't need time. I need to get back into my old routine. I think it's the only thing that will help." I've feigned post-partum depression and have been subtly planting the seeds since Kai's delivery, lobbying that a quick return to work will help me bounce back. I'm a year into my dream job and can't afford time off. Time off gives my co-workers a competitive edge, and I'll be damned if anyone gets an edge on me. Time off doesn't fit into my plans. The twelve to fourteen hour work days I thrive on is what fits into my plans. It's what makes promotions, raises, and titles possible.

He's inwardly sighing, I can see it, but he's also trying to be supportive of my fragile— fictional, unbeknownst to him— emotional state. "Are you sure this is what you need? That it will help?"

I nod. Damn right this will help. This is my façade and everyone's playing into it flawlessly. Seamus graduated with his degree two weeks before the baby was born on June first and doesn't start his high school counseling job until mid-August. He's doted on Kai twenty-four seven. I haven't touched a bottle, changed a diaper, given a bath, or gotten up in the middle of the night. All my choice, of course, but Seamus is over the moon happy to be a dad and do it. To pick up my slack. I knew he would. He's the goddamn patron saint of parenthood.

So, off to work I go. Leaving parenting to Seamus so I can focus on my career.

This baby stuff turned out to be a piece of cake.

Except the stretch marks, those sons of bitches are for life.

Forgotten and discarded, that pisses me off

Seamus

present

I'm watching Kai clutching my cell phone in his hand holding it to his ear. The grip he has on it is fueled by the anxious hope that she'll answer this time.

He's standing on the landing outside our front door on the W...E mat. I can see him through the window from my seat on the couch, and I can hear the silence of an unanswered call through the open window.

When the voicemail prompt directs him to leave a message, his shoulders collapse in defeat and my heart twists. His voice is shaky when he speaks. "Hey. It's Kai. Just checking in. Again. Looks like you're busy...or whatever. Again. Bye." And though I heard the muted sadness in his voice, I doubt she will.

It's been two weeks since she's talked to her kids. She's on her honeymoon in the south of France with him. She texted exactly fourteen days ago to inform me they'd just eloped and were on their way to Europe for three weeks. She said she'd check in with the kids every couple of days. I begged her not to make a promise she couldn't keep.

She hasn't called once.

Kai calls her instead.

He leaves messages when she doesn't answer.

Meanwhile, I bite my tongue. What I want to do is call her and say, "You're a selfish bitch and a horrible mother." Instead, I text her, *The kids miss you and would love to talk to you.* Or, when I want to scream into the phone, "You've ruined my fucking life!" I take a deep breath and text, *Please call your kids tonight. They need to hear your voice.*

My kids are beginning to feel forgotten. Discarded. That pisses me off.

Kai steps back inside and hands me my phone. "Thanks, Dad. I'm going down to shoot some hoops."

There's a basketball hoop attached to the side of the apartment building. I nod, but all I want to do is scream. For all of us.

Damn her.

"Want some company?" I ask. I know he doesn't. He's the type of kid that needs to be alone to process his feelings. We'll talk about it this afternoon.

He shakes his head and tries to put on a brave face. "No. I'm just working on free throws."

Scotch is for geriatric men

Seamus

present

Miranda's back from her honeymoon, apparently ready to make an attempt at parenting in person.

I'm sitting in my car watching her drive away with my kids.

I don't think of them as our kids anymore.

I think of them as *mine*.

I feed them.

I shelter them.

I talk to them.

And most importantly, I love them. Every minute of every day.

She left.

She hasn't been around to do anything for them, least of all love them.

Her feeble attempt at connecting over the phone has been pathetic.

I try not to dwell on it because then I demonize her.

More than I already have.

It exhausts me and chips away at the goodness that I used to think cocooned my heart. The dark ugliness of hate peeks through the recesses and blots out the light of decency. I wonder how long it will be before I transform completely into my hate.

I'm fighting it for my kids.

But it's a conniving bastard that doesn't fight fair; it fights dirty, a knife in the back of hope.

I shake my head to clear it and take a few deep breaths. She's here for twenty-four hours with my kids. It's eight in the morning on a Saturday. I'll pick them up in this coffee shop parking lot tomorrow morning at eight o'clock so she can make her 10:00 AM flight.

I don't know what to do with myself. I haven't gone twenty-four hours without a child in over eleven years. For a moment, I consider just sitting here in my car until they return in the morning.

But I crank the engine and drive back to my apartment.

As I climb the stairs, the panic starts to set in. It's similar to the initial feeling you get when you realize you've lost something important. The gripping, instantaneous fear associated with not only loss, but an incompleteness. As the panic rises and builds it becomes shockingly apparent how much of my identity is tied to my kids. I *am* my kids' dad. I *am* their caretaker. Everything else that used to make Seamus McIntyre, Seamus McIntyre, is gone. *I am a parent.* I don't know how to do anything else. I don't know how to *be* anything else. My chest hurts. The pain is alarming. Piercing. Am I having a heart attack?

"Seamus, are you okay?"

I look up and have to squint through the bright sunshine to make out the worried, sapphire-colored eyes staring down at me. It's Faith. I nod. I don't know if I mean it, but I'm nodding instinctively trying to calm her. Her expression is concern and fear. And it's then that I feel the rough concrete of the steps against my palms. I've fallen, in my panic or just as a result of my useless legs I don't know, but I've fallen. "I'm okay," I reassure her.

She places her hand on my back and whispers, as if to soften the message she's about to deliver. "You fell. You're bleeding. Let me help you up to your apartment."

"I don't need any help!" It's loud. And defensive. And condemning. Followed by a much quieter, "I don't need any help." A declaration that starts off annoyed...and finishes up embarrassed. When I look into her startled

37

eyes, I expect disgust and hurt, but what I see is empathy and acceptance.

She pats my back once before she grasps my forearm in her hands and prompts me to stand with her help. "We all need help. Human-ing is hard to do all by yourself," she whispers when my ear comes level with her mouth.

Inside my apartment, I want to apologize, but I head to the bathroom to wash up my bleeding knee instead. I feel like a jackass.

She's standing in the same spot near the front door when I return. I thought she'd be long gone. Because she's still standing here, I'm anticipating a motivational talk or a homily, so when she says, "Let's drink," I'm surprised.

I glance at the clock on the DVD player—eight forty-five. "It's a little early to start drinking, don't you think?"

She shrugs. "Nope. I worked all night. I go to bed in a few hours, consider it a nightcap." I don't know what she does for a living, but she doesn't look like she just got off work. Her dreadlocks are pulled back in a thick, low ponytail and she's wearing sweatpants and a t-shirt, not to mention that when she helped me on the stairs, she smelled like soap, clean and freshly showered.

I miss my kids like hell, and I hate my ex-wife with a passion and I can't see beyond that, so despite my mind screaming at me to dole out the obligatory rejection, I say, "Fuck it all, let's drink."

The smile that unfolds on her face is the most wickedly approving smile I've ever seen. I have a comrade. "Hell yes, Seamus! I knew there was a little bit of rebel in you."

Within two minutes she's run down to her apartment and returned with a bottle of cheap vodka and cheaper scotch.

We sit side by side on the couch, and I hand her a Pokémon plastic tumbler. She eyes it approvingly. "Pikachu was always my favorite."

"It's your lucky day then. Sorry, I don't have a lot of grown up glassware."

"No worries. It all goes down the same." She points to the bottles on the coffee table. "Pick your poison."

"Vodka. Scotch is for geriatric men."

She barks out a laugh and it loosens something inside me — tension and anger. "I happen to love scotch."

"How is that possible? You're not a sixty-five-year-old man."

"Quite right, a peen and age are not required to enjoy a glass of scotch," she says it with a straight face, which makes it funnier.

"A child's tumbler of scotch, you mean?"

She winks. "That's what I meant."

I pour scotch for her and vodka for me. We toast, "Cheers." Hers is heartfelt, mine is heartless.

We follow it up closely with two more.

And then I follow it up with another.

We sit as it dilutes our blood and our judgment.

"What do you do?" I ask. It comes out slowly, and I'm already slurring. I don't drink often, and when I do it's usually one beer. I'm verging on sloppy. I'm still processing everything, but it's cloudy.

She smiles, and her jeweled eyes look sleepy, droopy from the scotch. "Hmm?" she questions.

"What do you do? You said you worked all night."

"I work at a strip club." She raises her eyebrows when she says it, not as a seductive gesture, it's just an explanation. She's sharing information and waiting for me to judge her.

And normally I would judge her. I would judge the hell out of her. But, instead I ask, "You're a stripper?" The haziness has me curious.

She nods.

"Why?"

She shrugs. "Why not?"

"Touché. But you're a beautiful, smart, young woman. You could do anything. Anywhere. Why that?"

She sets her cup down on the coffee table and slumps back against the cushion and gets comfortable before she answers, "It's part of my research."

I feel my eyes squinting in quiet assessment. "What kind of research requires stripping?"

"Life," she says plainly.

When she says it, for some reason it makes some sense. It must be the vodka justifying the thought because sober, I wouldn't consider agreeing with it. I'm a high school counselor; I'm supposed to try to keep women off the pole.

She begins running a few of her long dreadlocks through her fingers. I don't know if it's a nervous habit, but she doesn't seem to be aware she's doing it. "For me, I can't understand something unless I've experienced it and I tend to be very judgmental by nature. But, it's very telling when you see the world from the other side of the lens because it opens the door to self-discovery. Perspective changes everything. I prefer empathy to sympathy if I have a choice. That's where the research comes in. I've packed a lot of life into the past few years trying to understand people and situations. Trying to make sense of my life. I have a lot to work through. My past is something that requires introspection and forgiveness. And that takes time. Research. When I feel like I've learned something about myself and grown as a person, I move on to the next journey. Hopefully with new perspective."

I don't know if that's admirable or crazy, but the vodka has freed my mind a bit, and I find myself saying, "That takes courage to scrutinize yourself so closely. Usually, people avoid taking a peek through that window at all costs. They keep the curtains drawn and hide behind them."

She shakes her head slowly and solemnly. I think she's going to retort, but she just stares at me instead. Tears fill and recede in her eyes and I'm transfixed, unable to do anything but stare back. I have a feeling there are demons to slay in her research. It's more complicated than she's letting on. I don't push, I let people share when they're ready to. She's not ready.

She glances to the bottles after several minutes of unspoken connection asking with her eyes if I want another shot.

I nod, and she pours.

Cups are clinked, but we skip the toast.

We drink.

When I sit back against the cushions, she stands, taking a moment to right herself on drunken legs, and leaves the room and walks down the hall toward the bathroom.

When she returns, she sits down next to me leaving no room between us. Our thighs and calves are touching. Then she rests her head on my shoulder and asks, "Are you married, Seamus?"

"No, why do you ask?"

She takes my left hand in hers and holds it up in front of my face.

"Oh," I say when I see my wedding band. "She's a bitch. And married to someone else now."

She lowers our hands but slips her fingers in between mine and doesn't let go as they rest on my lap. "That would explain why I never see her around. I thought maybe you were a widow because you always seem so sad."

I shake my head, even though she can't see it because her head is still resting on my shoulder. "I think you're mistaking bitter for sad. I'm thoroughly bitter, down to my core."

41

She raises her head and looks at me. She's staring again. And it's not a surface stare, Faith doesn't do anything surface, she's staring into the heart of me. I feel vulnerable and naked. I look away, but when I do I start to panic like I did on the stairs when it felt like I'd lost something, so I look back. And the feeling passes.

"How long have you been without her?"

"Miranda?" I correct myself quickly because Faith doesn't know her name, "My ex-wife?"

She nods.

"Physically? Several months. Emotionally? Several years. Maybe forever, hell I don't know."

She pulls her legs up under her, so she's kneeling on the couch next to me, but she's still holding my hand. I'm forced to turn sideways to face her. There's a pull I can't explain to keep my attention on her. She's one of those people that you couldn't ignore if you tried.

"You still love her?" she asks sincerely.

"She's a bitch," I answer solemnly. I mean it...and I don't mean it...in equal measure.

"Bitches need love too."

I don't know when we shifted from sloppy drunk to intensely drunk, but it's happened fully and completely. I laugh, but it's humorless because something's changing, I can feel it. "I don't love her."

"You're lying. You may not like her, but you still love her." She rocks back on her heels.

I huff out a breath and with it comes the truth. And it hurts, the piercing pain of an admission that doesn't want to be released. "I do." I shake my head. "How is that even possible?"

"Time, commitment, children, lots of reasons I'm sure."

I release her hand and stand and walk to the window to look out at the street. I have to hold on to the windowsill to steady myself. "More reasons to hate her, though."

42

"Tell me your story, Seamus. The story of Seamus and Miranda and your three adorable kids. I want to hear your story."

I turn my head and look over my shoulder. She's still sitting sideways with her butt resting on her heels. She looks patient and receptive. So, I begin. "I met Miranda in college. She was a senior, and I was a junior. I chased her for months before she gave in and agreed to go out with me. She was pretty and smart. So smart. She got her degree in finance and had several job offers immediately after graduation." I look back out the window lost in the memories. "Have you ever met someone who gets everything they want?"

"Yeah." It's the first time I've detected anything mildly hateful in Faith's voice.

"That's Miranda. Early on, I thought it was a result of hard work on her part and luck. A lot of luck. But, the longer I knew her, the more I began to see the manipulation. She talks a helluva good game. Always has. She's tells people exactly what they want to hear. And she seems to know what that is before they even do."

"That's a powerful gift to wield—a silver tongue."

I laugh a little at her word choice, but she's dead on. "It is powerful. And ultimately destructive."

"Was she a good mom? Is she a good mom?"

This is part of the story that always makes me sick with guilt and regret because we don't get a do-over. "No, not really. She worked all the time. That was her excuse. She was climbing the corporate ladder. She had her sights set on a vice president title by the time she was thirty. Which meant I was the present parent. The only parent really. She was more like an aunt who visited on the weekends for a few hours. She went to work before the sun came up, and I woke the kids every morning. I fed them. I got them to daycare when I went to work. I picked them up from daycare. I fed them. I bathed them. I played

43

Win. Motherfucking win.

Miranda

past

Over time, I got used to Seamus's love and attention being focused on the baby because I was winning at work. I'd battled my way into upper management before Kai's first birthday. Everything was on track. Pay raises came with each promotion. I'd quadrupled my yearly income in twelve months. The corporate world was my bitch. I was driving a brand new, leased Mercedes. We'd moved into our first home, which was solely in my name. The home was massive, a real statement piece.

I was winning.

Until I wasn't.

Another cunning *fuck you* handed down from the universe.

I don't know what changed, but I grew antsy and agitated. Suddenly, things weren't happening fast enough. I needed pace, I needed progression, and the world around me wasn't keeping up.

That's when I turned back to Seamus. I needed to conquer him again, physically and emotionally, and the easiest way to do that was sex. Sex fostered adoration in Seamus. He never disconnected during sex, it was always an act of love for him. And for the first time ever, I wanted it and the hole I hoped it would fill. I wanted him to rake my naked flesh with those dark, lust-filled eyes again. I wanted to feel the longing in his tight muscles and straining arousal. I wanted to feel his powerful body find the rhythm that brought me to a trembling, twenty-second high. I wanted to hear him moan out my name on a finish only I could grant him.

So, we fucked.

Often.

It backfired on me.

I liked it.

Loved it.

Craved it.

It was a sexual awakening for me.

That opened the door to digressions. There was only so much I could give and take from Seamus. I'd always been restrained with him, I liked the idea of my pleasure more than the idea of his, and achieving both came as a result of limited options on my end. But, now my mind was on overdrive, constantly aroused and weaving dark fantasies I wouldn't dare ask Seamus to fulfill. So, I turned outside my marriage to supplement, a young man fresh to one of the departments I oversaw as director. Stunningly good looking, built, and equipped with overblown confidence in those areas that proved him easily lured. I pandered initially to his ego, and he unknowingly fell under the guise of my interest and victim to his own naivety. The result was primal, animalistic, experimental fucking, whenever and wherever I wanted it.

Infidelity became my drug.

And Seamus continued to worship me.

Win. Motherfucking win.

My sex life was perfect.

Until it ended in my second pregnancy.

I'd been careless taking my pills. Seamus never used a condom. Thank God the sex toy always did, or I'd be up shit creek without a paddle. I had the poor fool laid off immediately under a fabricated downsizing initiative. He's of no use to me now.

Seamus was happy beyond belief when I told him I was pregnant. It was like watching Kai being born all over again. I deflated again. I've been replaced again. And I'm sure that when this little human is born there will be no room left in his heart for me.

The façade I was trying to create, and could control like a puppeteer, feels more like a mirage every day. Sometimes it's there. Sometimes it's not. The days it's not scare me.

The turncoat

Miranda

past

I threw myself into my work during the second pregnancy. Working even longer days and determined to ascend another rung on the corporate ladder before I was sidelined again.

The baby came early, four weeks to be exact. The labor was sheer hell. Blinding pain that came on so quickly they refused me the epidural I insisted on. They said I'd progressed so fast that I was past the point it could be administered safely. I think the nurses just took morbid delight in my agony. *Bitches.* I condemned every last person, unrelentingly and loudly, in the delivery room, Seamus included. No one escaped my wrath.

The actual birth was a heart-wrenching repeat of my first. "It's a boy," the doctor declared in the same congratulatory tone. A sticky, miniature life form was laid on my chest. I watched Seamus's eyes mist over and every feature on his face transformed into luminous love and pride. The cavern behind my ribs that housed vital organs for breathing and sustaining life instantaneously emptied, while Seamus's struggled to keep up with an overabundance of air being taken on by anxious, excited lungs and a racing, exultant heart.

I had been defeated again. By my own seed. Fucking little traitor. I lay there staring at Seamus, begging him with my thoughts, *Please look at me. Please tell me you love me.* Pleading. It didn't work. He only saw the turncoat cuddled up to my bosom.

"Do you like the name Rory?" He was smiling so sweetly that I would swear the two of them were having a telepathic conversation and had already bonded for life.

I didn't answer his question. I hadn't thought about names. I was in denial prior to the birth. And now that it was over I just felt empty.

"I'm sorry to cut your time with him short, but we need to get him checked out. Being premature, he'll need some extra attention."

Take him. Please. And while you're at it, I could use some fucking extra attention, I wanted to say. But I didn't. I was still looking at Seamus's beautiful face as it crumbled in the understanding that his little boy may have complications due to an early arrival into the world.

I should've been crumbling for the same reason, but I wasn't. I was crumbling for myself.

Rory spent four weeks at Children's Hospital before he was cleared to come home. I went back to work after the third week. Fortunately, Seamus was on summer break from school and took on parenting full time with both the boys.

The postpartum depression was real this time around. I avoided emotion at all costs and what overtook me was suffocating. I was medicated. It helped with my moods, but love never bloomed for my boys.

I saw the way Seamus looked at me. Questions like, "What do you need?" and, "How can I help?" were common additions to our limited conversations. I knew he genuinely wanted to help me, but I also knew that by helping me he thought he was helping the boys. Helping our family. Because Seamus was a family man, through and through.

I started to resent the fact that I was being silently judged, even if it was being done with good intent on his part. I felt weak and vulnerable. We all had our part to play in this goddamn façade, and postpartum depression was fucking it all up.

Kai is three now, and Rory is one, I've accepted the fact that I birthed these children, and that's enough. Their father loves them for both of us. I'm playing my get out of hell free card—Seamus. He will always deliver me from evil. Unknowingly atone for my sins. Thank God he hasn't left me. He's too blinded by his love for our boys to see me for who I really am.

The façade remains intact.

We needed a hero

Seamus

present

"Seamus!" It's the muffled cry of someone in trouble. Someone who needs help.

I blink the sleep from my eyes once and strip the covers back and bound from bed in one clumsy motion. I'm standing in the hallway outside the kids' bedroom trying to recall if the cry for help was female or male.

I'm only half awake, but my mind is leaning toward female when I hear it again, "Seamus!" accompanied by more knocking on the front door.

My heart's pounding in my chest, but there's a degree of relief when I realize it's not my kids calling out. They're safe and sound. I shuffle toward the door because tired legs paired with numbness don't make for a cooperative couple.

When I open it, Faith is standing on the W...E mat in wet pajamas. She's out of breath, and I can't tell if it's because she's just run up the stairs, or if it's because she's scared. "Thank God. Seamus, we need your help. A pipe broke in Hope's apartment, and The Lipokowskis aren't home. There's water everywhere, and we can't find the main water shut off."

I look down at my underwear, all too aware the time for modesty was *before* I opened the door, not now that Faith is standing in front of me asking for help. I'm sure she could care less if I walked downstairs naked at this point, as long as I shut off the water. Hope, however, I've never met. And underwear is not appropriate introduction attire, even during a crisis.

52

After I throw on some shorts, I instruct, "Stay here with the kids, please."

She nods quickly.

I'm walking down the stairs, just past midnight, trying to keep my balance. There's a recliner, small table, and dresser on the sidewalk in front of apartment one's door. When I knock on the unlatched door, it swings open a few inches. "Hello?" I call out loudly, not wanting to walk into a stranger's home unwelcome.

A tall, extremely thin woman walks out of what I'm assuming is the bathroom. Upon first glance, I can't take in anything about her other than despair. She looks like the type of person who's been beaten down by life so long that misery is a constant companion. "A pipe's busted. I don't know how to make the water stop."

I step into the apartment without introducing myself. "Where's the utility closet?"

She points to the door next to the kitchen.

I walk to the closet, and every step I take is wetter than the last. The carpet is saturated. The main water shut off for the apartment is located in the closet next to the furnace and water heater, just like in our apartment. Thank God for consistency.

When we hear the water stop running, she sighs. It's the audible release of stress. "Thank Jesus," she whispers, her eyes downcast.

I nod and offer my hand. "I'm Seamus. I live upstairs with my three kids. I'm sure you've heard us." I feel like I need to apologize for our noisiness. "We try to keep it down, but I'm sorry if the TV gets loud or you hear them chasing each other around."

She reluctantly takes my hand and her grip is slight, only her fingertips return my grasp. "I'm Hope," is all she says. She's looking at her damp feet.

"I see your furniture is all outside. I'll get my box fan and some towels and help you get this cleaned up." As long as Faith can hang out in my apartment with the kids, I can help Hope.

"I got a fan in the closet," she says. I realize she's offering a solution, but the way she says it is strange. Almost as if she's just making a random statement. It feels disconnected from the conversation for some reason.

"Good." And then I add, "Set it on the tile in the kitchen where it's dry and turn it on. I'll be right back," because I'm afraid she'll set it up on the wet carpet, plug it in, and end up electrocuting herself.

She nods.

I slosh through the soaked carpet to the door. When I step outside, I roll my shoulders a few times, close my eyes, and breathe in the humid night air. The tension in my body, created by the emergency-induced adrenaline coursing through me, is receding. And as it ebbs away, I find myself wishing all stress was that easy to release. The stairs taunt me, and the climb is slow because exhaustion is creeping back.

My apartment door is wide open, and Faith is sitting, cross-legged, in the middle of the living room floor, a palm resting face down on each thigh. Her eyes are closed, and I can see her chest rise and fall in a series of deep, deliberate breaths. Her lips are moving slightly as if she's talking to herself, but she's not making any sound.

It's an awkward situation; I'm not sure if I should interrupt her or wait to see if she senses I'm back in the room with her. I clear my throat; it's my way to deal with the impasse.

Her lips move for a few more seconds and then she opens her eyes and stands. "Well? Is the water turned off?"

I nod, but in my mind, I still see her sitting on the floor. "What were you doing? Meditating? Praying?"

"Both, I guess, though I don't like to pigeonhole," she says as she walks by. "I like to multitask." She winks.

I don't know if the smile reaches my lips because I'm tired, but on the inside, she makes me smile. "I need to grab my box fan and some towels and go back down to help Hope clean up."

"Why don't you give me the fan and towels and I'll help her? I don't mind at all. It makes me feel useful," Faith says.

"But I told Hope I'd be back down to help her," I argue because I hate letting people down, especially when I've promised something.

Faith smiles and I already know she's not going to let me win. "Your kids have school, and you have to work in the morning, I don't. Get some rest, Seamus."

"You're sure?" I feel bad backing out, but she's right. I have to get up for work in a few hours.

She nods.

I insist on taking the fan and towels down myself and explaining to Hope the situation and that Faith will be back down to help her. I also tell her to come up and knock if they need anything.

Hope nods in understanding but doesn't say a word.

Faith and I cross paths at my doorway.

"Thanks for helping Hope out tonight. Sorry I had to wake you. We needed a hero."

It's nice to be needed. "You're welcome. Goodnight, Faith."

She pulls the door shut behind her, but leaves it open an inch and whispers through, "Nighty night, Seamus."

Your knees are attractive; it's a shame to bloody them

present

It's seven o'clock on a Saturday morning, which is a guarantee of two things.

One: Kira is wide-awake and has been for over an hour now, sitting on the couch watching cartoons.

Two: I'm semi-awake, sitting on the couch next to Kira watching cartoons...through closed eyelids.

I haven't slept in past six o'clock in the morning for eleven years.

I'm not complaining. My kids are only little once. The boys sleep in now, and I'm sure she's not far behind them in making the shift.

"Daddy, are we going to the beach today?"

I answer with my eyes still closed, "Is it raining?" The weatherman on the local news last night said it's supposed to rain today.

She walks to the front door and opens it; I guess an accurate weather assessment requires immersion and not a simple peek out the window.

"What's this?" Kira asks curiously, looking at the ground outside the front door. Curiosity is not always a good thing when it comes to Kira. She's fearless. The kind of fearless that requires trust. Her trust is a bottomless pit. Trust that the world is good and nothing bad ever happens. But even when bad does happen, like getting stung by a bee when she was three because it looked soft and fuzzy and irresistible to tiny fingers, or bad like her mom leaves the family and moves out of state, she never loses her trust. She's still fearless.

I walk to the door for a close-up examination of the *this* half of *what's this*.

There on the W...E mat is a cane. It's wooden, and though it's not bulky, it looks substantial, like it serves its purpose and serves it well. And it's obvious it's had plenty of opportunity to serve well. The varnish and stain are worn away on the handle and the bottom foot shows some battle scars. There's an envelope underneath it, and my name is written on it.

When I see my name, a few things bubble up in me.

The first is embarrassment because someone thinks I need this. It makes my stomach lurch.

The second is anger because someone thinks I need this. It makes my stomach boil.

The third is foreign, a traitor that has invaded my bitter existence. It's relief because someone thinks I need this. It makes my stomach settle.

But relief only sticks around for a nanosecond because I'm a stubborn, thirty-four-year-old man. I refuse to use a cane.

Canes scream helplessness, weakness, and deterioration.

That's not me.

I may not be able to feel my legs from the waist down, except for occasional pinpricking pain, but I will not use an aid like an old man. A broken old man.

"Kira, darlin', can you do me a favor and put that in my room?" I want to douse it in gasoline and light it aflame on the W...E mat in a proper act of defiance and protest. I also can't help but find irony in the fact that it's been left on a mat that no longer says welcome. This cane is *not* welcome. The W...E mat just became the unwelcome mat.

She picks up the cane in one hand and the envelope in the other. "What about the letter? It has your name on it." She's looking at the handwriting, reading it.

"Just put it on my bed with the…" I can't even say the word, "with that." I point at the cane.

We spent the afternoon playing board games and watching movies on Netflix while it rained relentlessly outside.

The kids are in bed now. When I kissed and hugged them all goodnight, I saw three happy, content faces smiling back at me. I haven't seen them all smiling like that in a while. Too long. Even Kai was grinning. And Kai only does something when he means it. The honesty in him is born in his bones and seeps out into the rest of him, which means every inch of him is truth. When he feels it, it's projected. And today he was happy.

And that makes me happy.

I set aside the bitter.

Every last inkling of it.

Until I walk back to my room and see the cane lying on my bed.

And now I'm a jumble of emotions, pissed leading the charge. Someone's made a judgment of me. I let my mind go so far as to wonder if it was Miranda, which is crazy because she lives in another state. Unfortunately, it's not beneath her to rub my nose in something or to belittle me. She's always been good at belittling. Jesus Christ, what did I ever see in her?

I tear open the envelope and as I read the note the flash of relief I had earlier reappears.

So does the embarrassment.

But not the anger.

Seamus,

I was at the thrift store today and saw this. I thought it might save you another skinned up knee. I know you're a tough guy, but your knees are attractive, it's a shame to bloody them. And it makes me sad to see you hurt.
Faith

Faith. Of course, it was Faith. It was left with good intention. Not ridicule.

Even so, I'm not using it. I'm stubborn. I may as well wear a sign around my neck that says *I'm useless*.

Putting it in the back of my closet, I bury it along with the letter behind a stack of magazines and a pile of shoes. And when I can no longer see it the relief vanishes into thin air and all that remains is embarrassment. It jabs at me. Taunts me. And I don't know where it came from because it's a new kind of embarrassment. A branch that grows on the embarrassment tree, but not a limb I thought I'd find myself climbing on. It feels shaky and thin, too small in diameter to hold my weight. It's embarrassment tied to manliness and virility. Embarrassment tied to attraction and sexual prowess. It's the realization that men with health issues, men that need things like *canes* to function, especially at my age, aren't desirable and I feel like I've just lost something else to this disease. I feel like I've lost the ability to attract a partner, if and when I'm ever ready for that again.

I know when Faith used the word attractive she wasn't being condescending. But maybe it's the fact that she's an attractive woman, who used the word attractive in her note, that set off the avalanche of epiphanies leading me down the road of imagined lonely, celibate, lifelong bachelor. I know she meant nothing by it. It's just that sometimes a single word spurs thought. And thought can take the positive route when it comes to the fork in the road, or it can take the negative.

Lately, my thoughts always take a hard left and go negative.

Sometimes I'm irrational, I know I am, but even irrational thought feels very, very real when you're in the middle of shit.

And smack dab in the middle of shit is exactly where I am.

Shit.

Uneventful and normal, I want to be that guy

Seamus

present

The kids and I took a walk to the beach after dinner. Faith was standing on her milk crate giving away hugs again. Fear for her was still dominant when I noticed her. Regret was a close second.

Kira got her hug.

The rest of us didn't.

Faith and I haven't talked since the cane incident last week. I have trouble looking at her because I know how she sees me. I'm the guy who falls on the stairs and injures himself.

I don't want to be my MS.

I don't want to be my symptoms.

I don't want to be my limitations.

I don't want to be my pain.

I don't want to be my embarrassment.

I just want to be the guy who walks up the stairs, and no one thinks anything about it because it's uneventful and normal.

That's who I want to be.

Fuck the façade

Miranda

past

I always wanted the title of vice president before I turned thirty. Titles are important, they signify ascent. And with ascension comes power.

It's so close now I can taste it. My killer instinct is back. I struggled to keep my shit together the year after Rory was born, but I'm back with a vengeance and determined not to let anyone or anything derail my dream.

The vice president of Marshall Industries is scheduled to retire in three months, and interviews and scouting have begun for his replacement. He's an old codger whose time came and went a decade ago. For the past few years, I've done everything I could to make him look good while still taking credit for the accomplishments simultaneously. That's quite a task when you're performing as the conductor *and* the symphony, and you need the audience to be attentive and take notice of both. The audience noticed.

The president, Loren Buckingham, is a powerful man. He oversees Marshall Industries from his office hundreds of miles away in Seattle. No one ever interacts with him in person, unless they're summoned to him.

I was summoned last month.

He's twenty years my senior. Handsome in that dignified way that only excessive money buys and fosters. The glint in his eyes screamed *I could buy and sell you*, and that's dead sexy to me. Shaking his hand turned me on more than anything I've ever experienced in my life. The authority and command in his touch was a lethal transfer of voltage, erotic as hell.

The interview went well.

Dinner afterward went even better.

I returned home confident I'd made it to the next round.

The next round is here.

Seamus wished me luck this afternoon when I left for the airport.

I won't need it. I've got this. This is what I excel at. Closing deals.

Mr. Buckingham's personal driver picks me up at the airport in a blacked out SUV. When we miss the exit for his office downtown, I inquire.

"Mr. Buckingham's asked that I deliver you to his residence," he answers professionally.

I can't help the satisfied smirk that tips up the right corner of my mouth. I powder my face, freshen up my lipstick, and release the top four buttons of my silk blouse. I had breast augmentation surgery a few months ago because age and the pregnancies had taken a toll on the girls. They look phenomenal now, and I'm not beneath showing some cleavage to leverage advantage. Mr. Buckingham and I had some chemistry during our last meeting; I felt it. And you can be damn sure I'm going to use that to my benefit tonight. Let the vixen siege began.

His residence is what can only be called an estate nestled cozily behind an elegant iron fence and automated gate. The moment I lay eyes on his opulent home I'm sent into a daydream tailspin; visions of living here with him and reigning over his empire by his side involuntarily dominate my every thought. My mind and body are vibrating with need. A need that's completely driven by power and money. A need I will do anything to satisfy.

Fuck the façade I've been living, I want this instead. This is my destiny.

The driver pulls into the circle drive and ushers me to the front door, after which he hops back into the vehicle and disappears around the back of the house with my overnight and garment bags.

I'm greeted stiffly at the door by an elderly, regal-looking woman. She side eyes me, and I'm left wishing I had two additional buttons secured on my blouse.

That is until Mr. Buckingham joins us in the expansive foyer, and I notice as his eyes slowly run the line from my five-inch stilettos up my tanned legs to the hem of my unquestionably short, but tasteful, designer skirt before skipping to, and pausing appreciatively on, my cleavage, where he pairs a quick eyebrow raise with a sexy smirk. His eyebrows resume their natural position, but the smirk remains in place when his eyes find mine, and he addresses, "Mrs. McIntyre, so nice to see you again."

The elderly woman huffs her disapproval and walks away without a word.

Mr. Buckingham leans in too closely to be deemed socially acceptable and whispers, "My mother, please excuse her. She forgets sometimes."

I smile flirtatiously at his words and ask, "Forgets?"

"That though I'll always be her son, I am a grown man."

I nod. Still smiling.

"Who can appreciate an exquisite woman when he sees one," he continues with a wink. His stare is weighted with an intensity that has me trapped. Unable to move. This is a test. I can feel it. He's waiting for my reaction.

He's waiting for me to melt into a puddle at his feet, which is, I'm assuming what most living, breathing women would do. Accepting the compliment with such an overenthusiastic reception that they look a submissive fool by the end of the short, but telling, exchange. *Two can play at this game,* I think as I lift an eyebrow in challenge.

His smile is undeniably flirty, and he chortles in response. "I knew I liked you from the very beginning, Miranda. We're going to work well together."

My heart does somersaults. The position is as good as mine, and I haven't been here five minutes.

The rest of the afternoon is comprised of business related discussion. Poring over reports. Asking my opinion on several hypothetical, disastrous scenarios and how I would handle them if I were in charge. Asking what changes I would make if I had the full control necessary to do so. Discussing where I see myself in five years, ten years, twenty years. I answer every question confidently. I'm outstanding at my job and have a clear-cut vision of the direction this company needs to head to flourish over the next decade. I don't just want to grow the company, I want it to be the best in its field. I want to annihilate the competition.

He smiles approvingly while I speak. And it's not a smile to pacify and keep me talking, he loves what I'm saying. He can feel the passion in my words. They mirror his.

He asks me to stay and join him for dinner.

I do.

Then he asks me to stay and join him for a glass of wine.

One glass turns into two.

Then three.

Three leads to a not-so-innocent exchange on the settee in the living room: playful quips, flirtatious touches, and loaded glances coupled with telling conversation.

When talk becomes laced with brazen innuendo, he offers a fourth glass. I decline and boldly ask, "Are you trying to rid me of my inhibitions?"

I know the telltale signs of sexual desire in a man. I'm practiced in luring them out. The hungry eyes, nostril flare, deep breathing, muscle rigidity, not to mention his cock impressively filling out his dress slacks. He wants me so badly he'd take me right here on the settee in his living room. He licks his lips. "Maybe."

I flick one more button open on my blouse and whisper, "I don't have many, but I left them at the door when I came in today."

He doesn't ask me to stay and join him in bed.

But I do.

He tells me I'm his new VP the first time I make him come.

He calls out my name in pure ecstasy every time after.

I leave the next morning with my contracts signed in triplicate and Loren wrapped around my little finger.

Mission fucking accomplished.

She usually saves the sigh

Seamus

present

"I want full custody."

The words charge through the phone and to my ear like a physical blow that takes me to my knees. They steal my breath and make my vision blur. They make my thoughts halt and suddenly my head feels like it's filled with boiling, white-hot shock. That's quickly replaced with fury and a fierce need to protect what's mine, whatever the cost. "Over my dead body."

She sighs. Loudly. She usually saves the sigh. It's the exclamation point to emphasize extreme irritation. I'm surprised she's used it so quickly, which makes me believe she somehow thought this would be easy. That I wouldn't fight her.

Like hell I won't.

"Seamus, be realistic. You can't provide the life they need."

I'm still seething and at a loss for words because all that's raging through my head is a continuous, manic loop of "Fuck you." I can't come back with that because that's what she wants, so I settle for, "What?" until I can gather my thoughts and refute this.

She sighs again. But this sigh is different, there's an evil smirk behind it like she's been anxiously waiting to spew hate and degradation. "They're all sharing a bedroom. Kira was dressed like a vagrant clown last weekend. Rory is talking like an insane person. Kai is withdrawn and angry. You have them enrolled in *public* school—"

I cut her off because I can't listen to this. She's clearly only worried about her own image, not the kids' well-being. I still don't know what to say because *fuck you* still isn't an option, so instead I repeat a bewildered, "What?"

She continues as if I haven't spoken, "And physically you're not fit to parent. And we both know that will only get worse."

That's where I lose it. "*Fuck you*. I'm perfectly capable of raising my children."

"*Our* children," she corrects. "And no, you're not."

"*My* children," I correct through gritted teeth.

"Are you threatening me?" Her tone tells me the classic, evil smirk is still in place. She's not insulted; she's enjoying this.

"No, I'm stating a fact."

"You'll hear from my attorney." It's final. The line goes dead.

Of course, she got the last word. And of course, it was, *You'll hear from my attorney*. It almost wouldn't feel right ending a conversation without hearing it. Some people say goodbye. Miranda says, *You'll hear from my attorney*.

The passage of time changes people, many different influences come into play. They combine to perpetuate and escalate the enrichment, or erosion, of our ideals and personal code of ethics. Dominion and power have elevated Miranda, in her mind, to untouchable status. A place where decency is exempt and treating others like shit is her norm. It's ruined her. And I have a feeling it's going to ruin us all before she's done.

You might need your own sign

Seamus

present

Miranda is in town again.

She has my kids until Sunday morning, exactly twenty-four hours from now. I didn't want to let her take them because the nauseous feeling that started in my stomach seemed to bleed through my veins until it filled me, making me burn with the very real possibility that she may make some kind of screwed up play and take them back to Seattle with her. So, to quiet my fears, I followed her to the Hilton a few miles away. I considered parking my car on the other side of the lot and staying there to monitor her, but then figured that was probably a bit extreme and decided to leave and wait it out.

I drove straight to the beach and sat in the same spot on the sand until the sun went down. The water has always had a soothing effect on me. I don't know if it's the sound of waves crashing, or the sight of waves crashing that does it, but it's the reason I'll always live near the water. That and it makes me feel closer to my mom.

By the time I drive home, I feel like I've taken a sedative. I'm relaxed for the first time in ages.

I hear the buzzy exhaust of Faith's scooter pull up outside her apartment just as I hit the W...E mat. Stupid unwelcome mat. My hand is in my pocket searching for my keys. I don't know why but my heartbeat is beginning to gallop. Like it's in a race. Or trying to escape.

"Are you avoiding me, Seamus?" Faith yells, as she kills the engine on her scooter. I know she's yelling because I hear it loud and clear and she's a story below me.

69

The gallop holds steady at her words, but I don't answer. *Where are my damn keys?*

"Well?" That's closer, she's moving.

I hear footfalls on the stairs.

I stop searching my pockets, and my heart rate begins to slow as if someone's pulling the reins hard against the gallop. I stand and wait, but I don't turn around.

There's a hand on the center of my back. The touch is apprehensive and apologetic, so is her whisper. "I'm sorry if my gift offended you."

Normally, I would be quick to accept an apology. I'm the type of person who will accept an apology despite the genuineness of either the apology or of my acceptance of it. I'd say, *It's okay*, to get past the moment, even if it was *far* from okay. But, I'm still feeling some of the peace from the beach even though my racing heart interrupted it. It's enough peace to deliver honesty, not cruel, unfiltered honesty, but unguarded, truthful honesty. "I don't want to use it."

Her hand is still on my back. It's still apprehensive and apologetic. "But you need it. I've watched you struggle for a month now," she whispers.

"I don't want it," I repeat. I'm not angry; it's an admission. My back is still turned to her, making it easier to deliver the words.

"Why?" It's one of the softest things I think I've ever heard. Not soft as it relates to volume, but soft as it relates to comfort.

It prompts me to share one of my biggest fears. "There are stages to the progression of this disease. I feel like if I already give in and use the cane that the inevitability of a wheelchair isn't far behind. *I do not want to be in a wheelchair.* That scares the hell out of me." I've barely let that thought cross my mind; I can't believe I just verbalized it to another person.

"Don't let fear rule you." She's not whispering anymore, but there's no edge to her voice. It's still soft. Still comforting. A soft place to land if I fall.

"I don't." It sounds like a question.

A question that she responds to. "You do. It takes one to know one."

I huff out a laugh, if this weren't such a serious conversation, it would have been more convincing. "You're not scared of anything. I may not know you well, but I know enough. You're researching life for fuck's sake. You're engaged in it. You give new neighbors mangos when they move in, and you help the lady next door when her pipe breaks, and you give strangers hugs on the beach. You're not scared."

Her hand moves up and down my back slowly; it's soothing like the waves. "That doesn't mean I'm not scared." Her voice is raw. This is her being real, baring a piece — a very private piece — of herself to me.

"Why do you give free hugs at the beach?" I ask. I have a feeling her voice won't change.

"It started out as part of my research." She takes a deep breath. "Because everyone deserves love. A hug is a display of love that begins on the physical end of the spectrum but bleeds into the emotional end of the spectrum if you let it, if you give into it. It's the most innocent, pure form of physical human connection there is. It only takes two willing people, who don't even have to know each other, to participate. Two willing people who want that exchange. It's so easy, but there are people who never get them. *People who never get them*," she repeats softly, it's a confession.

The confession breaks my heart and prompts my next question. "You said it started out as part of your research, which leads me to believe that your hug research ended or it morphed into something else. So, why do you still do it?"

71

"Because, it reminds me I'm not alone." There's sadness and fear in her voice, something I cannot, and will not, ignore.

I turn and don't hesitate to fold her into my arms. "You're not alone," I whisper. She doesn't hesitate in wrapping her arms around me. I picture her in my mind holding Kira on the beach. I know what this embrace looks like, because I've seen this display, and it feels every bit as loving as it looked. It's strong, all-encompassing, and accepting on the outside and sweet and gentle on the inside. I feel her muscles flex because they take this seriously. I feel each inhalation and exhalation transfer peace and calm from her body to mine. Physically, I'm much bigger than she is, but she surrounds me with her being. With her energy. I hug my kids several times a day, but it's been years since I hugged an adult. Miranda was never much of a hugger.

When we part, perhaps a minute has passed, and Faith smiles at me through teary eyes. "Thank you. You might need your own sign." She sniffles through the smile and points at me. "People are definitely missing out. You're good."

That makes me smile. "Oh yeah?"

"I've hugged a lot of people, Seamus. You may have just dethroned and taken over the top spot." Her eyes tell me that was both truth and compliment.

I nod, and I want to tell her that aside from my kids, because their hugs are some of the most cherished things in my life, her hug was the best hug I've ever experienced.

The best.

I didn't know people could hug your soul with their soul.

Faith can.

He's not perfect anymore

Miranda

"Mrs. McIntyre, there's an urgent call from Seamus's school. I think you should take it," Justine, my assistant, says from the doorway of my office. Her voice sounds urgent and concerned.

I don't have time for urgent or concerned. "Take a message," I command.

"It's Seamus. They've taken him to the hospital." I look up, and she's piercing me with her eyes. She's always direct.

I sigh. The first thing that runs through my mind is, I'm going to have to leave work early and pick up the boys from daycare. And I don't even remember where their daycare is. Goddammit, I don't have time for this. "Put the call through," I huff.

"Mrs. McIntyre? This is Janet." She says it like I'm supposed to know who Janet is.

"I don't have time for chit chat. What happened?" I say while reading through an email on my laptop screen at the same time.

I hear her stunned irritation through the receiver before she answers, "It's Seamus. He's been taken to the hospital. He says he can't feel his legs from the waist down. He said it started this morning. He's scared and asked that I call you because he's left several messages on your cell phone today and you hadn't answered him."

I pick up my cell phone from my desk and look at the missed calls and voicemails. Twelve. All from Seamus. I toss my phone back on my desk. "I've been busy. Meetings. Trying to run a company," I offer flatly. How dare she try to call me out.

73

"He's at Mercy General," she adds.

I hang up without acknowledging the information and glance at the time on my laptop. Four o'clock. Daycare is open until seven o'clock I'm guessing. I tap the button on my phone for Justine.

"Yes?" Justine answers. She still sounds concerned.

"Find out what daycare the boys are at. And what time they close," I order before tapping the disconnect button.

Ten minutes later Justine calls. I pick up the receiver, and she immediately starts talking because she knows I don't like to waste time with greetings. "They're at Big Hearts Daycare. I have the address and phone number for you. They close at five-thirty."

"Five-thirty?" I question incredulously. "That can't be right. Call them back, there must be some mistake."

"I've just confirmed with them that they close at five-thirty," she challenges. Justine is feisty and outspoken, which I usually appreciate because she's using it on others in my favor. I don't appreciate it being turned on me.

"*Confirm. Again,*" I grit out.

Justine confirms with the daycare again. And then confirms with me again. Five-thirty. Fuck. I don't have time for this. I have emails to answer and a report to complete and get to Loren by midnight tonight.

I leave the office at five-thirty to pick up the boys.

It's six o'clock when I walk into Big Hearts Daycare. The woman seated in a chair holding a sleeping Rory in her lap greets me. "Can I help you?" She looks exhausted, but with a patience that only a loving heart can display to a stranger. *What a sap,* I think.

I point to Rory and say, "You're holding my son."

When I say it, Kai walks out of a door with signage that reads *Boys,* I'm assuming the bathroom, and looks at me with mild shock racing across his features. "Where's Daddy?"

"He's at the hospital. Get your stuff. Hurry up. We need to go." I know I probably should've softened that so I don't scare him, but I'm too irritated to censor.

"The hospital?" he questions timidly. Kai has always been softhearted. He's so much like his father, not an ounce of me in him.

"Yes. Hurry up," I repeat.

The woman holding Rory looks as if she's driving by the scene of a horrendous car accident, mouth gaping, eyes wide with alarm. "Oh my goodness, is Seamus okay?" she asks with a tremble in her voice. "I've been trying to call his cell, and he didn't answer, which is so unlike him. I tried the back-up emergency number, too—your cell number, Mrs. McIntyre—but there was no answer."

I think back on my phone ringing from my purse as I drove here. I ignored it. So, I lie, "My phone didn't ring. Must have a bad number."

"Is he okay?" she repeats.

"I don't know. I'm sure he's fine. It's nothing life threatening if that's what you're asking." Numbness hardly indicates he's on the precipice of death.

She looks at me oddly, judging me for my lack of concern I'm sure, and says, "I need to see some ID, please, to release the boys to you."

I look at the ceiling and shake my head as the frustration in me mounts. "Goddammit, I'm their mother. What do you need ID for?"

"Security purposes," she says as she stands with Rory in her arms.

I dig through my purse for my wallet and instruct, "Wake him up and put him down."

"Don't you want to carry him out to your car?"

I widen my eyes to reinforce the point that I'm done with this conversation. "No. I don't. He's three. He can walk."

She begins talking softly to him as she looks over my ID. His eyes flutter open, and a look of confusion momentarily takes over his sleepy eyes. "Sweetheart, your mommy is here to take you home. Can you wake up, honey?"

Rory blinks several times and then looks at me. "Mom?" he questions, as if me standing here is an impossibility. He's always been the straightforward, outspoken one of the two boys. No doubt this one's mine. He knows how to push my buttons.

"Yes, Rory. Let's go." The last five minutes of motherhood have already exhausted me; I don't know how Seamus does this shit every day.

"Where's Daddy?" he asks.

Kai answers, "He's at the hospital. We need to make sure he's okay." There are tears dripping down his cheeks as he says the words.

Rory wiggles in the woman's arms, and she puts him down. He immediately goes to his brother and hugs him, attaching himself to his side. This need to comfort is Seamus through and through. It's a good thing he's the one parenting or these two would likely be stabbing each other in the back instead of hugging it out.

When we get to the car, I open the door of my Mercedes convertible and push the driver's seat forward so the boys can crawl into the cramped backseat.

"What about our booster seats, Mom?" Kai asks.

"Shit," I mutter under my breath. I hadn't thought of that. They've never ridden in my car. "We're not using them tonight. Buckle your brother in," I instruct.

It's almost seven o'clock when we walk into the emergency room entrance of Mercy General. It smells like antiseptic, sanitizer, bodily fluids…and suffering. I hate hospitals. They remind me of my grandmother. She died four days after sustaining injuries from a car accident. I was driving the car. The front tire blew out and put us into a ditch. The passenger side hit a tree. A big, solid, centuries-old tree that wins battles against a cage of steel rolling at high speed.

I was fine.

She wasn't.

Fate is a fickle motherfucker.

Four days I sat by her side in the ICU begging her to stay with me, to fight.

Four days of the rank stench emanating from her mangled body and the room I was trapped in assaulting my nose, a foreboding indicator that death was coming...inescapable and diligent in its duty to claim her.

Four days of watching her suffer while life was forced upon her through tubes and needles and devices, her body rejecting every attempt to save it.

Four days of listening to her cry—my strong, ruthless grandmother weeping in defeat and saying her goodbyes.

I hate hospitals.

I would burn this building to the fucking ground if I could to escape those memories. They haunt me. Every day they haunt me. But here, inside the belly of the beast, makes them insufferable.

Kai is standing beside me holding Rory's hand.

After talking to the woman at the desk, I discover that Seamus is still undergoing tests with a neurologist. We take a seat and wait to speak to the doctor.

We haven't been sitting here five minutes before Rory announces he needs to use the bathroom and that he's hungry.

I make Kai take him to the bathroom while I buy them both a Pepsi, a bag of chips, and a candy bar from the vending machine. Mother of the year I am not.

We wait an hour before a nurse collects us and asks us to follow her. The smells grow stronger as we make our way into the depths of the hospital. I feel nauseous, and I'm not sure if it's a physical reaction or a psychological reaction driving the bile up my throat. The memory of my grandmother's cacophonous cries in my ears is so loud that my head starts to pound.

Seamus is propped up in a sitting position under the sheets of a hospital bed. He's in a cloth gown, and his right arm is exposed, the needle for an IV is inserted and taped to the inside of his forearm, but there's no tube running to it. I'm ashamed to admit that I'm taking everything else in so closely because I'm scared to look at his face. I'm scared that he'll look different than the perfect man I've been with for years. Because, now that I'm standing in this hospital room being barraged by horrific memories of my grandmother, I know in my gut that something is wrong. He's not perfect anymore. And he never will be again.

"Hi," he says quietly. The boys run to him.

I wait until the boys are at his bedside and he's talking to them before I scan his face. When I do, I ask myself when I did this last…really looked at him. It's been years. Most days, if I see him, it's in passing at home. We talk briefly, and my eyes pass over him. I might catch a glimpse of the graphic on his t-shirt, or the scruff on his chin if he hasn't shaved, or notice that his hair is in need of a trim, but I never really look at him. Not like I am now.

He's pale, washed out with worry. His eyes look like they've been open for days and seen nothing but disappointment. His hair is rumpled and in disarray. He looks older, defeated, though the sparkle that only the boys can bring to his eyes is there behind it all. Today, he's a shell, no longer vibrant. It plunges me back into the nightmare with my grandmother. My nightmare. I can't do this. I can't take this. Whatever it is, I can't deal.

I turn to walk out of the room, and he calls my name, "Miranda." It sounds like *please*, and *help*, and *I need you*. All the things I would usually run away from.

But I hear my grandmother in her last days, so I turn around and walk to his bedside. When he takes my hand, I ask, "What's wrong?" Tears are threatening. I haven't cried since my grandmother's funeral.

He shrugs. "They're not sure yet. They took blood, ran an MRI, and performed a spinal tap to try to narrow it down." He glances at the boys like he's not sure he should be talking in front of them and then swallows hard and shakes his head. "I can't feel my legs, Miranda. They're numb. I sat at my desk all day trying to figure out what was going on and trying not to panic, but it didn't pass." A tear escapes and he swipes it away. "I didn't know what else to do. I tried calling you." He swallows again. "I asked one of the teachers to bring me here. I had trouble walking. I didn't feel safe driving." He closes his eyes and turns his head away from me and tears seep through his pinched lids.

Just then a doctor walks in. He introduces himself and asks that Seamus spend the night for observation until all of the test results can be reviewed, interpreted, and corroborated.

We spend the night in the room with Seamus because I can't persuade the boys to leave him and come home with me. I work through the night on my laptop in the corner of the room while they all sleep in the twin bed.

Daybreak brings a diagnosis — Multiple Sclerosis.
A neurological disease.
No cure.
I was right, he's not perfect anymore.

My body was busy deconstructing itself

Seamus

present

I silence the alarm on my phone by feel, unwilling to open my eyes just yet and give in to the dawn of a new day.

But when I do it's darker than usual.

Something in the pit of my stomach tells me it shouldn't be this dark.

My thoughts are stirring.

It shouldn't be this dark.

As I stare at the ceiling and then track my eyes from one side of the room to the other, I feel icy terror rise in me.

I close my eyes and try to push the terror down, but it's lodged in my throat behind my Adam's apple and threatens to cut off my breathing as if my lack of confrontation and acknowledgment is being punished and bullied. My body was busy last night deconstructing itself; it wants to be noticed for its efforts.

When I realize the dread isn't going to pass, I open my right eye. Everything looks normal. Which should calm me, but it doesn't, because I know when I close it and open my left eye...

Nothing.

I see nothing.

Just the blackest darkness I can imagine.

If nightmares have a color it's this, darkness so black it blots out everything until there's...nothing.

And then I start whispering to myself, "Why me? Why me? Why me?" I repeat it and repeat it until I'm crying, unable to speak. Until the words are choked off by silent sobs into my pillow. I've perfected crying silently, keeping it all to myself. And when words become impossible my mind starts racing. *Why does my body hate me? What have I done to deserve this? When do I get a break? I just want a fucking break! I can't do this!*

When the tears stop, my mind goes into Dad mode. Even in the midst of health crisis, it's in Dad mode— problem-solving mode. I need to get in the shower and wake the kids up and figure out how to get them to school so I can deal with this.

After I'm showered and dressed, I wake the kids and set bowls, spoons, a box of cereal, and the gallon of milk on the counter. When I return to their bedroom Rory is already in the shower, Kai is dressed, and Kira is sitting on the edge of her bed with Pickles the cat under one arm and her eyes closed. She looks like she might be sleeping sitting up.

"Kai, I need to run next door to talk to Mrs. Lipokowski. I'll be back in a minute, but please make sure everyone starts eating breakfast. It's on the counter."

Kai nods. He's not a talker in the morning.

As soon as I step outside on the W...E mat I feel like a failure. Like I've failed at life. Being out in the open, out in the world, is scary. This is the place people label others. This is the place people notice when you're different.

Walking next door is hard. I don't know if it's my imagination and my legs are even less cooperative today, or if seeing the world through off-kilter eyes is throwing me off, but I feel drunk. Oh, how I wish I were drunk. Drunk out of my fucking mind would be preferable to this any day.

The knock on the Lipokowski's door goes unanswered. I'm sure they're down at the deli getting ready for the day's business.

Shit.

What the hell am I going to do?

Faith. I'll try Faith.

The walk down the stairs isn't really walking. My equilibrium is off, an unwelcome side effect of the nightmare in my left eye, and I don't trust myself, so I sit and inch my way down the stairs like a toddler. I'm beyond humiliated by the time I knock on Faith's door, and if it weren't for my kids I would probably lock myself away in my apartment and never come out.

I knock twice, and as I turn to walk away, she answers the door to my back. "Good morning, neighbor," she murmurs sleepily.

I don't greet. I apologize. "I'm sorry," I say it before I turn and face her.

And when I face her, her eyes are locked on my face, searching it, pulling every detail from the despair etched on it. She tilts her head and says nothing, but her gaze says it all. Sadness, mild shock, and the need to help are kindheartedly apparent. "What can I do, Seamus? Just tell me what you need." It's her soft voice, my place to land if I fall.

She's in her pajamas, just a large t-shirt that barely covers her underwear. It's old and the lettering on the front reads, *Our ribs will stick to yours. Rick's BBQ.* I'm momentarily distracted by how awful that tagline is, which makes me want to hug her because it's the first time all morning every cell in my body hasn't been tied up in this shitstorm.

Then I want to hug her because I have access to the world's greatest hugger standing right in front of me.

So I do.

I hug her.

And she hugs me back.

And I try not to cry.

But I fail and wet the shoulder of the awful BBQ t-shirt.

"Can you take the kids to school for me this morning and drive me to the hospital?"

She releases me. "Of course." She's nodding. "Of course."

I wipe the tears from my eyes quickly.

"When do we need to leave?"

I check my watch. "Fifteen minutes."

She's still nodding, I don't think she ever stopped. She's lost in thought. "Okay. Meet you at your car in fifteen minutes."

"Thank you." I've said thank you thousands of times in my life. Most of the time I mean it to some degree. There are times when I've said it and felt the gratitude behind the words wholeheartedly, but I don't think I ever understood what those two words truly meant until this very moment. Now I think I need a new phrase because *thank you* is insufficient in this situation.

She's still nodding. Still thinking.

When I reach the base of the stairs, I look at her door, and she's still standing there watching me. I don't want her to watch me walk these stairs, to bear witness to the struggle because it's not going to be pretty, so I stop.

"Seamus?" she calls. Her voice sounds lighter. "Remember that gift I gave you that pissed you off?"

I nod because now I'm thinking.

"I'm not telling you what to do, but if you didn't already chop it up and make toothpicks out of it, today would be a good day to take it for a test drive."

The nod continues because relief is pouring in.

The next several hours are a blur.

I explain what's going on to the kids in non-scary terms, even though I have no idea what's going on. Reality in non-scary terms is how I've always approached my kids with my disease. Basically, I tell them I'm having trouble with my eye, and that Faith is taking me to the hospital so the doctor can make it better. I'm not sure if it's true, but that's what I tell them.

I use the cane.

83

I call in sick to work.

Faith drives us and we drop my kids off at school.

Faith drives me to the hospital.

We wait in the ER for hours.

I see a neurologist.

He confirms MS is the culprit behind the blindness.

There's a good chance it's temporary.

But it could be permanent.

He consults with my doctor and writes me a prescription.

Faith drives me to the pharmacy.

The pharmacist gives me steroids in exchange for a swipe of my credit card that's almost maxed out.

Faith drives me to pick up my kids from school.

Faith drives us all home.

When she kills the engine, and the kids jump out and run up the stairs to our apartment, I'm not sure what to do next. I've spent all day with her and we haven't spoken two words to each other. She's done everything I needed without instruction or direction because I was lost in my body's breakdown. The last thing I said to her this morning was the thank you that wasn't thank you enough. And I want to say it again. But again, it's insufficient. So, I look at her and say the words I feel bone deep, "So much more than thank you."

Her confusion is evident when her eyebrows pull together, a crease forming between them. She has a very expressive face. I've watched it closely all day and seen a wide range of emotions. "So much more than thank you?" she questions.

"Thank you isn't enough to express my appreciation," I sincerely clarify.

Understanding lights in her eyes and the confusion crease disappears as a soft smile slowly spreads across her face. "So much more than you're welcome."

I can't help but smile, and then I let out a long breath.

"I have a few frozen pizzas. Mind if I come up and we have a Friday night pizza party?"

"I can cook, Faith. You've already done enough." I feel awful that I've killed her entire day.

"I know you can. This is me asking for a favor. Maybe I just don't want to be alone." She's still smiling, but a hint of sadness touches her eyes.

The tables have turned. I get to help her. I *can* help her. I unbuckle my seatbelt and nod once in all-out agreement. "Friday night pizza party it is. Let's do this."

The rest of the evening is spent in apartment three—the five of us eating pizza, Kira even tried a piece when Faith offered it, which is groundbreaking considering it's not one of her normal foods; singing karaoke, Kira's rendition of "Hello" by Adele was over the top dramatic and made all of us smile; and watching a Disney movie we've all seen dozens of times but still love.

It was the best ending to one of the worst days I've ever had.

She's kind of a bitch

Seamus

present

The chorus from "Evil Woman" by Electric Light Orchestra is blaring at me, unkindly waking me from a deep, somewhat enjoyable sleep. It's Miranda's ringtone. I know it's juvenile, I know, but it's an inside joke that takes the edge off and allows me to answer the phone with an unfeeling, "Hello," rather than an aggressive *fuck you.*

"Where in the hell are you?" she screeches.

I open my eyes and try to adjust to wakefulness, partial blindness, and verbal aggression all at the same moment. I have to admit I don't like any of them and close my eyes again before I answer, "What?"

"Where in the hell are you?" she repeats louder this time. "I've been waiting for ten minutes."

Shit.

Shit.

With everything that happened yesterday, I forgot about Miranda being in town this weekend for my kids. Think, Seamus, think. I can't let her know I forgot, or she'll use it against me, and I don't feel safe driving yet until I adjust to my vision change. "I was just about to call you. The battery must be dead on my car. It won't start. You'll have to pick up the kids here at my place."

She huffs. It's a huff that's so heavy with irritation at the inconvenience that I can practically feel it come through the phone and assault my cheek.

I rattle off apartment three's address and hang up without another word.

I wake the kids immediately and begin packing their backpacks with a change of clothes for each of them

86

while they get dressed. The pizza party ended late last night, and they're all struggling to get moving, but the longer I watch them their actions aren't slowed by sleepiness. I know my kids inside and out. This is a slow act of defiance, intentional or not; they don't want to go. The smiles from last night are wiped clean, replaced by an air of reticent duty.

"What's wrong, mate?" I ask Rory. He's my most forthright child, I know he won't hold back.

"I don't want to go with Miranda."

You would think with my low opinion of my ex-wife that his statement would make me happy. Ecstatic. But it doesn't. It breaks my heart. "Why?" I ask gently.

"She bloody ignores us, Dad. She takes us to a hotel. We swim. She works—yapping on her phone and typing on her laptop the entire time. It's bollocks. Why even bother?"

I look at Kai for confirmation. He nods.

"I'm sorry." I am. So very sorry. I want to say more, offer them comfort, but there's a knock at the door. I squeeze Rory's shoulder so he knows I hear him and I understand, before I have to transition them into Miranda's visit. "She's here. Better grab your bags."

When I open the door, prepared to face down hell, I'm offered a welcome reprieve. It's Faith. "Good morning, neighbor." She's standing on the W…E mat smiling.

"Good morning, neighbor," we all respond in unison. The cheerful greeting is executed with the uncheerful tone of a somber morning.

Faith frowns. "Maybe I should've just said morning and left out the good?"

We all step out of the doorway to offer her entry.

Kira perches on the arm of the couch with Pickles the cat hugged under her arm. "Mommy's coming to get us." Even my trusting, happy, little girl seems off this morning.

Faith sits down next to her and puts her hand on Kira's back. I know what she's doing, touching amplifies words. They're louder and more easily understood in your mind when two people are touching, even casual touch. It's a direct path for communication, fleshed out of one body and into another. "That's great, Kira. I'm sure your mom misses you very much since she lives far away and doesn't get to see you often."

Kira shrugs. It's not the shrug of a five-year-old. It's a shrug with some age, with the misgivings that only time and experience extend. It's deflating.

As if on cue, we all hear footsteps sounding on the stairs outside the open door. They're the precise, staccato taps of high heels scratching against concrete. Holding my breath, I brace for her appearance and this unwanted interaction.

And then there she is. My ex. Standing on the W...E mat.

It's the unwelcome mat again.

When no one moves and no one greets, Miranda clears her throat intentionally, to garner attention, even though every eye in the room is already on her. It's a smug act to establish dominance. As she stares at me, her presence brings on a rush of anxiety because I'm reminded that her threats of a custody battle have been lying dormant for a few weeks. A sleeping bear that I don't dare turn my back on. Or poke.

I turn to Kai standing next to me and pull him into a hug. "Be good, buddy. I'll see you in the morning."

"See you in the morning, Dad. Love you."

"Love you, too."

Rory and Kira are lined up when I release Kai and I repeat the hugs and words with them.

As they walk toward the door, Kira runs back to Faith and gives her a hug. The hug starts a chain reaction in Miranda's eyes. It's obvious she hadn't noticed Faith on the couch until now. Shock is the first emotion that registers given away by the widening of her eyes, which is quickly downgraded to surprise as they narrow, leading to jealousy in the squaring off of her shoulders, and finally, the look she settles on I can only describe as blazing hellfire. She's seething. "Who are you?" It's demanding and cutting. She's trying to intimidate.

Faith isn't easily intimidated. When the hug has ended, because Kira and Faiths' hugs are long and neither one of them cuts it short for Miranda's benefit, Faith stands and walks to the door, a friendly smile in place, and extends her hand. "I'm Faith."

"Faith is our friend and neighbor," I explain. "She lives downstairs." I feel the need to defend Faith and I don't want her to go at Miranda alone because Miranda will eat her alive given the chance.

Miranda flicks her gaze at the offer of greeting but refuses the handshake. With a roll of her eyes, she looks to my kids instead. "Let's go," she commands.

The kids file out the door behind her and down the stairs.

When they're all in the car and it drives down the street and out of sight Faith looks at me. "Seamus?"

"Yeah?" The air in the room feels corrupted, brought down by Miranda's attitude.

Her mouth twists to the side as if she's debating what she's about to say. "She's kind of a bitch," she finally says, apologetically.

My mouth quirks up in a semi smile as I nod. "No kind of about it."

An incoming text alert comes from my pocket. It's a few notes from the Darth Vader theme song.

Faith raises her eyebrows in question.

"Miranda," I answer.

She smiles and nods in agreement at my dark, evil choice of alert.

The text reads, *Are you fucking her?*

I laugh. Out loud. Longer and harder than I've laughed in a long time.

Faith is smiling at me.

"What?" I ask.

"You have a great laugh, Seamus. You should unleash it more often."

I'm still smiling though the laughter has faded. "She's delusional." I turn the screen on my cell to face Faith, so she can read it and be included since she's the subject matter of Miranda's jealous accusation.

I shouldn't have done that.

I shouldn't have shared.

That much is glaringly obvious by the look of devastation and humiliation on Faith's face.

Her eyes drop from the phone to the floor for a few seconds before they meet my eyes. She steps through the open door onto the W…E mat before she speaks. "Funny." It sounds anything but funny. "I gotta go. See you later, Seamus."

She's down the stairs before I can catch up to ask what's just happened. "Faith!" I yell.

It's met with a door opening and closing below me.

I walk out and sit down on the top stair contemplating my next move.

Miranda is jealous because she thinks I'm sleeping with Faith.

I found Miranda's jealousy funny. Not because of the subject matter, but the idea of her being jealous is asinine because she has no right.

Faith thinks I found the idea of her and I having sex funny and downright crazy.

Jesus Christ. Now I'm staring at the text again feeling like an asshole for the miscommunication and mix-up. And I'm also zeroing in on the words *you fucking her* and thinking quite literally what exactly that means. I've never let myself go down this road…fantasizing about Faith. Because Faith is my friend. And because I don't know how old Faith is, but I know she's too young for me. And because Faith is beautiful. And because Faith is healthy and energetic. And because Faith deserves more than I could give her.

But now, sitting on these stairs, I close my eyes and let myself go *there*. Her naked. Me naked. In my bed. God, she's gorgeous lying beneath me. Her breasts are full and heavy with the weight of desire, cupped in my hands. Her skin so soft to the touch. Our kisses' intensity and passion matched by the pace we're keeping. I'm buried inside her, she's tight, and her hips are meeting each thrust of mine. It's the rhythm of two partners pleasing each other and themselves at the same time. Sex like I've never known it. My name escapes on a sexy moan between kisses. *Fuck*. It's coming...coming...coming.

Shit.

I'm about to come.

In my fucking shorts.

On the steps in front of my apartment.

And I didn't even touch myself.

Shit.

It's been too damn long since I've been with a woman if a vivid, mental fantasy can bring me this close to the finish.

I was going to walk down and try to talk to Faith, but maybe this is a sign that I just need to go inside and give us some space. An embarrassing sign.

The unwelcome invader invites new obsessions

Miranda

past

I dive even deeper into work with Seamus's diagnosis. He makes no changes to his routine and accepts whatever his body dishes out. He struggles, trying to act like nothing's different. He cares for the boys. He works. I let him.

Honestly, I try to ignore it. Deny it away.

But I can't.

It's there in our home like an unwelcome invader. It's warped our image, warped the façade.

In turn, I throw myself at Loren. Making up any excuse to get away to Seattle and spend time with him.

"Mr. Buckingham will see you now," Loren's busty assistant says as she rises from her chair and moves to escort me to his office.

"I know the way," I say, efficiently stopping her advancement and putting her in her place as subordinate.

Loren's on the phone when I enter his office and lock the door behind me. He smiles appreciatively, carnal excitement sparking in his eyes, as he watches me undress before him. His conversation, all business related, continues though he picks up the receiver, eliminating the speaker phone as an auditory witness to our explicit activities.

He mutes the conference call, to say hello and give me a peck on the cheek while I unzip his pants. Our sexual encounters have taken a bold turn. Seduction has become my new obsession and I've mastered it. I can entice him into a quickie anywhere these days.

"Carry on," I say with a sexy smirk as I return him to his call, releasing the mute button.

He stiffens in his chair when I wrap my lips around him, but it's only minutes before the phone is on mute again and he has me bent over his desk. Quick and dirty, just the way he likes it. And without a condom, just the way I like it.

I've stopped taking my pills. I have a new plan. I'm determined to have his child, determined to make him love me. Getting pregnant nabbed me a husband once. I'd bet money it works again.

I don't want the façade, it's broken and no longer appealing. I want Loren and his empire; it's my destiny.

And I always get what I want.

Flypaper

Seamus

present

"Seamus, would you mind coming to the office?" It's Janet, the school secretary. She's called my desk phone, and she sounds nervous.

"Sure. I'll be right down."

I walk as fast as my legs and cane allow, and when I step through the door of the school office, I'm met with a consolatory smile from Janet and a loud voice, which matches the stranger's, who's standing at her desk, demeanor. "Seamus McIntyre?"

I'm confused.

But I'm not.

Flashbacks of being served divorce papers, standing in this exact spot, not so long ago spring to my mind. I feel hot and sticky, like flypaper attracting bad news.

"Sign for this, please." It's too loud. Why can't he speak quietly? Everyone in the office is staring at me now. Janet looks like she wants to put up a shield around us and deflect the attention.

I sign, and the first thing I notice is the return address on the manila envelope. I recognize it as Miranda's lawyer.

The other shoe just dropped.

And it felt like an atomic blast.

She's done it.

She's pursuing full custody.

That bitch.

I'm the punchline

Miranda
past

I'm pregnant!
Hallelujah!
It's Loren's.
I have obligatory sex with Seamus once a month, but never when I'm ovulating. Hell yes, I keep track of that shit. That's when I visit Loren and make sure he fills me to capacity with baby-making potential.

I deliver the pregnancy news to Loren delicately.
He doesn't receive it delicately. He rages at me. It's a fury I'm sure will ignite the air around us and burn us both alive. "How did you fucking get pregnant?! You're on the *fucking* pill!" He rarely curses, he's beyond angry.
"The pill's not one hundred percent," I say quietly. I hold back that it's zero percent effective when it's not taken. I feel like a child being chastised for their stupidity. I've never felt so small and weak. I don't like it.
He looks me dead in the eye and commands without blinking, "Have an abortion. I don't want children."
My heart drops to the soles of my feet. I can feel my blood growing cold and pooling around it in my shoes. "I can't do that. I want the baby." I don't want *a* baby. I want *his* baby. I need this link to him. He'll change his mind. He'll come around. Someday, he'll realize we belong together.
He smiles in disgust and shakes his head. "Fine. Keep the baby, but my name's not going on that birth certificate," he threatens. "Put your husband's name on it. He can raise it."

95

His words hurt. I'm the punchline to a joke that no one delivered. It wasn't supposed to go this way.

But, I'll take it. At least he didn't say it was over between us. I'll never lose. I'll make him see things my way one day.

Goddamn pathetic sponge

Miranda

past

Baby number three is delivered under a heavy administration of drugs, and I feel nothing but pressure, no pain. Two pushes, because this isn't my first go at ridding my womb of an invader, and a belting cry saturates the room.

"It's a girl," the doctor says. Well, that's new.

I know I should look at Seamus, it's what I did with the other two. I watched his reaction, even though it crushed me. But this time, I look at the baby when the nurse lays her on my chest. She's covered with a layer of goo that makes me want to gag, and she's squalling like she objects to the outside world and wants back in where it's warm. Her obvious displeasure makes me smile a little; it sounds like something I'd do. Then I look over the features on her tiny face, even with her mouth open in rebuttal and her eyes squeezed shut, she looks like me. This warms me to her a bit; finally, I got one who looks like me.

"Hey, baby girl, don't cry," Seamus coos.

She hiccups in air, and the cries lessen as if his voice is soothing her. Of course it is, he's a saint.

His large hand is on her little back, he's already her protector, when he speaks again, "We're so happy you're here and we finally get to meet you, darlin'."

She settles completely at his words and blinks her eyes wide.

"She looks like you, Miranda. She's beautiful." His voice is thick with emotion.

I smile at his words and think *Jackpot! This is how I'm supposed to feel after giving birth! I'm supposed to feel at least some sort of connection. And he's supposed to show me admiration. Finally!*

"What should we name her?" he asks.

With the other two, I was unable to speak after birth, choked off by negative emotion and jealousy. Not this time. "Kira. After my grandmother." Seamus doesn't know anything about my grandmother, other than she raised me. Not because he hasn't asked, but because I've always kept her to myself and refused to talk about her.

"Kira is perfect," he agrees.

But as soon as Seamus picks her up and cradles her in his arms and the nurse says, "I don't think I've ever seen a prouder daddy," my temporary happiness comes crashing down around me.

She's not his.

Loren should be here with me to share this moment.

This whole dramatic, picture perfect scene is a fallacy. An illusion.

She's mine.

Not ours.

Just mine.

And that's terrifying.

What if Seamus finds out before Loren warms up to the idea of us, and I'm left to raise her alone?

I feel sick. My head is caught up in the undertow of deceit. Usually, I can breeze my way through shit like this, but today is different, maybe it's the hormones.

And then the whole twisted plot is only made worse as I watch Seamus holding my daughter. He's talking to her so softly I can't hear him, but I can see his lips moving, and I know by the look on his face that every word he's uttering is a promise. Promises he'll keep until the day he dies. I can feel the love rolling off of him in waves. And it's all for her. All of his attention. All of his commitment. Another child has captured his heart.

And she's not even his.

If I had a conscience, I'd tell him.

Instead, I let the full weight of losing, not what's ours, but what's mine, my dream of a new life with another man, to him. And I feel more alone than ever.

Sonofabitch, I'm relieved I asked them to tie my tubes now that this production is over. I refuse to go through this mindfuck again for any man.

I request the postpartum depression meds the minute I'm deposited into my recovery room. The nurse tells me she'll need to consult my doctor. I tell her, "Fuck the consultation, bring me drugs," with a growl in my voice and narrowed eyes. She exits swiftly, and Seamus returns immediately from the nursery, I'm sure at her urging.

I send him away for a cheeseburger and fries from the fast food restaurant he likes that's miles away. I never eat that shit, but today I'm going to indulge in every guilty pleasure I can. Speaking of guilty pleasure, the moment Seamus leaves the room I pull my cell phone from my purse next to the bed and dial Loren.

"Miranda." His voice always makes my belly flutter; and it's trying to, despite all the trauma it's been through the past several hours: baby expelled; all the baby housing, gelatinous accoutrement expelled; traumatized, stretched skin sagging in relief; and internal plumbing irreversibly altered to ensure this doesn't happen again.

"Hi." It's a single, pathetic word that sounds flimsy and tinny. Suddenly I'm on the verge of tears. Not an isolated, pitiful tear, but a painful, hysterical breakdown.

"Justine said you weren't at work today. Is everything all right?" I want to hear compassion and concern in his voice, all I hear is urgency. He's busy and wants to end this call. I do the same thing…with everyone but him.

I take a deep breath to keep the deluge of emotion at bay and answer, "It's a girl. She looks like me."

Silence. The news is met with silence.

"We're well," I add, wishing he'd asked the question, instead of offering the answer unsolicited.

More silence.

I swallow hard twice. "I'll let you go. I just wanted you to know." I end the call before he hears the sob escape my lips.

I'm still wailing when Seamus returns. He drops the bag of food on the table and crawls into the bed and holds me.

He holds me like I'm worth comforting.

He holds me like I'm not the devil incarnate.

He holds me like he loves me.

All of which I probably don't deserve, but I soak it up like a goddamn pathetic sponge.

And I think, *Fuck you, universe.*

All that's left is we

Seamus

Miranda just picked up my kids from apartment three for her visit today. I refused to deliver them to her. Truth be told, I wanted to barricade us inside the apartment. And not let her in. Or put the kids in my car and drive far away. And never come back.

A court date is set up for two weeks from now to discuss custody. I know she thinks I'm going to give in to her and sign the papers she had delivered to avoid a battle because she knows I don't have the money to hire a lawyer. I would sell my fucking soul to fight for my kids. Miranda's always been self-absorbed, selfish, but it seems the more power she gets career-wise and the more money she makes, the more unreasonable she is. She can't relate. Everything is a competition...that she counts herself the winner of before it even gets underway. Fuck the opponent—half the time they don't know they've been screwed, and should've been fighting with everything they have, until it's too late.

It's not too late.

I'm fighting.

I'm stir crazy. Trapped by four walls. I need to get out of this apartment for a few hours. I decide a sandwich from Mrs. L's deli is in order. I haven't had one in a few weeks. I've been living on peanut butter and jelly sandwiches for lunch. They're cheap. And cheap is what sustains me these days. But today I'm splurging on a foot long roast beef with extra spicy mustard and banana peppers. Maybe it will help soak up the misery I'm feeling.

101

Mrs. L sold me a foot long for the cost of a six-inch. I feel like a king. And my mood is lifting slightly. The sunshine begs for my company as I walk out the door of the deli. Its warmth is a hug.

Hug.

And now I'm thinking about Faith as I take a seat at the table in front of the deli. And I'm missing her. And her smile. And her good nature. And her brightness — not just her boldly colored hair, but her presence. Everything about her is colorful like a rainbow set against a backdrop of gray.

My world.

Gray.

She's contrast. She shines effortlessly, unknowingly imploring me to take notice. It's an attraction I wholeheartedly feel but have unconsciously tried to deny.

Faith doesn't answer when I knock, so I write on the deli receipt in my pocket, and tell myself this is not a date.

Dinner? Apartment 3. 7:00.

The ground under the apartment building is settling and there's a slight gap under the right side of her door, so I slip the paper underneath.

Returning upstairs to my apartment, I lay down on the couch and in no time I'm asleep. It's sleep I desperately need — making up for all that was lost to worry this week.

Rap *rap*...rap...*rap* rap.

It's Faith's trademark knock, random and improvised. It's never the same sequence.

I blink away sleep, but the pace of my heart is so erratic it has me sitting and reaching for my cane before consciousness fully engages.

"Coming!" I yell, even though we can see each other because she's peeking in through the front window next to the door.

When I open the door, she's standing with her feet centered between the remaining letters on the W...E mat looking down at them. "We," she says. "Do you think it means something?"

I'm pretty sure I'm awake now, but the question catches me off guard. She lifts her chin and trains her blue eyes on me. I'd forgotten how deep they are, her eyes. "What do you mean?"

She doesn't move. "I mean the rest of the letters are gone. As if removed purposely. All that's left is 'we.'"

Her words ring in my ears. *All that's left is we.* Her. And me. I shrug. "I suppose that's true. All that's left, tonight anyway, is we. You and me." She smiles, and I feel the acceptance of my apology before I even say it. "I'm sorry. It was a misunderstanding. I was laughing at her jealousy, not at you. I should've come to you sooner. Life's been—"

She cuts me off with a finger held to my lips and repeats, "We." And then she steps off the mat and enters my apartment. "What's for dinner, Seamus?"

As she follows me to the kitchen, I scratch the back of my neck, wondering the same thing. "I'm not sure. We'll have to make do. I haven't been to the grocery store in a week."

She shrugs. "I'm easy to feed." She's always agreeable, and I wonder if that's a direct reflection of her parents and how she was raised, if it's just her, or if it's something she works at.

I open the cupboard and the refrigerator and survey. "Looks like ramen, mac and cheese, cereal, oatmeal, or bologna sandwiches. Oh, or toast. Or any combination of the aforementioned."

Looking over my shoulder to gauge her reaction, I find her smiling. "How about mac and cheese bologna sandwiches?"

"What do you mean, mac and cheese inside the sandwich?"

"Yeah," she confirms. "I've never had that. But we have to fry the bologna. I don't like cold, dirty meat. It makes me gag."

I bark out a surprised laugh because that could be interpreted many ways and I don't want to dive straight into the gutter, but I can't help it. "Dirty meat?"

She laughs with me, blushing a bit, but standing her ground. "Yeah, dirty meat. Bologna, hot dogs, pepperoni. You never really know what's inside. It's dirty meat."

Her rosy cheeks are adorable. "Gotcha. Please don't mention that to Kira. She lives on bologna and hot dogs, and I can't afford to cut any foods out of her limited diet."

Faith fries the bologna while I make the mac and cheese. We even toast the bread, so everything about the sandwich is hot.

When we sit down on the couch with our plates, Faith assesses her sandwich. "Seamus, we might be on to something here. This is classy on a budget."

Raising my eyebrows, I look around the room. "If you hadn't noticed, that's how I roll."

She laughs as she bites into her sandwich and talks only after she's swallowed. "Oh, I noticed. Me, too," she adds with a wink.

While we eat, I decide now's a good time to find out a little bit more about her. "Where are you from Faith?"

"Kansas City," she answers.

I stop chewing and look at her because surely she's kidding. She doesn't look like a Midwesterner. "Really?"

"Really. I grew up there. I moved here a few months ago."

104

"What brought you to California? You're a long way from home."

She smiles at me like she knows I'm going to be amused by what she's about to say. "Research."

I smile in return. "Ah, of course, research. Do your parents still live in Kansas City?"

She shakes her head as she chews a bite of her sandwich.

"Where do they live?"

"I grew up in foster care."

The words, even though there wasn't negativity behind them, concern me. I'm familiar with the foster care system due to my job. Counseling sheds light on all facets of my students' lives. Most foster care parents are loving, giving individuals who want what's best for the child. But, like anything else in life, there are always the bad apples. The ones responsible for tarnishing the reputation of the good. Those are the ones who stick out in my mind. The ones who shouldn't be allowed around other human beings, let alone children. "How was that?" My stomach twists as I wait for her answer.

"Let's just say, some families were better than others." She takes in my worried eyes and adds quickly, "Some people are really good at making you feel valued. Like you're worth something. And some people feed and house you." She shrugs. "I survived. And it made me that much more grateful for the ones who cared. Gratitude isn't a gift to the receiver, it's a gift to the giver."

"How old are you, Faith?" I'm more curious than ever now.

"Twenty-two."

"How'd you get so wise in twenty-two years?" I mean it, she's a deep thinker.

"Old soul." She winks. "Growing up in and aging out of the foster care system is like dog years. About two to your one. Technically, I'm forty-four."

I love her sense of humor. "Good to know. Should I start calling you ma'am? That's how I address my elders."

She shakes her head threateningly. "Never. Even when I'm ninety, no one will be allowed to call me ma'am."

I'm finished with my sandwich—which was an unexpectedly tasty combination—and wait for her to finish before I ask another question. "How old were you when you went into the system?"

"Two."

"So, you don't remember your birth parents?"

She shakes her head to let me know I've missed something or that I have the story all wrong. "Long story short, my mother gave me up for adoption at birth. My adoptive parents...weren't exactly up to the task of parenting after the newness wore off and they figured out babies, toddlers, were work."

My heart aches. It aches because I can't help but think of my kids. "Do you know the circumstances behind you going into foster care in the first place?"

"My caseworker shared my file with me when I turned eighteen. The neglect and abuse was all there in black and white. I'm glad toddler's memories are purged as we mature." She looks at me. "That's one of the best gifts I've been granted in life, not remembering the worst. But it did make sense of some of the scars I have."

I cringe at the pain she has no doubt suffered. "I'm sorry."

Shaking her head, she says, "Don't be sorry, Seamus. I don't remember it—"

"That doesn't excuse what they did," I interrupt, feeling protective. I can see Faith in my mind giving hugs to strangers on the beach with a kindness that should've never been tainted.

"I'm not saying that because I don't remember it excuses it. They both did jail time. I've never spoken to them. I'm just saying that not being plagued with the

106

awful memories was a sympathetic act the universe bestowed upon me. An act that saved me a lot of money on therapy."

I smile at her positive take on her life. "You're pretty incredible, you know that?"

She shakes her head. "Nope. I'm just a girl who fought like hell for her name."

"What do you mean?"

"When I was eighteen I legally changed my name to Faith Hepburn. And before you ask, it's after Audrey *and* Katharine, because they were both amazing women. And it's a pretty name."

"That it is," I agree. "Are you religious? Is that why you chose Faith?"

"Nope."

"Faith in what then?"

Her eyes are bright, but slightly aged when she looks at me and answers, "Life."

I nod. Of course. Everything is about living life to her, experiencing it.

"What about you, Seamus? What do you have faith in?" Before I answer, she adds quickly, "And you can't say your kids. That's obvious."

Damn, that's exactly what I was going to say. The only other answer that comes to mind is too depressing to verbalize.

"Well?" she prompts.

"I don't know," I lie, not wanting to bring this conversation down. "I can't think of anything."

"You have an answer," she challenges. "I can see it all over your face. I can see it in the way your posture slouched. I can see it in the way your eyes dropped."

I turn my head and look at her and then I sigh and slump back against the couch cushion behind me. "I have faith in decline; the decline of my health, the decline of my sanity, the decline of my happiness. Miranda's going to make sure I hit rock bottom with everything she's got.

She's going to strip it all away. I hate her, Faith. I really, truly, hate the woman." She narrows her eyes as if she's trying to figure out what's going on and I answer the question. "She's taking me to court in two weeks to fight for full custody."

"What? She can't take your kids."

"It's all up to the courts. It's not fair, you know? That total strangers are going to decide my future and my kids' future. All because Miranda has a hard-on for revenge and power and flaunting her money. Have I mentioned how much I hate her?" The last sentence I mix malice with sarcasm because I'd rather do that than cry. Or scream and punch a hole in the wall. And I'm on the verge of either now.

"You have to fight. With everything you've got." She looks determined. The kind of determined I want to feel in my heart, that leaves no room for doubt.

I have too much doubt. It's the bastard child of fear. I hate fear. So doubt sidles up next to determination in my heart. It doesn't outweigh it. They coexist.

I nod in agreement with her. "I can't lose them, Faith." My voice is thick with the sadness and frustration that's clogging my throat.

"You won't," she assures me. And then she stands and walks to the front door and opens it. She bends over and picks up the W...E mat, steps back inside, and closes the door behind her. Then she walks toward me and sets the W...E mat down on the floor directly in front of me. And after she steps onto it she smiles and says, "I need to hug you. Now."

I take her hand she's extended to help me up.

She looks down at the mat we're both now standing on and back up to my eyes. "We," she says. "You're not alone, Seamus. I'm here."

I hug her, and I let everything bad drain out of me. But I don't give it to her. I let it siphon down from my head through my torso and legs and out my feet, just like

108

opening up the drain in the bathtub. I can feel the fear and tension escape, if only for the moment.

And I feel her doing the same thing. The hug that started out strong, more physical than emotional, as if we both needed to prove that we were here and present for each other, lessened in grip and shifted to something more emotional and supportive. And it feels every bit as intense in strength.

"So much more than thank you," I whisper in her ear.

"So much more," she whispers back. And in those words I hear my soft place to land again, but I also feel a change in both of us. That wasn't just acceptance of my appreciation, it was also an admission. A desire.

I'm at odds with my conscience. All too aware of the *woman* pressed against me. A woman I want to get lost in, if only tonight. I'm mapping out boundaries and lines in my mind. Lines I shouldn't cross. And then my mouth is working on the specifics without me. "Do you have a boyfriend, Faith?" I ask it softly, like a wish, into the indentation of her collarbone.

"No," she whispers.

I hear the word. I understand its meaning. But what makes heat thread through my veins is the hesitant, sadly hopeful tone of her voice. Hope that pleads for consequences...immediate consequences.

Consequences that have me arguing away lines and boundaries and touching my lips to her skin. Her shoulders lift slightly into the contact before settling out on a silent sigh.

I chase the sigh with my lips...and then with the tip of my tongue, tracing the hard line of her collarbone to the base of her neck.

Her hands twist up the back of my t-shirt in response.

I've always romanticized that physical intimacy should be a conversation. A loving exchange back and forth. I've never had a partner who was a willing conversationalist.

Until now.

Fingertips brush faintly up the backside of an arm, wrist to shoulder, raising goosebumps in response.

Warm breath against skin, exhaled on a patient pause between kisses below an ear, elicits a shiver.

A shifting of stance tucks one leg between two, the two hug it in return.

The initiation of a kiss, soft and tentative, is welcomed by parted lips.

A shirt removed is reciprocated with the shedding of the other.

Touch for touch.

Kiss for kiss.

Heart for heart.

Trust for trust.

It's all traded until the line I drew in my mind earlier is approached, if not mildly crossed already. I don't retreat, but I don't take it any further. She doesn't push it either and seems perfectly content to continue the conversation without the introduction of sex.

Even when we move to the couch and she sits on my lap straddling me, all of the conversation happens from the waist up. The pace and intensity vary like the waves of the ocean I love to watch. Some swells are low, no break, just a gentle ease. And some swells are high, all whitecaps, intensely crashing in with passionate frenzy. The ebb and flow is so natural that I obey every instinct without hesitation. Hesitation requires doubt or uncertainty, neither of which are possible when I'm touching Faith.

An easy hour passes, and as it does our bodies begin to meld with each other as the blissful, satisfying blanket of exhaustion envelopes us. Slowly, so slowly, we're pulled under until her head is resting on my shoulder, my head tilted, her forehead against my neck, our torsos contently accepting each other's touch as the precursor to a final hug. And the last thing I hear before we both fall asleep, is a whisper, "So much more." It sounds like an appeal to my soul.

Botox, overcoats, and destiny

Miranda

past

Seamus goes through ups and downs with his MS. It appears to subside and then returns in a furious, vicious, illogical circle. Not that I'm a supporter; I bear witness to the struggle when I'm home, which isn't often. The feeling returned in his legs but was replaced by pain. He doesn't complain, but I see how it affects him when he moves, when he walks. His gait isn't fluid, there's tenderness and a tentativeness that gives him away. It's unattractive. I know that sounds callous, but even though his face still looks like a goddamn model, I can't get past the incompleteness I know exists physically.

For the year after Kira was born, I turned to Seamus because Loren backed away from me sexually. I ignored the lack of attraction because in the darkness of our bedroom his performance was never lacking. I could have sex with Seamus and think of Loren.

That didn't last. After months of wallowing, I took charge; Botox and a personal trainer have me looking better than ever, and when I show up at Loren's front door wearing only an overcoat, he wastes no time in stripping me of it and taking me right there in harsh form up against the wall of his foyer.

I stay two days. I think the news that I'm sterile turns him on. His appetite is insatiable like he's been starving for a meal only I can serve up for months. I'm on my way, my destiny back on track.

I throw up another middle finger to the universe as I pull away from his estate in a taxi. I'll be back to stay someday. With a new last name. Or I'll go down in flames trying.

112

Blackmail sounds so harsh

Miranda

past

I'm thirty-three years old.

I'm successful beyond belief career-wise. I'm vice president of a tech company that's increased its profits tenfold the past several years — all thanks to my direction and leadership. My reputation in the industry precedes me. I've constructed it with precision, an intricate master plan at work: money, titles, power.

I am fearless.

But more than that — *I am feared.*

My grandmother would be so proud.

The money is rolling in. My salary is exorbitant, though I always lobby for my next raise. I stash it all away in bank accounts and investments that Seamus doesn't, and will never, know about. My day is coming, and when it does he'll be sorry he was stupid enough to sign the prenup I insisted on all those years ago, stating that all of my future earnings would remain with me should there ever come a time we should split. Let him keep his measly forty grand a year. That shit's gone the minute it goes into his account anyway, spent on utilities and food and insurance and his meager car payment and whatever the kids need. The thing about Seamus is, he'll probably be okay when he's living hand to mouth someday. Money doesn't mean anything to him. He's all about the kids, and helping people. Fool.

Despite my successes, I'm at a stalemate.

I'm still with Seamus. Still with the kids. The façade intact.

I'm so fucking tired of the façade.

113

I thought the façade would sustain me. A good husband, two point five kids, and a white picket fence looks good. It's the layer that society expects and grants you merit points based upon. Merit points, even fictitious ones, offset my ruthlessness. Even if people think I'm a bitch, they'll say, "Oh, but her husband and children are lovely, she can't be that bad." It balances me out. And it worked until my eyes were opened to bigger and better. My destiny, it's the façade on steroids. Remove goodness and insert excess. Excess, what a magnificent word.

I need my destiny.

It's long overdue.

Kira just turned four.

Loren still hasn't met her. Acknowledged her.

I fly to Seattle a few times a month. We have sex like rabbits, and then I come home. Empty. Even while I'm with him, I'm empty, because I know I'll just be cast out when it's done. I don't want to be cast out. I deserve to be there with him. The motherfucking queen to his king.

I used to think I loved Loren, the man, and I think to some degree I did, but what I love most is the idea of Loren, the things that make up Loren. I love his estate. I love his money. I love his power. I love his business prowess. I love his cold, calculating confidence. I love his winner-take-all attitude. He's basically me with a penis. And who wouldn't love that. Put us together. Combine our assets. It's the wet dream of wet dreams, a fucking financial fantasy.

And it's time to take it because it's clear that Loren isn't going to buy the cow when he gets the milk free.

It's late, after eleven in the evening. This trip was last minute. Instead of going home from the office, I went to the airport and hopped a flight to Seattle. I'm in a taxi on my way to his estate to show him just how much this bitch's milk is going to cost him.

114

The Louis Vuitton bag hanging from my shoulder contains the ticket to my future, my destiny. I'm tired of waiting. I need action. I'm bored with the lack of upward mobility. The documents housed in the files inside have been painstakingly crafted over the past few years, just in case I needed a firm hand to make him see things my way.

As the driver turns onto his street, I dial his cell phone from mine.

He answers on the third ring, "Miranda?"

"Open the gate. I'm here," I tell him. He loves it when I give commands. He does the same to me. It's a sparked, charged, battle of wills; a twisted mating ritual.

"You're here?" he questions, though he doesn't sound surprised. It's Friday night, this happens often.

"Right out front," I say as the driver pulls up to the gate.

"I'm just leaving a business dinner that ran late." Business dinner means sex with a high-priced escort. I hired a private investigator to follow him. I know what he likes: dark hair, big tits, and kink. I have photographs. Unbeknownst to him, he also has a proclivity for underage girls. Though they look mid-twenties, a lot of them are under eighteen. He's been a very, very naughty boy.

"Take your time," I say with a smile.

"I'll call the housekeeper and have her let you in. Make yourself comfortable while you wait." *Make yourself comfortable* means *get naked*.

"Like I said, take your time," I repeat.

The gate retracts moments after I end the call, and his housekeeper greets me by name at the front door when I'm dropped off.

After she takes my coat, she says, "Mr. Buckingham will arrive shortly. He asked that you wait for him wherever you like." She nods politely and walks away.

"I will," I say to her retreating figure as I watch her ass sashay in her short skirt. When I move in I'm firing her and replacing her with someone older and less attractive. Someone whose ass sashaying is past its prime.

I walk directly to his office and close the double doors behind me. Everything about this room excites me. The overall masculinity is overwhelming and makes my lady parts tingle. The rich wood, the leather, the dark colors, and the faint scent of cigar are a pheromone.

After pouring a snifter of his finest cognac, I remove all of the paperwork and photographs from my bag and spread them out in a showy presentation on his desk. I've been busy creating a scandal; the massive desk is covered. After that I strip down to my lace bra and thong, leaving on my stilettos, and take a seat in his oversized, leather desk chair, patiently sipping my drink. I ponder masturbating because this high I'm riding has me uncomfortably at the edge of release, but I wait because I want him to relieve the ache before I crush him. Fuck him before I fuck him, if you will.

When he finally opens the door, he smiles approvingly at my lack of clothing. "You're my favorite houseguest, you know that?" He's removing his clothing, letting each article fall piece by piece as he walks toward me. His naked form is something I've always admired. He goes to the gym and runs obsessively; his body looks good if he were half his age.

I stand and remove my thong and bra. I do it slowly, a striptease to wind him up.

He's watching me with rapt attention as I lie down on his desk atop my masterpiece.

"My favorite," he whispers as he mounts the end of the long desk prowling toward me on his hands and knees.

When his hands land on either side of my waist, I halt his advance, "Stop right there."

He does.

"You've kept me waiting," I purr.

He glances down and smiles. I know he smiles for his whores exactly like that, it's not special anymore.

"Me first."

His smile widens as he looks up and licks his lips. "You first?" he questions teasingly.

"Now," I command.

His descent is slow, keeping his eyes locked on mine. It's part of the buildup with him. The slow pace, the control, he gets off on it. And I can't deny that I do too.

His mouth devours me. Lips, teeth, tongue — the way they work together is blissful. He throws in a few fingers, and I'm on fire. My hands grip his hair tightly holding him in place while my hips choose to increase the pressure and pace as needed. I'm giving him orders, talking absolute filth and loving it. He's groaning into me, intoxicated with the act he's engaged in. "Miranda, I need inside. Now," he begs.

He begged. The scenario I've built up here just keeps getting better.

"Me first," I remind him.

And that's when it happens, the most exquisite orgasm I've ever experienced. The combination of the trap I've set, his submission, and his talented fucking mouth created a trifecta that will never be replicated. I ride it out long and hard, screaming, "Fuck you!" repeatedly, which only serves to turn him on more.

The moment I still and open my eyes, he sits back on his heels and takes in the view.

I smile. "You like what you see?" I ask.

His eyes are dark. His chest is heaving. His dick is pleading. "Very much," he says.

I wink. "You haven't seen anything yet." He grins greedily as he watches me climb off the desk and sit in his chair. "I rather like this chair," I say, stroking the leather arm with my fingertips. "It makes me feel powerful."

He's stalking every inch of me with his eyes while he steps down off the desk and stands in front of me.

117

"Down on your knees." The way he says it would normally leave no room for negotiation.

"Not tonight, Mr. Buckingham." I lean back in the chair, cross my legs, and steeple my fingers. *Why don't you get down on yours?* I add with a smile sent straight from hell and gesture to the scattered array of evidence on his desk.

"What's that?" he says pointing to the papers.

"Oh, those? Those are your balls, my dear," I say sweetly as I bat my eyelashes. "I've got you by the balls. And you know I'm never gentle. This may hurt a bit."

His face grows red with anger before his eyes begin reading the words, flitting from one paper to the next. Then his head is shaking side to side, it's supposed to be defiant, but I know terror when I see it. As the color starts to drain from his face like sands through an hourglass, I can't help make the analogy...his time just ran out. He's still shaking his head in denial when he looks at me. "What is all of this? What do you want?"

I tilt my head. "I want us." That's as simple as I can make it.

His face blanches. "No, I don't think you do." He points to the papers and stutters, "This...this isn't love."

I roll my eyes. "Who said anything about love?" The irony of us having this discussion naked with the scent of arousal still floating in the air around us isn't lost on me.

He blinks several times. "Isn't that why people generally get married?" He's stunned. "Are you blackmailing me?"

I tap my pointer fingertip against my lips as I think over my answer. "Blackmail sounds so harsh. Let's call it relationship negotiations."

He walks to his pile of clothes and yanks on his dress pants before shrugging on his shirt. He stares at me for a moment; it's disbelief, and then disgust. "Put some goddamn clothes on."

I look down at my breasts. "You didn't seem to mind me naked a few minutes ago when your mouth was between my thighs."

He runs his hands through his hair in frustration before he pulls a handful of it and shouts, "*A few minutes ago you weren't a fucking psycho!*"

I frown. "That's no way to talk to your fiancée."

His eyes lock with mine, and the fear is plain and transparent.

I begin gathering up the papers and putting them in a neat stack. "I'm filing for divorce as soon as I get home. Seamus will be served Monday. I'll be moving in here the day the divorce is finalized. I'm going to hold off for the sake of appearance, we don't need people talking."

He huffs out a stunned laugh. "Well, aren't you thoughtful? We certainly can't have people talking. That's the least of our problems, Miranda. You're certifiable, and that's the one I'm focused on at the moment."

I wave him off. "This is all for the best. You just don't see it yet. We're good together."

He scrubs his hands over his face repeatedly. "How in the hell did I get myself into this mess?"

"Hmm, let's see...insider trading, money laundering—"

He cuts me off, "I didn't do any of that. You obviously did, though, and forged my signature."

I laugh. "I didn't forge anything. You should know better than anyone that you shouldn't sign anything you haven't read over closely. That kind of oversight could lead to incarceration for the rest of your life. We wouldn't want that, now would we?"

He's shaking his head again. "My business dealings are clean. I've never done anything illegal."

I cluck my tongue and raise my eyebrows. "I beg to differ. Your dick would probably back me up, too. Last time I checked, paying for sex in the state of Washington was still a no-no. I know this is a progressive state, but..." I

119

trail off and then add in a mocking tone, "Especially the underage ones, pretty sure that's still frowned upon."

"The agency guaranteed me they were all over twenty-one."

I smirk. "When did you get so naïve, Loren? People lie."

He pinches the bridge of his nose and blows out a breath, but I see by the set of his shoulders it does nothing to calm him. "They sure as hell do. What do you want? My money? I'll pay you. Name your price."

I shake my head. "I told you. We're getting married. That's what I want."

He looks completely bewildered, but I can see the gears turning, he's weighing his options. He knows his neck is in a noose. "Fine. But you're fired. I'll pay you a severance package. I don't want you anywhere near my business. Are we clear?"

My heart shudders initially, but then I realize I can go anywhere and get a job after I move to Seattle. "Fine."

"There will be a prenup."

I nod, I don't know how my ultimatums turned into negotiations, but if I'm honest I'm a bit surprised this is all going so well, so I'm participating in them. "Fine."

"And I saw the paternity results in your pile of exploitation. I need your word that no one ever finds out Kira is mine. I don't want children. Her father is raising her as far as I'm concerned. Your husband can have her. She's better off with him." He huffs. "They're all better off with him. I hope you know that. You shouldn't be a mother."

I'm not a mother, I think, *they're my façade.* "Okay." I'm agreeing today. Little does he know I'm just giving him time to adjust to the idea of marriage before I move the kids in with us. I don't want them here, but for appearance's sake it's necessary. I still need to be surrounded by sheep. And no one loves women who abandon their sheep. I also need Loren to bond with Kira.

120

Eventually, he'll soften to her and claim her and then he'll thank me for giving that gift. That's how I'll redeem myself in his eyes, by giving him the one thing he didn't know he wanted. I'll get to Loren's heart through Kira. Who knew sheep would make such ideal pawns?

A lovely shade of *I will annihilate your soul*

Seamus

present

I know stress isn't good for me. It's a lion that prowls the recesses of my brain waiting to attack and when prodded, it's a man-eater. It feasts on my well-being, rationality, and health like a gluttonous savage.

Sometimes stress can be backed into a corner and controlled with mental reassessment and a change of perspective. Some problems aren't as big as I initially make them out to be. And sometimes they aren't even problems at all.

But what I'm facing now with Miranda and the prospect of her taking my kids to Seattle, it doesn't get more real than this.

I can feel the stress, physically feel it. In the numbness of my legs. In the blindness of my eye. In the loss of appetite. In the insomnia. In the fatigue of my muscles and the headache crashing like cymbals between my ears. It's bleeding through me, too thick for my veins, filling me like a bloated balloon on the brink of bursting.

I'm sitting in the reception area of Miranda's lawyer's office. Everything about the room is orchestrated to scream dominance: from the masculine, oxblood leather sofas; to the dark wood paneled walls and bookshelves, to the artificial musky scent in the air. It's a testosterone fest. I'm sure if they're defending you it offers a sense of security, like being cocooned in Superman's cape. But if you're on the other side, staring down an unknown future that's in their hands, it makes you feel two inches small…to their ten feet tall. Mission accomplished.

This meeting was called out of the blue a few days ago. It was presented to me as a civil offering with a mediator to settle the issue. I'm hoping Miranda came to her senses and is reconsidering, but my gut and the pounding in my head tell me that's impossible.

"Mr. McIntyre?" The voice is professional. It's the veil that cloaks the bared teeth and claws that hide underneath.

"Yes," I answer without meeting his eyes. It's an intentionally evasive gesture to set the tone. Bitterness has me standing at the edge of sanity looking down into the deep, dark pit of future regret. I fear my mouth may get the better of me this morning. Sleep deprivation has put my sense of decorum and tact through a grinder and left me with shredded remnants of sensibility and preservation. I need to keep myself in check. I grab my cane and stand to follow him down the hallway to a conference room.

Miranda is already sitting inside. She's wearing a black tailored suit jacket and a crimson silk blouse. The color red represents power. It's her favorite...color to wear and distinguishing trait.

I take a seat where I'm instructed, directly across the wide table from her. She's five feet away, but I can feel intimidation tumbling at me in violent surges of aggression. I blaze my eyes in return to let her know I'm not taking her shit today.

Her lawyer, Dean Bergman, clears his throat to break the silent pissing match we've already begun, and says, "Why don't we get started?"

I'm drunk with rage. I raise my eyebrows in challenge. "Why don't we?"

He slides a neat stack of papers across the table toward me. They're deliberately neat like they've been tapped on all sides on a flat surface several times to ensure perfection and add to the overall presentation of superiority.

I take them heavy-handedly, jostling them into disarray and erasing the posturing they're vying for.

Revision of Custody
Kai McIntyre
Rory McIntyre
Kira McIntyre

Those are the only words I see on the page. My sight shifts in and out of focus and suddenly I can *hear* my headache. Hear the cymbal crashing with each beat of my heart as if the blood rushing through me is keeping time for the disaster unfolding. I defiantly squeeze my eyes shut and will the world, and everything in it, except for the names on the paper in front of me, to burst into flames and burn white hot until they're reduced to ash.

"Mr. McIntyre?" Bergman wants my attention.

I rub my temples with my eyes still closed, silently cursing his existence. "Yes."

"Would you like me to summarize the document?"

No, I wouldn't. "Yes." I pry my eyes open, and Miranda is staring at me, her expression unreadable.

"Mr. McIntyre, Mrs. Buckingham is —"

I cut him off because his voice clashing with the thundering in my head creates a dissonance I can't bear. "I changed my mind, I'd like a few minutes to read through this myself. Can I have some privacy?" Mutiny from within is upon me. I'm beginning to sweat, a light sheen that's the predecessor to nausea. As soon as I think the word, I swallow hard and fast because my morning coffee is preparing for emergency evacuation. Backtracking the way it came in, rather than completing the journey to the traditional exit on the other side.

"Of course," Bergman says politely.

Miranda takes her time standing to leave. I'm sure I look a mess, and she's taking pleasure in having a front row seat to my unraveling.

124

The solid door shuts with an echoing click that signals privacy, and I turn in my chair just in time to grab the trashcan behind me and spill the liquefied contents of my stomach into it. My body purging it with authority like it's trying to extract the evil I'm immersed in. My body relents and when it does I feel like the hate has been temporarily exorcised. The room smells. The unmistakable odor of undigested food mixed with stomach acid and an insufferable ex-wife. I tie off the bag and turn my attention to the papers.

My vision is blurry. I can't see through my fury. It takes longer than it should to read them.

When Bergman and Miranda walk back through the door, I'm seething. My thoughts alone could rip them to shreds. They take a seat across from me. Bergman is on his game; he's wearing a compassionate, but disheartened expression, just short of a predatory smile. Miranda, on the other hand, isn't holding back. She looks triumphant and celebratory.

I know she's waiting for me to shout and spew vengeance. I want to. I want nothing more than to crucify her to the wall behind her, driving my words through her flesh until she bleeds out and pleads for mercy. But I don't. Because she would love that. Instead, I say the only thing that I know will speak to her power hungry attitude, "How did I *ever* fall in love with you?"

Miranda loved the way I loved her. My love was unconditional and absolute. She never loved me that way, she's not capable of it, but she relished in the knowledge that she was the keeper of my heart. She treated it like a caged circus animal. Praising and feeding it just enough to make it perform despite the pain she put it through. My love fed her insatiable ego.

Miranda is the master of control, but she felt my words like a slap in the face. I saw it in the minute recoil of her body as she absorbed them and by the pinched look in her eyes as she tried to reject them. It's confirmation that I

125

no longer love her, something I'm sure she never thought would happen. She's delusional enough to think my love is undying.

Bergman clears his throat. Whether he's trying to gauge the atmosphere or prompt someone to proceed, I'm not sure.

I don't speak. There's nothing else for me to say. It's all there in black and white. An intricate web of lies and a few truths spun until they mix into a damning portrayal of an unfit father...in black and white. She hired a private investigator who's been following me since she left for Seattle months ago. There are dozens of photos: me holding Mrs. L's joint, Faith and I half clothed making out on my couch, Kira hugging Faith. The photos are followed by affidavits confirming the decline in my health, exaggerated in large part, and time I've missed at work due to it; the names are all made anonymous to me, of course. Detailed lists of what my kids eat, what they wear, how they act, including a letter from an independent psychologist Miranda must've hired, stating his "concern for the children's mental and physical well-being" and "signs of neglect." This is all bullshit. How much is she paying these people to lie? But the next photo in the stack is the one that stops me dead in my tracks, it's a photo of Faith topless on a stage. What the fuck? It's followed by affidavits from multiple men stating, in detail, sex acts Faith has performed in exchange for money. Again, their anonymity protected, of course. My first instinct is to deny because Miranda is so damn good at fabricating untruths.

The shocking finality of my dissipated love has passed as Miranda remembers why she's here and the crimson color of power stains her pale, stricken cheeks to a lovely shade of *I will annihilate your soul*. An evil smile creeps back in. "It seems you've been busy, Seamus. Dating a prostitute —"

126

"She's not a prostitute. And we're not dating," I say angrily through gritted teeth. I don't know if any of my words are true or not.

She laughs haughtily. "Oh, I'm sorry. Are you paying for her services?"

I inhale deeply, and I can't speak because I want to yell, and I feel like anything I say will dig me deeper into this imaginary hole of doom Miranda has created.

"You have my children spending time with a prostitute and a drug user." She eyes me disdainfully. "Not to mention, you're smoking marijuana."

I roll my eyes because I can't help it. "I didn't even take the hit when she offered it to me."

Bergman speaks up, and his voice carries an air of authority that I'm sure is convincing in the courtroom when he's defending something that a high-priced fee for his representation has justified into defendable and right. "Seamus, Miranda is only looking out for the children and their best interest. She has hired a caretaker, who's already moved into their home, and has registered them at a private Catholic school with an excellent reputation as one of Seattle's finest educational institutions."

"*The kids aren't even Catholic.* Neither are you," I pronounce in stunned confusion.

"They begin their studies Monday," Bergman continues as if I hadn't spoken.

"Monday?" I question. The shock is so heavy I don't sound like myself. Today is already Friday.

"My flight leaves this evening. I'm picking the children up from school and taking them with me," Miranda clarifies, sinking the knife in deeper.

"What?" It's a word released on a punch to the gut, a pained gasp of breath.

Miranda looks at Bergman, who nods, and then returns her gaze to me. "Don't fight me on this, Seamus." That was a threat, bold and immoral.

"Why not?" I challenge.

127

She picks up her cell from the table and looks at it thoughtfully. "It's hard to parent, even on your limited holiday schedule, from prison."

"What?" The pounding in my head is all-encompassing, it's trying to blot out reality, to dampen her words out of existence.

She raises her eyebrows. "There's enough marijuana in your bottom dresser drawer to put you away for twenty years, my dear. All I need to do is make a call, and the police will have your apartment searched before you can limp out to your piece of shit car."

I shake my head in disbelief. "You set me up?"

She smiles. It's broad and bright and toothy, and all I see are rows of shark teeth gleaming razor sharp and deadly back at me.

Anger is rising in me, pure and irrationally dangerous. I picture myself leaning across the table and strangling her with my hands. Delighting in the sensation of life draining out of her beneath my grip. My body is vibrating with an undeniable need to exact retribution. And when the anger is so strong that it's erased ethics everything goes quiet. Everything goes black.

I wake lying crumpled on the floor like a balled up, discarded piece of trash. Bergman and Miranda are standing over me like royals ruling over a peasant.

"Mr. McIntyre?" Bergman asks.

I side-eye him in response and have the urge to punch them both in the ankles.

"Are you all right, Mr. McIntyre? You passed out. Do you need me to call paramedics?" The amplification of his words hints toward genuine concern.

I heave my body into a sitting position and test out my failing faculties. Everything's in order though I feel like throwing up again. "Get her out of my sight," I grind out through gritted teeth.

Miranda leaves the room.

128

I sign the papers under duress blinking back tears and gather them up into a neat pile. I hold them in my hand and look at Bergman standing across the table from me. "You just handed three precious lives over to the devil herself. I hope your conscience eats you from the inside out, you bastard. This isn't the last you've heard from me. I'll get them back or die trying." I throw the papers up into the air and watch them flutter down in a flurry. I look him hard in the eye. "Oh, I almost forgot. One more thing. *Fuck you.*"

I march out stabbing at the ground with my cane.

I drive straight to the kids' school and park in the lot in a visitor's space near the front doors. School doesn't get out for another forty-five minutes, but I'll be standing here waiting for them.

When they exit, Miranda is standing twenty feet behind me with her arms crossed. It feels like she's hovering over me. I pull my kids aside and explain to them that they're going to have to go live with their mother for a while. I break it to them as gently as I can and try to put a positive spin on it despite the words burning like acid on their way out. It kills me to watch their reactions. Kai goes stone-faced. Unblinking. He's shut down and crawled into his cave where he mulls over things that kids his age shouldn't have to contemplate. Internalizing them until they're a cancer on his soul. Rory pins Miranda with a stare that's contempt. He's already blaming her with his eyes for an unwelcome future and then he yells, "No!" That's all he says. And my little girl, she cries. She cries like I've never seen her cry.

And my heart shatters for the second time today. It's blown apart into so many pieces, the shrapnel spread so far and wide, I know what remains will never fit back together again. Puzzles don't work when you only have half of the pieces. Same goes for hearts.

I hug all three of them at once because I can't fathom excluding any of them while I hug their sibling alone. I hug them. I kiss them. I tell them all I love them more than anything else in the world, and that's when my eyes fill up. I'm trying with everything in me to hold back the tears because they're already scared and sad, and I don't want to stir up any more heavy emotion in them. But I can't help it, I feel like Miranda took an ax to the top of my head and split me in two. You would think everything inside me would feel dead, but it's the opposite. Everything inside me is exposed nerves, all raw, tingling, unmistakable pain and agony. It's emotional torture.

Her words are like salt poured in an open wound. "Come, children. We need to get to the airport. We have a flight to catch."

I sniff back the tears and wipe my eyes before I turn to look at her. "Follow me to my house so I can pack their things."

She shakes her head. It's hard; I swear there's no softness in this woman. "We don't have time. I'll buy them everything they need when we get home."

Kira's face loses all color. I've seen joy vanish temporarily from someone's eyes when a happy moment passes, but I've never seen it flushed entirely out of someone before. Kira just lost her innocent joy. It's gone, snatched away carelessly and thoughtlessly. "I need Pickles." Trepidation is rising in her voice. "I can't leave without Pickles."

Miranda looks at me in confusion. She didn't just see our daughter lose her innocence. She's annoyed that her schedule's being delayed. I explain, "She needs her stuffed cat. She can't fall asleep without it, Miranda."

Miranda shakes her head impatiently again. "We don't have time to get it, Kira." She says Kira's name but she's looking, she's talking, to me. "We'll get you another tomorrow."

Kira screeches in horror, "I don't want another one! I want Pickles!"

130

I struggle to kneel down on the ground, afraid I'll never get up again, take Kira's tiny hand in mine and kiss the back of it before I rub it to console her. "I'll mail Pickles to you, darlin'. I'll make sure you have her first thing in the morning. I promise."

The tears continue to stream, but she quiets for several seconds as she thinks over my solution. "Okay, Daddy."

I kiss her hand one more time and echo, "Okay."

And then I hug my kids again. I kiss my kids again. I tell them I love them again, and then I tell them, "I'm sorry. So much more than sorry." And I mean it with everything I am.

And then I watch them walk away with their mother.

And I feel myself die inside.

Everything wilts. Emotions, organs, thoughts, memories, hope…it all wilts. Like a leaf wilts due to lack of water or sunlight, they all turn in upon themselves until the edges are curled grotesquely and shriveled into something unrecognizable.

I walk home, partially because I fear driving would put others in danger — I'm enraged — and partially because I want to punish myself. I want my body to be forced into the action it rebels against. I want my muscles to struggle and my legs to protest. I want my head to throb angrily. I need to fight something, to fight someone, and since I'm the only one available, I'll fight myself.

After checking my dresser drawers and finding them weed-free, I grab Kira's stuffed cat from the couch and head right back out, down the stairs and to the post office three blocks away. I fall twice, even with my cane. There's a hole in the knee of my pants, and I could care less. They're khakis. I only wore them for the court related matters today because they're conservative and look like something Middle America would wear, which should earn me brownie points in the parental department. It

131

didn't today, obviously. The palm of my left hand is also bleeding from the run-in with the rough concrete. But I get Pickles into a Priority Express box for overnight delivery five minutes before they close.

And then I walk out and sit on the bench outside. The sun sets before I rise again.

I stop at a convenience store and make an impulse buy that is driven by soul-searing anger, along with a stick of beef jerky, and a cheap bottle of wine. I shove the angry purchase in my pocket and eat the beef jerky, chasing it with swigs of red on the walk back home.

I'm buzzed by the time I round the corner in front of my apartment complex, and I don't want to go upstairs. I'm too tired, so I sit under the tree, and I nurse the bottle until it's empty. And then I fall asleep like a proper wino, on the ground under the canopy of Mother Nature. I hope Miranda's private investigator is still watching because I'm putting on one helluva show tonight. I hoist my hand, middle finger raised, into the air before I let sleep pull me under just in case I have an unwelcome audience.

I'm awakened by the sound of Faith's scooter pulling up in front of her apartment. When she kills the motor, the world goes quiet. I hear her keys jingle followed by her door opening and closing.

That's when I struggle to my feet. My head is swimming in alcohol, and my legs don't just feel numb, they feel like they're made of lead.

Walking to her door is slow.

Knocking is clumsy.

She answers in her horrendous Rick's BBQ t-shirt, and I can't help but think how beautiful she is before I remember how much I'm supposed to hate her for her part in the *Shit Father of the Year* award I was presented earlier today. "Seamus, what's wrong?"

"Everything," I mutter as I stumble my way in. "Close your curtains."

She shuts the door behind me, draws the curtains closed, and watches me cautiously. Her apartment is a studio, just one room, and there's nowhere to sit except the futon cushion on the floor that has a blanket and pillow on it. I turn and glare at her remembering why I'm here. "Are you a prostitute?"

She narrows her eyes at me, but the shock I see in them is all the answer I need. It's innocence. "No. Why would you ask that?"

I pinch the bridge of my nose in frustration; anger is rising in me. "Have you ever *been* a prostitute? Ever taken money for sex? I'm begging you to be honest with me right now, Faith. What remains of my sanity depends on it."

She shakes her head and takes a step so that she's standing directly in front of me. "No. What's going on, Seamus?"

I believe her. She's just another pawn in Miranda's game. Any ill feelings I felt toward her disappear, but the anger is still bubbling within me, like a volcano preparing to erupt.

I reach out and run my fingertips along her cheek. A light touch and the restraint is physically taxing. Smashing things would relieve stress and anxiety; softness only makes it roil. When I get to her mouth, I switch to my thumb and increase pressure. Her bottom lip drags under my touch.

"Seamus?" she whispers my name. Her chest is rising and falling visibly now, and my mind is too fucked up to tell if it's fear or lust filling her lungs so purposefully.

I lower my forehead until it's resting against hers. My hand moves to the back of her neck. It's a gentle movement, caressing the skin there.

Her hands are on my chest now. She's not pushing me away. She's fanning her fingers apart and then squeezing them together tightly. It's the blatant, repetitive motion of someone restraining herself. Stalling until she's given permission.

"I need to forget it all for a few hours, Faith. Make me forget who I am."

I see a flash of understanding in her eyes. Sadness emerging. Demons of her own. Empathy. Agreement. She needs this too.

Our lips crush together. There's desperation in the union that makes kissing impossible. It's a battle to purge the hurt and assuage it simultaneously. Confusion reigns supreme in the clash. Tenderness is lacking. It's feasting and biting and sucking.

Buttons are torn from my shirt in an effort to remove it quickly. The swift release of my zipper sounds like a cannon in the silent, small room.

"I hate this shirt. It's fucking cheesy," I tell her as I rip it over her head.

"I hate these pants. Khakis are fucking boring," she counters, as she pulls down my pants and boxers in one swift jerk to my ankles.

There's a temporary truce in the war as we stand, looking each other up and down. She wasn't wearing any panties. We're both naked—physically and emotionally.

"I *hate* her," I hiss.

"I know," she says, willingly absorbing the venom.

"I need to get this hate out. I'm so full of it I can't breathe." The hate and anger is so intense I swear I can see it, touch it, smell it. It's driving me insane.

"Give me your hate, Seamus," she whispers. "And I'll give you mine."

"Deal," I say the word against her lips.

And just like that, we're at each other again. Mouths and hands are greedy. There's no trading of affection, no taking turns. We're just two people vying for their own bodily pleasure as if it's a hazard instead of gratification. Stimulation, touch, is reckless and rough. And though the wine has freed all my inhibitions, I feel like a different person. We're feeding each other, off of each other. My mouth is moving its way across her chest. Her teeth are skirting the hard edge of my ear. My hands are mapping out her body like they're memorizing the path to the Promised Land. She's touched every inch of me from the waist up and currently has a firm grip on me below the belt. Pulling the pin out of a grenade is how this all going to end, one giant, mutual explosion between the two of us.

"I need to lie down." My legs are unsteady and everything rushing through me isn't helping.

I grab my pants from the floor and pull my angry purchase, a box of condoms, out of the pocket and tear one end open. Pulling a strip from inside, I let the box fall like an afterthought before moving to her bed on the floor.

I'm on my back when she curls up next to me on the mattress, watching intently as I tear the packet open and sheath myself. When I roll on my side, she presses up against me. Her eyes and fingertips are slowly and affectionately tracing the features of my face. Calling on connection. Urgency is gone. What has been, up to this point, animalistic, just turned intimate. And the intimacy governs my hate, taking control and diluting it with Faith's innate goodness until all that remains is the need to pour love into this woman. The need to show her how she deserves to be loved.

And over the next hour, I learn something important.

Love is an act.

What we just did. The way our bodies and minds partnered to please each other — to put the other first — was making love. I'm in awe as I lie here beneath her, her body still trembling from aftershocks, my body slack from my release only a moment ago.

The kissing.

The careful attention shown.

135

The connection.

The words spoken.

The pace.

The quiet assurances.

The rhythm.

The climax.

Every last detail was an act of love.

I've never been given this gift.

I've never given this gift, not like this.

Which makes me treasure it even more because even though we're not in love, the transfer of love was so damn real.

I smile at her when she looks at me. "You took my hate and turned it into love."

She smiles back. "Gladly. You took mine, too, Seamus." It's her soft place to land voice.

I take a deep breath to calm my racing heart and initiate an embrace.

We wrap each other up in a tangle of limbs.

The hug lasts hours.

It endures deep sleep and emerges intact on the other side.

"Morning, neighbor." I know she's smiling before I open my eyes.

"Morning, neighbor." I'm smiling, too, until my hangover announces its intention to ruin my day. My stomach is queasy, and my head is ferociously reminding me that it doesn't like wine.

After I use her bathroom and dress, I sit down on the corner of Faith's bed. She's wearing the horrendous BBQ t-shirt again. I stare at the letters when I speak. I stare so hard that after a few seconds they're not letters any longer. "Miranda took my kids. They're gone." My voice is hollow, like my heart.

When she doesn't say anything, I pry my gaze from the blur of color on her shirt and meet her eyes. They've turned to liquid, sliding down her cheeks. She shakes her head. "How?"

"Lies. She's an evil bitch."

"What kind of lies? You're a great dad, Seamus." Her voice is calm, but the tears are still flowing.

"Apparently, I'm a drug user who's dating a prosti−" I cut myself off because I can't say it. I don't want to drag her into my nightmare.

She takes a deep breath and lets it out before she finishes for me. "Prostitute. She thinks because I'm a stripper, I'm a prostitute."

I nod. "It's worse. She's has signed statements from men who claim they've paid for sex. With you."

The tears are no longer silent. A hiccup sets off a deluge. "I've never, Seamus. You have to believe me. It takes everything in me to dance in front of strangers. *Everything in me*. It's degrading and makes me feel like an object, rather than a human being. I could never have sex with a stranger." She squats down in front of me and puts her hands on my knees. She's looking at me through mascara smeared eyes. "Last night was only the second time I've had sex, but it was the only time it mattered. What I gave you last night was special. You have no idea how special. I wouldn't do that with some random guy."

I hold her face in my hands. "I know, Faith." I do know. What happened between us last night was special. "I'm sure she paid people to write the statements. Or, hell, for all I know she wrote them. Like I said, she's evil." Faith's so fragile, so pure; I still can't erase the image of her topless on a stage from my mind. It doesn't reconcile with the person I know. "Why do you do it? Strip, I mean. I know you said it's part of your research, but there has to be more."

"I need the money." She sounds a little ashamed and a lot determined.

"Get a roommate," I challenge.

She looks around the room. "Where are they going to sleep? Not too many roommates like to share a bed, Seamus. This space isn't exactly conducive to more than one bed."

I nod. "Move somewhere else and get a roommate?"

She shakes her head. "My lease is almost up, but for now, I need to be here." She's adamant.

"Why?"

"Research," she says simply.

I shake my head at her evasiveness. "Research is not the answer to everything."

She closes her eyes as if she's frustrated. "It's my everything. I'm trying to find my birth mother. I thought maybe I could save some money and pay someone to help me search. I need to figure out who I am."

I scrub my hands over my face and mutter in agreement, "I need to forget who I am," before I look at her and say, "And you need to keep searching for your mom. That's important."

"You know who you are, Seamus. Don't forget. You need to fight for him. You need to fight for your kids. Get them back. They belong with you."

I nod. And then I huff. "It sounds so easy, doesn't it? Get them back." I huff again and run my hands through my hair. "Short of driving to Seattle and kidnapping them, it feels impossible." I look at her glare and correct myself, "It's not *impossible*. I know that, but it's daunting, you know? Like searching for your birth mother. Miranda has me by the balls. And she has money. I don't. That makes the fight that much harder."

She nods.

"I want them back *now*. I want to walk upstairs and see them sitting on the couch. Waiting another week to see them is too damn long, let alone Thanksgiving." Tears are threatening now. "Jesus Christ, my life is so fucked up."

She smiles sadly. "I'm sorry your children's mother is the Antichrist," I nod in agreement, "but you'll figure the rest out."

I nod.

"In the meantime, it sounds like my company is doing nothing to help your situation." It's an apology that comes before the apology...that comes before the delivery of bad news.

I narrow my eyes.

She smiles sweetly, but her eyes are already welling up. "I'm sorry, Seamus. We can't be together, we both know it. You'll never get your kids back if we are." She looks up at the ceiling blinking rapidly, but it doesn't dam the tears. They break free and roll down her cheeks. She's still not looking at me. "You have no idea how much it hurts to say that. It fucking kills me." She drops her chin and lines her eyes up with mine, and I feel the words in her stare. "I've moved around a lot in my life. I've met a lot of people. I like your heart, Seamus." She cups my cheek, kisses me softly on the corner of my mouth, and whispers, "My heart *really* likes your heart."

She's right.

I don't want her to be right.

But she is.

Goddammit.

I stand up with her help. And we have a long conversation with our eyes. I tell her everything my mouth can't say because words are futile and don't have a future beyond her front door.

And then I ask her for another hug.

The embrace is everything we just said with our eyes. Every promise we couldn't make. I don't want to let her go. Her t-shirt is balled up in my fists in a desperate attempt to wring every last bit of Faith out of this moment and take it with me when I walk out that door. Her tears have soaked the front of my shirt by the time we part. And when I walk out neither one of us says anything, because there's nothing left to say.

Jesus, Mary, and Joseph

Seamus

present

My desk phone rings as soon as I unlock my office door.

"This is Mr. McIntyre," I answer.

"Seamus," Janet clears her throat, "can you please come to the office to see me immediately. I'm sorry." The way she says it makes me uncomfortable. I like Janet, but I'm beginning to hate it when she calls.

I walk slowly as if the bad news will diminish or disappear by the time I get there if I take my time.

It doesn't.

Janet waves me into an empty office to the right of her desk and closes the door behind us. I don't know what she's about to say, but I'm already thankful for the privacy she's provided. She hands me a form. "They want you to take a drug test this morning, Seamus. You'll need to leave right now to make the appointment." She's biting her bottom lip like she's sorry she has to deliver the news, and she hopes I'm clean, all in one worrying gesture.

"Who's they?"

She looks around like we aren't alone and then she lowers her voice, "I'm not supposed to say anything, but administration called Friday afternoon to inform me of the screening appointment." She stops and nervously licks her lips. "And earlier in the day, a manila envelope was delivered to Principal Brentwood from your ex-wife's attorney's office. It wasn't sealed, only clasped," she closes her eyes when she admits her wrongdoing, "and I opened it and read the documents inside. There was a letter stating your suspected drug use and a photo—"

I stop her. "Jesus."

"Mary and Joseph," she says under her breath. It's a statement of solidarity. She knows I've been through hell with Miranda. "Seamus, this is serious. Any suspicion of drug use results in immediate testing, you know that. And if found positive, there's a zero tolerance policy, you would be terminated." She's asking, without asking, if I can pass the test.

I hold her gaze and plead with her, "I don't do drugs, Janet. You have to believe me. It's not what it looks like."

She nods her head in relief. "I believe you, Seamus. Now, take the test and prove it to them."

I took the test.
I was clean.
Fuck you, Miranda.

No one measures up to a saint

Miranda

past

True to my word I filed for divorce, and had Seamus served with papers Monday while he was at work.

He didn't see it coming.

He's waiting up for me when I get home late. The kids are already in bed, as usual. I should've gone to a hotel, but the house is big enough for all of us to live in and continue to avoid each other.

He's sitting, facing the front door, in an armchair he's dragged in from the living room, when I walk in. He's clutching a bottle of beer in his hand. There are five identical, empty bottles lined up at his feet. "Who is he?"

I'm irritated that he's not letting me set my purse down or take my jacket off, before he starts attacking me. I don't answer him right away.

He waits patiently and takes a long pull from the bottle.

"Who is who?" I ask innocently.

"The man you're leaving me for?" His voice is quiet, which worries me more than if he were yelling. And the white-knuckle grip he has on the bottle in his hand tells me anger is at the surface, barely contained.

"I just can't do this anymore, Seamus." I don't know why I feel like I need to keep this vague. I've been waiting years for this day, working toward my destiny, and now that it's finally here it's harder than I thought it would be.

I have to trade in my get out of hell free card.

Fuck.

"Does he have more money than me? Is that it?"

Loads, I think.

"Is he better looking?"

No. Good looking, but no one's better looking than you.

"Drives a fancy car?"

Someone drives him around in a fancy car.

"Buys you expensive gifts?"

Not in years.

He's firing questions at me, his voice rising. I'm not answering any of them out loud. And then it turns personal, his voice biting and accusatory. "Does he love and care for your children?"

He doesn't want children. Not even his own.

"Does he look after you when you're sick?"

He'd ask the housekeeper to do it.

"Does he bring you food when you pull an all-nighter at work?"

He wouldn't think of it.

"Does he get up before the sun comes up on your birthday and make you pecan pancakes with extra butter and syrup because they're your favorite?"

He doesn't cook. Or know that I love pecan pancakes.

"Does he know that you like your back rubbed when you can't sleep because it relaxes you and makes you tired?"

He's not one to comfort.

The truth in his questions, and my undisclosed answers, has me wanting to run for the door to escape this confrontation. I wanted to tell him I was leaving. And for him to quietly accept it. He's not supposed to fight me on this. He's not supposed to make me think. I can taste something hurtful and mean on the tip of my tongue.

"What is it about him that makes him better for you than me?!" he bellows.

"He's not broken!" There it is. The worst thing I can say to him. The thing that will destroy him. Because he believes it. He knows he's a good father, husband, counselor, human being. He knows that and never doubts

144

it. His health he can't change, and he wishes so badly he could. It's his Achilles heel. And I just used it against him.

I'm going to burn in hell atop the hottest pyre for all of eternity.

Because the truth, everything else aside, is that no one's better for me than Seamus. In the deep, dark recesses of my mind, I know that. And it's not his MS that's driving me away. Do I like it? No. Does it make him less attractive in my eyes? Yes. But does it make him less of a man than Loren? No. It's everything that goes along with Loren that I want. Seamus can't be the king to my queen.

Because he's a saint.

And no one measures up to a saint.

He doesn't refute my claim. He doesn't fight me. He stands, drinks down the rest of his beer, tosses the bottle on the floor with the others, and walks toward the hall. Before he turns the corner, he looks back. He holds me in a stare that has my emotions folding in upon each other until my stomach aches. When he finally speaks, it's low and clear. I forgot how much I loved Seamus's voice all those years ago when we first started dating. The first time he spoke to me butterflies fluttered in my chest. "He'll never love you like I do."

And then he walked away.

I felt the connection we'd had for over twelve years snap like a rubber band.

Another *fuck you* from the universe, and I can hear it laughing at me this time, too.

Choking on thick smoke

Seamus

One month rolls into the next.

My eyesight returned. Slowly, and deficient from what it once was, but I'm not complaining, I'll take what I can get in the vision department. Feeling is somewhat returning to my legs again, the numbness replaced by tingling, pain, and easy fatigue. I've lost weight; my appetite just isn't there. I don't dwell on any of it. At this point, I've forgotten what a healthy body and mind feel like. I exist, that's about the extent of it.

Work is work, a job that used to be fulfilling is now just a job. I take the kids I work with seriously, and do everything I can to help them, but my motives are obligation and duty, my heart's no longer driving it.

I don't talk to anyone outside of work except Mrs. L once a month when I drop off the rent check. She's good at asking loaded questions meant to flush out substance and emotion. I recognize the approach, I'm a counselor. She's so kind and caring that I find myself swallowing back the honesty that wants badly to escape and replace it with vague evasiveness that pacifies instead.

I miss Faith. I miss her so much. I used to watch her come and go from her apartment. Studying the way she walked, the way she carried herself with such graceful, unassuming confidence. And admiring it because I know it's not a product of her upbringing. She invested in herself and manifested it. That's remarkable, a thing of beauty. I don't watch anymore because studying her soon felt like stalking her. The torture of not being able to have her in

146

my life distorted observation into forbidden leering. I'm not a creeper.

I call my kids every evening. Sometimes I get to talk to them, and more often than not there's an excuse as to why they aren't available. It makes me furious that Miranda has this control. My fury should be calmed with words, talking to someone I trust but that person is Faith, and I can't, so most nights I calm my fury with alcohol and a sleep aid my doctor prescribed. It doesn't dispel, it only erases consciousness for a few hours. I'll take that. And when I do get to talk to my kids my body is on such a rollercoaster I feel exhausted when I get off the line. I'm happy beyond belief to hear their voices, but they sound distant, the kind of apprehension that's a reaction to sadness. That breaks me. They used to tell me they wanted to come home, now time and complacency to circumstances beyond our control has worn them quickly until all of their hard edges, their personality traits that made them so distinct, are being smoothed over to blend them into Miranda's bland, strict world—a world where children don't exist as children. There's no fun, no creativity, no fostering of individuality because none of those things serve you well in a world of money-focused, soul-sucking, career-driven existence. Rory's dropped his accent. Kira's sweet chatter is gone, so is Pickles the cat. And Kai is silent; silence not related to introspection, but the scary silence that is the surrender of self and motivation.

She's sucking the life out of my kids.

I keep the conversations positive, encourage them with every word whether they acknowledge my comment or not. Talking to them this way was second nature all their lives, even if I felt like shit or my mind was muddled in the chaos of adulting in Miranda's world, talking to them was always easy. They were my light, my fire that I never wanted to dwindle. I wanted it to grow stronger, brighter, bolder, so I fed it by the day...by the hour...by the minute. Because that's what parents do, without even thinking about it, *that's what parents do*. They fill their children with love and understanding and compassion and knowledge so that when they're adults no one can extinguish them. They'll burn so bright they can't be brought down.

Feeding now takes effort because their fire has been reduced to a small flicker leaving only an ember that I feel like I'm trying to ignite with water-sodden branches and soggy newspaper.

And it's generating only thick smoke.

That I'm choking on.

So are they.

I used to write them a letter every day and mail it. They never saw them. I know because I asked. I'm sure Miranda's housekeeper intercepted the mail and gave the letters to her. I even sent a few certified. A signature was refused, and the letters were returned to me. I still write the letters I just don't mail them anymore. Instead, I keep them in a shoebox that I'll give to my kids when I see them next. She can delay communication, but she can't shut it down entirely.

Sulking in the cesspool of villainy

Seamus

present

Thanksgiving.

It's finally Thanksgiving.

My first visitation since Miranda stole custody.

School's out the entire week, so I pack up the car on Tuesday morning with a suitcase of clothes, a cooler of food and water, the shoebox of letters to my kids, and a heart full of hope I've missed for so long, and I drive north.

I drive eleven hours before I give up and stop at a rest area and let sleep consume me for several hours making the final few hours of driving possible.

My legs ache when I pull up to the gate in front of Miranda's address, and eyestrain has launched the indignant insurgency taking place inside my skull, a violent thumping.

The pain is easily pushed aside by excitement, though. My kids, *my kids*, are on the other side of that fence, inside that house, waiting for me.

I call Miranda's cell. No answer.

I call her house phone and the housekeeper answers, "Buckingham residence." Her accent is thick.

"May I speak to Kai, please?"

She knows it's me on the line, but she keeps up the air of formality, even through her broken English and heavy accent. "Kai not here."

Something feels off, even with the formality. "What? This is his father. I'm here to pick up my kids."

She clears her throat and delivers the death punch with an assertiveness I'm sure even Miranda would

149

admire. "Mrs. Buckingham and kids on vacation. They be back Monday."

My anger is delayed by disbelief. Disbelief is short-lived. Anger implodes, gutting me before it explodes on her. "Where in the hell are my kids?" The words come from the bowels of that deep, dark place where hate is born.

The line goes dead on my rage.

I throw my phone on the seat next to me and climb out of my car. Before I know it I'm beating on the iron gate with my cane, hurling obscenities at the oversized, pretentious structure that is supposed to house my children.

A stout, steely looking woman emerges from the front door and stomps toward me. The look on her face is a mixture of annoyance and fear. She's waving her arms in front of her urging me to be quiet.

To hell with quiet.

"Where are my kids?" I yell again. Projecting my voice isn't necessary, she's standing six feet from me, but my rage won't allow civil volume. "So help me God, if you don't tell me where my kids are —"

She cuts me off, "Quiet," she hisses. "They not here. I told you." Her eyes are darting back and forth, never falling on me; she's assessing the street to see if my commotion is drawing any attention. She looks nervous now, the vibrato she exuded over the phone is gone.

I take in a deep breath through my nose. It's a nostril-flaring intake meant to quell anger. It doesn't. I take another. Still nothing. So, I dive back in speaking through clenched teeth to moderate the volume. "Where did they go?"

She shakes her head emphatically, her words hurried like she's trying to speed up my departure, "I not know. They no tell me."

I'm staring into her eyes, trying to read her. I see nothing but fear now. She's scanning the street again. I turn my back on her and slam my fist down on the hood of my car. "Fuuuuuuuuck!" It's a long, drawn out release of frustration, rattling out on all the air my lungs will hold. And when it's purged it hangs heavily around me, as if I'm surrounded by hate so tangible I can touch it. Punch it. Strangle it with my bare hands.

Arguing with her is useless. The ache in my chest tells me she's not lying and that my kids aren't here.

The stubborn side of me tells me to wait it out, in case she's lying, and see if they either come out of the house or return home.

I wait.

I eat two peanut butter sandwiches and drink a bottle of water from my stash.

After the sun goes down, I pee behind Miranda's high hedges next to the gate.

I doze off around three in the morning and sleep for an hour.

I pee behind the hedges again before the sun comes up.

I eat an apple and another peanut butter sandwich and drink my last bottle of water.

After twenty-four hours of sulking in the cesspool of Miranda's villainy, I relent and leave.

I drive straight through, only stopping for gas.

My body, mind, and spirit are wrecked by the time I get home.

I write my kids a letter telling them about every evil thing their mother has ever done. I tell them how much I hate her. And how much they should hate her. And how sorry I am that she's in their life. And how I wish she would die and rot in hell.

And then I crumple it up and throw it in the trash because my kids don't need my hate.

They need my love.

So, I pull out another piece of paper and I write:

November 28

Kai, Rory, and Kira,

I love you so much. Every second, whether you're with me or not, I love you. Always remember that.

Dad

I fold it in half and tuck it in the shoebox with the others.

And then I drink some tequila and skip the sleeping pill because I'm already so tired I can't see straight, and I fall into a state of rest so solid that it takes fourteen hours for me to deconstruct it and emerge on the other side.

When I do my chest still feels hollow, like Miranda took a blunt spoon to it, emptying the cavity of my life force and ability to love or see the good in anything.

Shedding regret like snakeskin

Miranda

I'm standing in what was, up until an hour ago, my master bedroom. It belongs to someone else now. I shouldn't be here. I signed the closing paperwork and handed over the keys this morning. But I kept one so I could come back and say goodbye.

The room is empty. There are indentations in the carpet where the four-poster bed and dresser stood. An imperfect reminder that there used to be life in this room.

Now it's quiet.

And cold.

Like me.

The divorce is final. I've been in Seattle with Loren for weeks. Living my new life. The life I wanted.

That's what I keep reminding myself—it's the life I wanted.

Loren and I were married last night. He arranged for a minister to come to his house to conduct the ceremony. It lasted five minutes. I lied to Seamus and told him we were headed to Europe this morning for an extended honeymoon. There won't be a honeymoon; we didn't even go out for dinner afterward.

I close my eyes and let grief and loss and regret overtake me, something I never do. Something I never allow. But that's why I'm here. It's been eating at me, and I hate it. I feel like a snake trapped in skin I'm trying to shed, but it won't fall away. It sticks with me, itchy and uncomfortable. I need to release it so I can move on.

I can see Seamus in my mind, so handsome. Hair as dark as midnight and eyes to match. Eyes that didn't just look upon me, they looked into me. Golden brown skin he

153

received from his mother and a tall, broad frame that could swallow me up when he wrapped me in it.

And now that I can feel his touch again, there are tears in my eyes. He's the only man I've ever been with who made love to me. Even if I didn't return it, he gave me all of him, his body and his heart, because that's how he did everything. I took it for granted. I gravitated toward the physicality of sex with others because it was need driven, solely to satisfy an itch. I couldn't reciprocate love driven. But I realize now how much I loved receiving it.

I traded in love for power.

It wasn't a fair trade.

Not even close.

I always thought I was the one in control where Seamus was concerned. Fooling him to ensure he participated in our love. I told myself the attention I showed him was brokering. I gave an inch. I gained a mile. Disproportionate, that's how our relationship functioned. He never noticed, or if he did he never let on because I married a giver, not a taker. He was content receiving a compliment here and there, or a loving touch when I could spare it, or the occasional deep conversation. Seamus was easy, quality over quantity. Presence enthralled him and he made the most of every minute. At the time, I thought I coaxed it out of him with skillful manipulation. Sitting in this room, mired in regret, I wonder if my skillful manipulation was nothing more than Seamus coaxing actual feelings out of me. While I thought I was inciting compliance with orchestrated attention, I was merely reacting to his attention. Craving it, however sparingly.

I'm going to sit in this room and I'm going to cry myself out.

I hate crying and the longer I cry, the angrier I become.

Angry with me. Angry with Loren. Angry with Seamus. Angry with feelings I don't want to feel. Angry with depression that's threatening to smother me. Angry with the helplessness and loneliness that's become my constant companion.

Just fucking angry.

And I want everyone else to feel it with me.

Sometimes a blessing is disguised as despair

Seamus

present

Sometimes I drive to our old neighborhood. I never drive by the house Miranda and I owned. I go to the library and mill around. Or I sit in the park and watch toddlers feed stale bread to the birds. Or I go to the grocery store and buy a jar of pickles.

Today I'm doing all three because it makes me feel closer to my kids. I picture them so clearly in my mind when I'm in a familiar setting we used to go too often. I hit the library and park first, and I'm walking into the grocery store when a voice stops me, "Seamus? Seamus McIntyre?"

I turn and don't recognize the woman staring at me until she smiles. It's a smile that turns a puckered, sour, resting face into something friendly and warm. I nod. "Justine, it's good to see you." Justine was Miranda's assistant for years. I talked to her a lot, mostly on the phone because she was the easiest way to relay messages to Miranda if I needed her while she was at work. Justine was audacious and outspoken, which is probably the reason she kept her job, Miranda recognized and liked another viper in the pit. The thing she failed to notice was that Justine had a heart behind the tough exterior. It wasn't a soft, endearing heart that gained her friends and admirers; it was an honest heart that was selective about what, or whom, it showed concern. And that concern was hard-edged, sometimes hard to hear, but untouched by evil intent. She always asked me about the kids when I called. When I was diagnosed with MS, she fussed over me like a domineering mother during every conversation.

156

And the last time I talked to her, the day after Miranda told me she was leaving me, Justine said, "Sometimes a blessing is disguised as despair." I was shell shocked by Miranda's announcement and didn't give Justine's words much thought, but they're echoing profoundly from my memory now.

She shakes my hand. "It's good to see you, too, Seamus." It's firm and professional, but she adds a pat on the back of my hand to soften it. I've always imagined the pat was her attempt at connection. Her no-nonsense temperament hinders physical interaction; it's like a barrier to ward off the unwanted. Which makes the pat that much more genuine, because I have a feeling it's hard for her to translate her heart into her actions. I think back to Faith alluding to growing up never being hugged. I wonder if that's how Justine grew up too. "How are you holding up? You look like hell. Tired. You're not taking care of yourself, are you?" There it is, the caring heart blended with no filter.

I shrug. I can't lie to her. She can smell bullshit like a bloodhound.

She shakes her head. "How are the kids doing?"

"They live in Seattle with Miranda." The words feel traitorous coming out.

She looks knocked for a loop; her face has never been one to hide a reaction. She blinks several times before her eyes go wide and she asks, "Pardon me?" The question isn't asked to clarify the information I relayed; it's an exclamation of shock.

I nod in agreement. "Yeah. She fabricated a nice little case against me and took my kids a few months ago. I haven't seen them, and she barely lets me talk to them." I swallow hard because I haven't talked to anyone about this, except myself when I have too much to drink late at night.

Her eyes are still wide. "I could never understand why a man like you put up with a woman like her."

157

"What do you mean?"

Her eyes have settled into the motherly expression she usually reserved for me. "You're good. She's not. Like water and oil, you never should've come together."

"She did give me three beautiful kids." I'm not defending her, not in the least, but it's true.

She pulls both of her lips in between her teeth, and her eyes are looking just over my right shoulder like she's thinking something over. Something important that she's not sure she should share. When she meets my eyes again, her mouth is drawn into a hard line. "May I have your address, Seamus?"

My eyebrows draw together in confusion, and I question, "Why?"

There's resolve in her eyes, but there's sadness too. "I need to write you a letter," she says it like it explains everything, so when I don't react or answer, she continues, "There's something you should know."

I'm still confused, and I can't deny the heat creeping through me, uneasy pulses generated by the twisting that's begun in my stomach. "Tell me," I urge her. My voice sounds stronger than I feel.

She shakes her head and the motherly smile returns, but it's crestfallen and apologetic. "I can't. My heart might be made of stone, but I have some compassion. This needs to be delivered in privacy, not standing in front of a grocery store for the world to see. You deserve that."

"Tell me," I plead again.

She takes a deep breath, and her lips drop into a frown that matches her eyes. "I don't..." I think that's where it's going to end, but it doesn't, "want to see your reaction. I don't want to be the one who hurts you, Seamus."

"But you're just the bearer of bad news."

"It doesn't matter whether I'm the one who did the act, or I'm only the one informing you of the act—the bearer of bad news is always the unfortunate person to absorb the shockwave of intense emotion immediately after impact. I don't do well with intense or emotion. I'm sorry, Seamus. May I have your address?"

I suddenly feel nauseous. I reach into my pocket and pull out a gas receipt, scrawl my address on the back, and hand it to her without another word.

She takes it from me, folds it precisely in half, sticks it in a pocket on her purse, and then extends her hand to me.

I take in the shake, hand pat and all. I know it's an apology.

"Take care of yourself, Seamus. Your kids belong with you. See what can be done to make it happen. And have some faith."

I don't say anything. I can't say anything. When her hands leave mine, she enters the store. I decide I feel too sick to look at pickles and turn around and walk to my car.

And I drive home and wait for a letter that I'm sure will break my heart.

Again.

Compressed wood pulp and bad intention

Seamus

Present

Two days later I'm standing on the W...E mat, favoring the E half when I pull three items out of the mailbox next to my door.

The first is my cell phone bill.

"Next," I say out loud, as if by flipping to the next piece of correspondence this phone bill will be erased from existence.

The second is a flyer for a Chinese restaurant down the street. My mouth waters at the sight of the sesame chicken photo on the front until I remember that their food tastes like shit and looks nowhere this appetizing.

"Next," I say, swallowing down the rancid reminder of a bad meal I had weeks ago.

The third.

The third is...

I drop the papers in my hands as if their heart-wrenching contents, words written on compressed wood pulp, have already singed my hands with their bad intention.

My mail is now lying on the W...E mat, perfectly placed between the W and the E.

Justine's handwriting is scowling at me. The letters each written deliberately, pressed deeply into the paper by the point of a pen with purpose. They scare me.

I know I should think of the mat as the unwelcome mat again, but the truth is, all I can think about is WE. Faith and me. I can't read this letter without her.

So, without giving it any logical thought, because logic would tell my heart to shut the hell up, I pick up the

160

letter and make my way downstairs to her apartment and knock on the door.

She doesn't answer, so I knock again in desperation because anxiety is starting to fill my lungs like water.

Tears accompany the silence that follows the unanswered knock.

I lean my forehead against the door and beg, "Faith, *please answer the door*. I need you." And then I cover my mouth to cap off the sound and I sob.

I never thought I had a type

present

Seamus.

Seamus McIntyre.

The first time I laid eyes on him, he literally took my breath away. That's never happened. I stopped breathing for several seconds, as if it was physically impossible for me to draw air into my lungs until my brain let the imprint of his perfection settle in and develop into a memory I'd be able to recall at will when I needed something beautiful to focus on. I never thought I had a type. Apparently that's because I'd never met Seamus McIntyre. As soon as I saw him, I didn't want to look away. Ever. He was tall, the kind of tall that denotes a definite presence, but the way he moved and postured himself signaled a kind and laid-back nature. His dark hair was short but looked like he was overdue for a cut, the perfect mix of untamed and messy that a little extra length creates. It also hinted that he wasn't the kind of guy who was hung up on his appearance—the worn out jeans, scuffed up Doc Martens, and simple white t-shirt backed up my theory. Everything about his face, the set of his jaw covered in days old scruff, high cheekbones, strong nose, and dark, deep-set, mysterious eyes, was a contradiction. Intensity versus gentleness. Youth versus wisdom. Strength versus vulnerability. I'd never seen such an expressive resting face. And after getting to know him, I realize it's because he doesn't hide anything— it's all there written all over his features.

The first thing that attracted me to Seamus, the man, was when I watched him squat down on the sidewalk to talk to his little girl, Kira. She was crying, a hiccupping, distressed howl. The transition from standing to kneeling isn't a big deal for most people, but for him it is. He could've patted her on the head or just talked to her, but he didn't. He struggled to get down on his knees, the progression slow and painful, but also beautiful to watch, because I knew at that moment, that he would do anything for his kids. *Anything for his kids*. It was so simple, but so telling. And that's when I realized that being attracted to someone happens at a visceral level. It happens when you see and feel the other person's heart and your heart twinges in your chest in reaction. I watched him get face to face with his daughter, so he could look her in the eye while he consoled and then hugged her. That's when my heart decided it liked Seamus McIntyre more than any other person I'd ever met before.

The first time I kissed Seamus, my mind went blank and ran wild all at once. I was stunned by physical sensation. And decided that though other men's mouths had moved against mine, I had never been kissed until that moment. Seamus's lips told a story. A story I wanted to live in. Forever. A realistic story that was sprinkled with darkness, but that always came back to light. A light that made me believe love exists. Pure, intentional, forgiving, enduring love. Bone-jarringly beautiful love. He took his time, pace was part of the allure and signified sincerity. There was presence and intent in every movement, every sigh, every moan. Seamus's kiss was a kiss within a kiss...within a kiss...within a kiss. Layers upon layers of Seamus assaulting my senses in the most satisfying, impassioned way.

The first, and only time we had sex, Seamus gave me a gift. He didn't know he was giving it to me. He doesn't know my past because I haven't burdened him with the truth, but he vanquished some of my demons that night. He made love to me. It was everything he'd previously poured into a kiss amplified until it was pure bliss. A deep connection of mind, body, and spirit I didn't think could exist between two people, especially within the confines of sex. Only Seamus. That's the night I fell in love with him. All of him.

The first time I said goodbye to Seamus, my heart shattered. It was a blast that obliterated me, leaving only dust and making the task of putting the pieces back together impossible. But through it, my mind kept going back to something he told me, *so much more than thank you.* So. Much. More. Seamus was so much more. He needed to fight for his kids. They were, and should be, the most important things in his life. And I needed to find and fix myself. I call it research, and it's far from complete. I like to think that given another place and another time, we could've turned into something more. We could've been a *we.*

My time here is up. I gave myself six months to find my birth mother. I knew it was a long shot, I don't even know her name, but I thought faith, not me but the incredible, unseen force, would lead me to her. An invisible force in the universe would grant me my wish because I believe in miracles. I believe everyone gets one in their lifetime.

I guess it's not time for mine yet.

I said good riddance to my job last night and vowed to never do it again. I'm walking away with some perspective, though; everyone does what they need to do to survive. Some of the girls were single parents trying to raise a child on their own. Some girls were students trying to put themselves through college. Some girls were drug addicts trying to numb a pain no human being deserves. We all stripped to survive, it's only the *what we were surviving* part that was different.

I talked to Mrs. L early this morning and thanked her for her hospitality. I told her I might be back in a few weeks. I won't. I think she knew. She gave me a toasted pastrami on rye and the tie-dye scarf she was wearing as a parting gift. The sandwich was delicious, and the scarf smells like patchouli.

I visited Hope this afternoon. I took a bag of groceries, mostly fruit because she eats like shit otherwise, and told her goodbye. I hugged her like I always do when I leave. I don't think she understands that she'll never see me again, that's what goodbye means this time. It means I won't be back tomorrow to say hello and check on her, even though I worry about her and want to. It means I won't bring her leftovers, even though I worry she doesn't eat regularly and she's too thin. It means I won't bring her clothes when I find something in her size at the thrift shop on sale, even though I like to replace her threadbare, worn out, dirty clothes, with something new to her and clean. It means I won't watch her favorite movie with her again, even though it makes us both laugh every time we watch it. It means I won't buy her toothpaste or deodorant when she runs out, even though she needs the reminder sometimes, and I don't mind being that reminder.

It means I'll miss her. I'll miss her dry sense of humor that peeks out when I least expect it. I'll miss her mismatched outfits and her rumpled, constant bedhead that she won't let me brush. I'll miss her obsession with the pop radio station and her need to randomly sing at the oddest times. I'll miss that look in her eyes she gets sometimes that makes me think she sees things the rest of us don't.

I gave Hope an envelope with Seamus's name on it and asked her to give it to him. It's a letter telling him I'm leaving and that I'll miss him, and asking him to watch out for Hope. I don't know if she'll do it, but I'm hoping that her delivering the letter will ease them into interaction. She's standoffish at first.

Sadness I didn't expect overtook me as I walked out of her apartment. I tried to hide the emotion, but Hope felt it. There are a lot of things she doesn't understand — she's a simple woman — but there's almost a sixth sense about her. She always knows what I'm feeling. I told her goodbye a second time. She told me she loved me. I told her I loved her too, and that's when the tears fell and I had to leave. No one's ever told me that.

It's late now, way past dark. I'm sitting under the tree in the spot that Seamus and I ate our first picnic. I'm watching his front window, the light's still on. I'm waiting for him to go to bed, but until then I'm soaking up this last of our time together. I'm recalling every memory, every conversation, every smile I shared with him and his kids. And I'm wishing for their future, a future together and happy because they all deserve it. I've been waiting for it for hours, but when, in a fraction of a second, light blinks to dark, it's jolting. The inevitable turned into a surprise. I hate surprises.

I also hate goodbyes.

That's why I'm walking up the stairs to his apartment, and I'm not going to knock on his door. Instead, I stand on the W...E mat, right in the center, and I kiss the number three on his door. "So much more, Seamus. So much more."

French onion dip and damage control compost

Seamus
present

Three more days pass until I'm able to pick up Justine's envelope again. It's Friday night, or more accurately Saturday morning, just past one o'clock. I've had a few beers, and I don't want to take my sleeping pill. I'm restless. It's restlessness that demands action of some sort or another. I've paced the living room. That wrapped up quickly because my legs hurt. I watched a movie on Netflix that was so unimpressive I can't recall the plot thirty minutes after finishing it. I ate the rest of the French onion dip I had in the fridge with the crumb-sized pieces of chips left in the bag in the pantry. The French onion dip expired last week, I'll probably end up with the runs; it wasn't my best judgment call. I'm blaming the alcohol.

I need something, anything, to occupy me.

And then my eyes land on it and I'm backpedaling, taking back the word *anything* and just leaving it at *something* to occupy me; it's Justine's letter.

My name and address are still scowling.

I pick it up from the end table and walk into the kitchen to drop it in the trash. It lands amongst today's still soppy coffee grounds and the mostly empty dip container. I watch as the stark white paper greedily wicks up the moisture from both, tinting one side deep brown and speckling the other side with spots of creamy curdle.

Satisfied I've stripped the letter of all its dignity, I return to the couch and flip through the Netflix menu. The futile act distracts me for about five seconds before I walk back to the kitchen and pull the disgraced envelope from the trash. Wiping the coffee grounds off of it with my hand, I open it over the bin and let the envelope fall back to its fate as compost.

The letter is only a single sheet of paper. Unlined. Each word, just like on the envelope, written purposefully with a heavy hand, as if the pressure used to write the words would translate into a dramatic delivery stressing the importance of the message. The stationary is lightweight, but the slickness in texture notes its high quality. It's dry and unblemished on the right side, and the left side is a blotchy watercolor of various shades of brown that make the paper translucent, though still legible.

I walk to the sink and stand over it while I begin to read. I don't know why because the paper isn't wet enough to drip. Maybe I just need the counter to lean against and prop me, and my sanity, up.

Dear Seamus,

I'll keep this short because drawing out the delivery of bad news just makes it hurt longer.

A year before Kira was born, Miranda was pregnant. She never told you. She didn't want another baby. Her exact words that I will never forget as long as I live were,

"I've given Seamus two; I'm not going through that bullshit again. I'll be off Friday, put the appointment on my calendar and title it damage control." That was her flippant response when I handed her a phone message I'd taken while she was in a meeting—it was an appointment reminder. I recognized the name because it was an abortion clinic that made the news a few years prior when a protest turned violent.

She had the abortion and then spent the weekend at a spa in Malibu. I have no idea what sort of lie she fed you.

I'm sorry,

J.

168

I would say I'm reeling from the news, but to reel you have to feel. And I feel nothing. My blood has gone stagnant in my veins. My heart seized mid-beat and decided function was no longer necessary. All synapses, in a split second, boycotted in unison making thought and action impossible.

Nothing.

Nothing slowly transforms, setting off an insidious barrage of emotion.

The shock and betrayal is staggering as if my entire body and mind have been concussed by the news, and I'm now left to process her actions with a shock-induced, modified conscience. Right and wrong are glaringly obvious in my judgment of her. Right and wrong blur noxiously in my reaction to her. I'd love nothing more than to exact revenge. Revoke her life, for revoking my child's.

The hate blazing through me is making it hard to breathe. I feel claustrophobic. I need to go outside.

The air outside is considerably cooler than inside, but it does nothing to ease emotion. There's too much and it feels like it's gnawing at my insides. Feasting and gorging until soon I'll just be a shell filled with nothing but rage.

Panic starts to set in, and the only person I want to talk to is Faith. Fuck Miranda if she still has a PI following me. "Fuck you!" I yell as I descend the stairs. "Fuck you!" I yell again as I conclude the stairs.

I knock on Faith's door. It's loud, both due to the absence of most other sound because of the late hour, and to my angry, heavy hand.

"She don't live there no more." The voice is quiet, meek, but nearby.

So nearby that it startles me out of my solitary focus. It's the woman from apartment one, Hope. And then her words hit me, and I'm questioning and denying her statement all in one word, "What?"

169

"The girl, Faith, she left a few days ago." She sounds mildly sad, but for the most part the words are delivered void of attachment or feeling like she keeps everything buried deep inside.

She's sitting on the ground just outside her open front door smoking a cigarette. I walk toward her but stop when I'm several feet away remembering how skittish she was the only other time I talked to her. "Where did she go?" I ask.

She shrugs while she takes an ugly pull from the cigarette, her cheeks drawing in exaggeratedly, and due to her frail appearance she looks like skin stretched over a delicate framework of bones.

"Did she tell you she was leaving?" The inflection I put on certain words makes them sound accusatory, like a mouthy teenager who doubts the validity of what they're being told.

My tone doesn't change her demeanor. She's no less timid, and no friendlier, than normal. She nods, still sucking on the cigarette like it's a lifeline.

I shake my head, annoyed with her wordless responses, and turn to go back upstairs.

She speaks when I'm only a few steps away. "She's the only person I talk to besides Mrs. Lipokowski. Faith," she adds as if clarification is necessary. "The only friend I got."

Maybe if you weren't nuttier than squirrel shit and came out of your apartment more often people would talk to you, is what I almost say, but then I realize that's the rage in me talking, and it's mean. So, I say, "Yeah, Faith was special," instead.

She doesn't agree. She doesn't disagree. She just looks at me with her dead eyes and says, "I got to walk to the convenience store down the street. You wanna come?" The way she says it I know she won't be disappointed if I say no, and she won't be happy if I say yes, either answer will elicit a neutral reaction out of her.

170

Which is one of the reasons I say yes—no pressure. The other is I'm out of beer. I check my pocket for money and my keys and nod.

Without a word she steps inside her door, slips into some worn out, dirty flip-flops, and grabs her wallet off the floor. I notice she doesn't pick up the keys on a key ring lying next to her wallet and a thick stack of mail.

When she begins to close her door, I ask, "Don't you need your keys?"

"No," she answers blandly.

"But you'll lock yourself out," I warn. I feel like I'm talking to a child.

She shakes her head. "I never lock it. I ain't got nothing to steal."

I want to argue her logic. This isn't a small, rural town—crime happens—but I don't because she's a grown woman. Though the more I talk to her the more indecisive I am about her mental state or capacity. Socially, she's awkward. Obviously, she's a hermit, but I don't know what's driving it. And although being around her makes me uneasy, I feel like I'd go mad if I had to go back up to my apartment alone, so here I am shopping with the crazy neighbor at two o'clock in the morning.

We walk there in silence. She walks slowly and matches my pace, which I appreciate and tell her so.

She doesn't acknowledge my comment, and I didn't expect her to.

When we reach the convenience store I buy a six-pack of the cheapest beer they have and a stick of jerky and tell Hope I'll wait outside for her, but to take her time, I'm in no hurry.

She doesn't take long, five minutes tops, and meets me out front carrying four plastic bags. The weight of the bags is dispersed unevenly and has her walking off-kilter as if she's developed a limp under the weight.

"Let me help you," I offer.

She doesn't hesitate to hand me one of her bags. It's full of canned goods: soup, Vienna sausages, and baked beans. I take it and couple it in my grasp with my bag.

As we start walking, I look at her other bags: cigarettes, chips, cereal, bread, and milk. She grocery shops at the convenience store. I don't know why this makes me so sad, but it does. As if her deviation from the norm is hindering her somehow, limiting her choices to live a well-balanced life. Not to mention this food isn't exactly healthy. And then I glance at my bag and think about my dinner tonight, and I disregard all judgment.

"Do you shop here often?" I ask. It's small talk, but I have a feeling it's the only talk that may turn into a conversation with her.

She's staring straight ahead as if the journey is a task that needs all of her focus, and her eyes don't veer off her course when she answers, "Every Saturday and Wednesday morning at two o'clock."

"Why do you go in the middle of the night?"

"Less people. Everyone's sleeping," she says matter-of-factly.

We don't speak for the duration of the walk. It's a bit uncomfortable for me, but she doesn't seem to mind. I hand over her bag at her door. She nods to address the exchange and then she shuts the door without another word.

My mind is muddled. Weary with tonight's fucked up events. When I get to my apartment, I put the beer in the fridge, the jerky on the counter, and I go to bed and let sleep take me before I analyze anything further.

Because tomorrow I need my brain fresh.

The epicenter of hell

Present

I swore I would never do this.

Never go back.

Never.

Never say never.

My lungs feel like they're punishing me for overturning my promise, my breaths are short and stunted. The compression of fear isn't allowing for enough air. I haven't had a panic attack since I've been in California. I'm convinced now that they were geographically induced. Kansas City is the epicenter of hell.

My legs are soldiers marching up the steps onto the Greyhound bus, determined to carry out their mission. By the time I take a seat near the back, the pain in my chest is swelling. It's already reached that critical mark that brings the heel of my hand to press against it, praying for relief. My full backpack is sitting in my lap. I hug it tightly to my chest with my free arm and bury my face in the top of the rough canvas, and then I let the tears fall. And I hope the people sitting around me ignore my meltdown and let me muddle through it in peace.

They do.

I don't know how long it is before the assault lessens and relents, but I'm exhausted in its wake. I sleep through a few hundred miles. I decide I like the unconscious approach, even though each time I awake it's like a time warp that places me closer and closer to my adversary.

When the bus pulls into the Kansas City station, my body aches. Every muscle is protesting at the tense posture I've held the entire trip. Even while I slept I didn't relax. I wait for everyone else to exit the bus and only at last call do I rise. My legs carry me out on a militant charge, and the thought briefly crosses my mind about developing blood clots in my legs from prolonged sitting and how that wouldn't be such a bad way to go if it took me quickly before I stepped off this bus.

There are no blood clots.

Only numbness, that's flushed mercifully through my torso and limbs in a deluge as if it's being carried intravenously in my bloodstream.

The sidewalk feels more substantial under my feet when I land upon it. I huff under my breath. Everything is less forgiving here, even the concrete. The air is biting and cold, the sharpness of it pricks the lining of my lungs, and I tug Mrs. L's scarf that I already had wrapped around my neck up over my mouth to repress the attack.

My fingers are shaky as I dial a number I haven't thought about in years, Claudette, my caseworker.

"Hello?" her answer brings on the same rush of relief it always did. I always thought of Claudette as my guardian angel because she was the woman who rescued me.

"Claudette, this is," I hesitate because I haven't said my birth name out loud in years, "Meg Groves." The words are acrid, and I swallow repeatedly trying to rid my mouth of the awful taste they've left behind.

"Meg," she says it the same way she always did, soothing, setting the stage for what is about to unfold. She lived her life in crisis management mood, obviously she still does. "It's been a long time, dear. How are you?"

"I'm good," I lie. I've learned that lying when my well-being is concerned is easier than trying to navigate the truth. Nobody wants to hear, *I'm not good*. That just makes everything uncomfortable and then the fact that I'm not good would need to be addressed or ignored. Either option makes people squirm, so I lie. *I'm good. I'm always good.* Deep down I'm so scared I want to cry, but I continue. "I've been in California, and I just came back to Kansas City for a visit. It's kind of late to get a motel room, and I was wondering if maybe I could stay with you, just for tonight?"

The pause that comes brings tears to my eyes. The silence sounds like denial.

"Never mind, it's okay. I shouldn't have called."

I'm ready to press the button on my phone to disconnect when she calls out loudly as if she senses my looming escape, "No! No, of course you can stay with me tonight. I apologize for the hesitation. I think I'm just in shock hearing your voice. The good kind of shock, but still shock."

She gives me her address and I Uber a ride to her apartment. It's the same apartment she's lived in for as long as I can remember. The same apartment that offered me refuge all those years ago.

Stepping inside, and into Claudette's open arms, settles my nerves. She looks the same; her black hair smattered with silver and her reading glasses perched on the end of her nose. I've always thought of her glasses as a sharp underscore to her intense owl-like eyes. She's short in stature and heavy set in build. She's a safe place. The only safe place in this city as far as I'm concerned.

Time yields results, even against the defiant

Seamus

present

Justine's letter is wavy and rigid now that it's dry. It feels brittle, like the words it contains.

I read it again this morning as soon as I woke up. I think I was hoping it was all a nightmare.

It wasn't.

If anything, it hurts worse in the daylight.

Last night it gutted me with intense anger.

This morning it gutted me with sadness—mourning what could have been.

What could have been…

I know Justine isn't expecting a response—that she's probably hoping against one—but I feel like I need to write her.

Justine,

Thank you. Though the news is impossible for me to come to terms with, I know it was also difficult for you to share. Thank you for putting truth ahead of any loyalty you may have had to Miranda. I appreciate it very much.

Seamus

I dig her envelope out of the trash—it reeks with the days old decay taking place in the bottom of the dark, moist bin. I jot her address down and quickly discard it again. I transfer the address to an envelope and place my folded letter inside. I'll mail it tomorrow on my way to work.

I glance at the time on my phone; it's just after eleven. The deli is open, so I head down to see if Mrs. Lipokowski has any forwarding information on Faith.

The place is crowded with the early lunch rush. I buy a six-inch roast beef and ask her if she can stop by apartment three when she closes up this afternoon because I don't want to take up any extra time while she's swamped in paying customers. She agrees.

And at three o'clock she knocks on my door. "Hi there, Seamus."

"Hi, Mrs. L. I won't keep you, I know you're on your way home to relax. Hope told me last night that Faith left."

She raises her eyebrows. "Hope talked to you?"

That isn't the information I want to focus on, but I answer to move along to the important stuff. "Yeah, I walked with her to the convenience store."

"Huh." She looks perplexed.

"Faith moved out?" I ask because I'm done with the Hope talk.

"Her rent is paid until the end of the month, but she didn't know if she would be back."

"I was wondering if she told you where she was going? Or if she left a forwarding address? You know, in case she doesn't return?"

"She didn't. She seemed preoccupied when she stopped by to talk to me; like in her mind she was already someplace else. I felt bad for her. She's a determined young lady, but I have a feeling her decision was weighing on her heart."

None of the words I've just heard make me feel any better about Faith leaving. I was hoping she would tell me Faith found her birth mother and moved closer to her. Or that she got a new job, in a new city that would complement and embrace her potential. Instead, I'm left with uncertainty tarnished with negativity. I hate that for Faith. "Okay. Please let me know if you hear from her."

She smiles softly; it's a gesture meant to comfort. "I will, Seamus."

"Thank you." The words don't feel appreciative. They feel like I'm begging her to deliver good news to me. Sooner than later.

She nods and turns to walk toward her apartment. "Have a good night."

After Mrs. Lipokowski leaves, my mind goes back to Justine's letter. It's a presence in the apartment, like another person occupying the space. I don't pick it up. I don't read it again.

I don't need to. I have it memorized word for word.

Heartbreak floods in again with a brand new intensity. I've been heartbroken for months. First, by the divorce, which I thought monumental and that nothing would ever top it in the heart wrecking department. And then she took my kids. That took the storm I was besieged by and ratcheted it up from a tropical storm to a hurricane. This latest news was like adding a tsunami wave, one giant destructive swell, within the eye of the relentless storm.

How could she have made a decision so important to both of us without consulting me? Without including me?

I've always thought of each of my children as a miracle. Because in essence, they are. Every child is a miracle. I understand the whole process of conception and a baby growing within a womb is scientific and physiological, not a rare occurrence. But I can't wrap my head around the fact that one day there's no baby, no separate life existing within another, and then nine months later a tiny human being is delivered to the world. A human being that is unique in make-up and perspective. A human being unlike any who's lived before. That is miraculous. And the fact that these tiny human beings have the ability to own your heart even before you meet them, touch them, feel them, and then when you meet them, touch them, feel them for the very first time, that love you already felt explodes into something so strong and protective and nurturing. The English language should have a word for it. Though the new word would lack weight and defining presence. Because that love you feel the instant you lay eyes on your brand new tiny human being is indescribable. It's a love so instantaneous and so intense that it defies logic. Just like babies do. It's all miraculous.

And given that I consider each of my children a miracle, the question that keeps surfacing is so disturbing. Why did Miranda carry Kira?

179

As soon as the question sounds loud enough to demand my attention, I want to turn my back on it because it's so ugly. I want to tell it to shut up and go away and never return. Kira exists, and that's all that matters. Any question that involves a hypothetical answer that varies from reality is torturous. And even though I don't want to know the answer, I want to hurl every question and accusation at Miranda and watch her grapple with her unearthed secrets. I want to watch her squirm. Her conscience wouldn't make her squirm—she lacks one—but she prides herself in winning, right or wrong, because she thinks she deserves it. Entitlement is a sickness festering within her. It's slowly transformed her into the devil she is.

I need to get my kids back. Time yields results, even against the defiant. It's a subtle opponent. It partners up with other forces, like environment and people, and erodes.

My kids are eroding and changing. Miranda and the new elements at play in their new lives are affecting them all while they fight them.

I've started calling Miranda's home several times per day. I know the housekeeper is annoyed with me because she usually answers, but I also feel like there's a peculiar, resistant mutual respect for each other's bullheadedness emerging, which seems to be working in my favor because I usually win and get to talk to my kids at least once per day. Miranda and her husband work late hours and aren't home most nights, so I bet she figures it's easier to let me talk to my kids and not tell Miranda, than to keep answering the phone. The kids all like her too, which eases my mind a bit, since they're in her care most of the time.

I need to start making a case for myself. I've never believed in painting another party to be the bad guy to get what I want, but in the case of the custody of my kids, one of us is bad. I need to start documenting everything. So, I grab a notebook and I start writing down everything I can remember about Miranda and our relationship from the very beginning until now. It takes hours and when I'm done I'm exhausted, like I've physically exerted myself. I also start emailing lawyers, pleading my case and asking for their opinion and representation.

I need to get my kids back.

Batman angels

Faith

present

Last night, Claudette made me some chamomile tea and insisted I get some sleep. The sleep she tried to tempt me toward never came. And even though I felt safe in her home, I was restless. I was trying to put together a game plan, or trying to talk myself out of one. The pattern and path of my thoughts changed minute to minute.

I'm sitting in her small kitchen eating a bowl of Rice Krispies and watching her pour water into the coffee maker. My thoughts are cloudy and unfocused, as if the reality of what I'm about to do is blurring rationality.

"How've you been, Meg?" Claudette asks as she waits for the machine to brew her morning addiction.

"I go by Faith now. And I've been good." It's my trained response. *I'm good. I'm always good.*

She smiles, apparently practice makes perfect and she believes me. "Good. And I like Faith, it suits you. What brings you back to Kansas City, Faith?"

I sniffle against the runny nose that's plaguing me this morning. It seems I picked up a cold along the way. I can't imagine how, the bus was a cornucopia of germs, complete with hacking coughs and snotty noses. I'm trying to decide how much information I want to share with her. She knows more about me than anyone else. She knows my secrets. I need to be honest with her. "I'm looking for my birth mother. Or father. Either, really," I answer vaguely.

She sits down in the chair across from me and stares unblinkingly with her discerning eyes. "The time has come?"

182

I nod and sniff again. "I need to figure out who I am. I don't think I can do that until I have some answers, you know?"

She nods. She knows. "Did I ever tell you I grew up in foster care?"

"No, you never told me that. Is that why you do what you do?"

She smiles thoughtfully, but sadness tugs from deep inside trying to dissuade it. "Yes. I was nine when I went into the system. I remember my parents. I know who they were, and I wish I didn't." She takes a deep breath. "My foster parents were my salvation. They cared for me until I was eighteen. I believe there are superheroes walking amongst us. Or maybe they're heavenly angels. I'm a Batman fan, so I tend to lean toward superheroes. They're dressed in skin to look like you and me, but they have an exceptional ability. My foster parents had it."

"What is it?"

"They had the ability to make someone who felt unseen, unwanted, and unloved feel special. They saw me. They wanted me. They loved me."

My mind goes to Seamus. He's the only person I've ever met, who made me feel that way.

"And I feel like it's my responsibility to do my part in trying to make those connections for children in need: the unseen, the unwanted, the unloved. And it's also the reason I take it so hard when I fail a child like I did you."

I shake my head. "It wasn't your fault, Claudette."

Tears are spilling quietly from her eyes as she shakes her head. "I'm so sorry. You have no idea how badly I feel about what happened. Still."

I don't want to talk about it, but I also don't want her to feel in any way responsible for what happened. "Claudette, you know I don't talk about that day, but I will say this, you're a Batman angel. He was an evil bastard."

She nods and switches topics. "Your birth parents' names were undisclosed, even on your birth certificate. It was all part of the private adoption, which we know wasn't on the up and up. The only information provided was that your mother was under the age of eighteen."

"I know. I went to California hoping against hope that I'd find a needle in a haystack. I lived in the neighborhood near the hospital I was delivered in. It was a small beach community just up the coast from Los Angeles. A quiet place, lots of mom and pop businesses, and a nice stretch of boardwalk that attracted a kind crowd. It was laid-back and welcoming. I know it's stupid, but I prayed that I'd run into her." I huff. "My mom is probably long gone. She probably doesn't even live there, but it was the most painless attempt I could make. And it offered escape from here. From hell."

"So, what's the next step?"

"I need to talk to Trenton Groves. He and his wife were the ones who adopted me at birth. Maybe he can give me details about my birth mother."

She's unblinking again. "Are you sure you're ready for that? Are you sure you want to face that monster?"

I nod, more to myself than anything. "I need to. I have a gut feeling that he's my only hope of finding my birth parents."

"Where is he?" she asks hesitantly. She already knows I know or I wouldn't be here.

"Prison. In Springfield, on drug charges. I've been keeping tabs on him. It's been easy, he's usually incarcerated."

"Oh. I suppose I shouldn't be surprised."

I shrug. "Yeah, I wasn't surprised either. He's not exactly an upstanding citizen." A few years ago I read the transcripts of the trial that convicted he and his wife of my abuse and neglect. Decent humans don't do that to a little girl.

"You'll need to get him to add you to his visitation list and make an appointment to set up a visitation time," she coaches.

"Done. Tomorrow at ten in the morning."

Her eyes dart to the side. She's not looking at anything, she's thinking. "I'll drive you. I'll go with you."

I was praying she would. I don't want to do this alone. "You're sure?"

"This is how I begin to make amends," she says solemnly.

I want to tear my pages out and run away
with them like a thief

present

The building is cold. The concrete, the steel, even
the fluorescence of the abundant overhead lighting is stark
and house an inherent chill. I'm still wearing my coat,
scarf, and gloves, and there are goosebumps covering
every inch of my skin under all the layers of clothing.

Claudette is holding my hand with her left and
fiddling with the clasp on her purse with her right. The
fiddling is a passive attempt to speed this along, silently
chiding the sluggishness of the process.

"Faith Hepburn," a guard's voice booms through
the small holding room we're seated in. It rattles me like
two giant hands clutching my shoulders, a stiff jerk
forward and back. I look around the room and feel heat
light on my cheeks like a beacon exposing my
whereabouts.

Claudette hesitates at my new-to-her legal name,
but rises first, and I follow her lead.

We walk wordlessly behind the guard through a
maze of secured doors before we're seated in front of a
reinforced window with an old school phone receiver on
each side. The chair opposing ours is vacant, but only for a
moment.

The orange jumpsuit-clad midsection of a body
comes into view. He's moving slowly, indicating physical
ailment, stubbornness, or laziness; I guess when I meet his
eyes they'll tell me which. His wrists are cuffed, his fingers
interlaced. His hands are rough, knuckles calloused,

186

gnarled by years of mistreatment or hard use, and covered in poorly executed tattoos.

I don't have the courage to look up at his face, but our eyes lock when he drops laboriously into the chair. And at once, all three become glaringly apparent: physical ailment, stubbornness, and laziness. He also looks like a first rate asshole.

He's scowling at me with cold eyes. They're dark like they died years ago. His head is shaved, and his skin is pale, except his cheeks. They're ruddy but lined with broken capillaries that weave across each other like roads on a map.

We both pick up our phones.

He doesn't talk.

I clear my throat.

"What do ya want?" His voice cuts like a file and makes me flinch.

I clear my throat again.

Claudette takes the receiver from me. "Mr. Groves, this is Meg Groves, the child you adopted twenty-two years ago. She'd like to ask you a few questions about her birth mother and her adoption."

His eyes widen before they narrow back into their scowl. "I ain't got nothin' to say to you." He glances at me before resting back on Claudette. "That little bitch put me in jail."

Claudette squeezes my hand. It's both reassurance for me and anger at his choice of words. "Mr. Groves, the circumstances behind your incarceration were no fault of a child. We don't care to take up too much of your time. Do you remember any details regarding the adoption?"

He grunts, "Nope."

"You don't remember anything? Names? Places? Dates?" she presses.

"Nope." He smiles at me when he says it. When he agreed to the visitation, he didn't know who I was, but now that he does he's enjoying denying me.

187

"What about your wife? Maybe her memory is better than yours?" Claudette asks. She's trying to remain calm, but I hear impatience driving her questions.

"Doubtful. She ain't real talkative these days," he says.

"Why is that?" she asks.

"She's dead. Died ten years ago," he says it with no emotion like he's talking about what he ate for dinner last night, instead of the death of his spouse.

The news is disturbing and quiets Claudette.

"We done here?" He's done, that much is clear.

"Is there anyone else we can talk to who may have some information? Another family member, perhaps?" It's Claudette's last ditch effort to salvage this trip.

"Nope. The old lady did the deal. Ain't nobody else involved but her and she took it to the grave." He hangs up the receiver, stands, and lets the guard remove him from the room.

Just like that, I watch him walk away. With *my* secrets. Whether he remembers them or not, my secrets are there. People who aren't capable of harboring our memories with integrity, shouldn't be allowed them in the first place. I've never wanted to open up someone's brain like a book and start reading—looking for answers in his memory bank—until now. I want to tear my pages out, run away with them like a thief, and greedily read them over and over until I memorize every word. Until every word becomes *mine*, instead of *his*. That's what I want.

You don't always get what you want.

Even if you want it more than anyone's ever wanted anything.

The calendar is now sacred

Seamus

I've contacted several lawyers. Most declined interest in representing me based on the current custody arrangement and accompanying incriminating documents calling it futile. Futile is a label I put on the passage of unproductive time and complacent existence. Futile is not my kids. Futile is not our situation. So, I kept searching until I found a lawyer who sees the potential in righting the wrongs and doing what's best for my kids. Futile is not in his vocabulary. He's building a case, putting together a solid fight, and hoping to initiate proceedings in mid-January, which is a month from now.

The calendar is now sacred. I mark off each day with newfound determination.

Fool me twice, fuck you

Seamus

present

I'm supposed to have my kids for a week during Christmas holiday according to the current custody arrangement — pick them up Christmas Eve and drop them off New Year's Day.

After Miranda's Thanksgiving stunt, I don't trust her to not run off with them again.

Which is why it's December twenty-first and I've just pulled up to the gate in front of her house.

Fool me once, shame on me.

Fool me twice, fuck you, Miranda.

I smile as I think the thought and dial my phone.

The housekeeper answers on the third ring, out of breath like she's run to the phone. "Buckingham residence."

"May I please speak to Kai?"

"Hold," she replies and sets the phone down on a hard surface.

Kai picks up the phone seconds later. "Dad?"

Everything inside me is smiling, because not only is his voice in my ear, but I know the rest of him is inside the house in front of me. "Hey, buddy. Can you do me a favor?"

"Sure," he sounds confused. This isn't how our typical conversations go.

"I want you to hang up the phone and get Rory and Kira and walk out to the mailbox together. I sent you all a surprise, and I'm sure it arrived this morning."

"Can we just talk for a few minutes first?" Kai asks, he sounds hurt I'm rushing to end this call.

"I promise we'll talk in a few minutes. I'll call back after you check the mail."

"Okay," he says still sounding disappointed. Gifts, material things, have never meant much to Kai.

"Talk to you soon. Love you."

"Love you, Dad."

What's most likely a minute at most, feels like an hour, before the front door opens and I see my kids.

My kids.

I'm standing in front of my car, one hand wrapped tightly around the decorative iron bars on the gate and one wrapped tightly around the grip of my cane, both steadying me. I want to scream their names, but my throat is closing in on itself with overwhelming emotion. I knew I would be happy to see them. I had no idea it would be so overpowering. They say absence makes the heart grow fonder. It doesn't. It's more, so much more. This is like witnessing their birth all over again. I'm in awe. They've grown so much over the past few months. And while I want to mourn the time I've lost with them, I can't bring myself to it. My happiness won't allow it. It only allows the present, everything else is irrelevant.

They haven't noticed me yet. Kai and Rory are arguing, or more accurately Rory is arguing with Kai, and Kai is ignoring him watching the ground pass beneath his feet. Kira is trailing behind. She's still in her pajamas even though it's almost noon. She looks tired. Until she sees me waving at them and then all hell breaks loose. It's probably the most noise that's filled the air on this street since I was here last. "Daddy!" she screams.

Kai and Rory stop walking at the sound of her scream, and she races past them. Their delay to process what's happening is only a second or two before they're running across the lawn after her.

Kai reaches the gate first and enters a code into a keypad to open it. The gate retracts slowly, and they all three try to push through, unsuccessfully, at the same time. Within seconds, they're all bundled together in my arms. Kira's arms are wrapped around my right leg, Rory's arms are waist height, and Kai's are chest height. I almost forgot what this felt like.

When I look up, the housekeeper is walking toward us like she's on a mission, but she's smiling. "You full of surprises, Mr. McIntyre."

I decide now is a good time to attempt a truce, so I smile in return. "Hi, Rosa." This is the first time I've ever called her by name. I only know it because the kids say it so often.

"What you doing here?" she asks, but her tone isn't confrontational like the last time we did this.

"I needed to see my kids."

"They need to see you too," she says quietly as if the admission is a betrayal of her employer that she refuses to contain, but doesn't want anyone to hear.

Rosa ushers all of us inside with the practiced efficiency of someone who's served others for years.

I call Miranda's cell. She doesn't answer, so I leave a message.

Rosa calls Miranda's cell. She doesn't answer, so Rosa leaves a message.

Rosa prepares lunch and feeds us while we wait out Miranda's ire. She tells me it's a traditional dish her mother taught her to make when she was a young girl in Mexico: potatoes, onions, and tomatoes, inside homemade flour tortillas. I'm shocked as I watch Kira eat it.

Rosa is firm with my kids, but there's a gentleness that suggests she enjoys being with them. I can see it in her eyes when she watches them, and they don't know it. She's fond of them. She's bonded with them. She's protective of them. I'm guessing she's old enough to be their grandmother. I'm glad my kids have her here.

Hours later, Loren arrives home and Miranda isn't far behind. She releases the kids to me days early, at

192

Loren's prompting, and we pack their bags and leave on our very own Christmas adventure. I don't know where we're going yet, and I don't care as long as we're all together.

Miserably imperfect saccharin happiness

Miranda

present

"Miranda, we need to talk," Loren calls through my closed bedroom door. It's late. We have separate bedrooms. He won't let me step foot in his in all the months I've lived here.

My heart beats double time in reaction to his voice, his words. It makes me angry that his attention can still set off a Pavlovian response, especially after the way he's been ignoring me, but that's all it is—an unconscious response. It's not desire. It's not need. It's a physiological chain reaction that begins and ends with my loneliness.

I pull back the covers and crawl out of bed, cloaking my naked form with a silk robe. It's tied loosely in front, but the two halves aren't drawn closed when I meet him in the hallway.

He sighs when he looks at me. It's not the sigh of irritation I've grown so used to. It's sympathy, sadness, something I didn't think him capable of. "Can I come in?" he nods his head at my door.

My heart has squashed the synthetic excitement and is beating rationally again. "It's sad you had to ask that question," I mutter as I turn and walk into my bedroom. He trails behind, both of us weighted by the uneasiness of our fucked up situation. Two adults, three children, one housekeeper: all living separate lives under one giant, dividing roof.

I walk to my bed, prop the pillows up, shed my robe, not in an attempt to seduce, but in an attempt to return to my prior comfy state, and crawl back into bed. With the covers pulled up to my chin, and everything else hidden underneath, I look at him sitting in the antique

194

wingback chair in the corner. "What do we need to talk about, *Loren?*" His name is an abrasive exclamation point.

He's sitting forward, his elbows resting on his knees, hands clasped. He's still wearing his dress pants and shirt, but his tie is gone, and the top several buttons are undone. "This isn't working. You know this isn't working. I know this isn't working."

I nod. This isn't working. I thought forcing my way into his life would make things perfect.

It's not.

It's far from perfect.

It's miserably imperfect.

"You're depressed," he states.

I don't answer. I've been on medication to treat it for weeks now. It's not helping.

"You need help." I meet his eyes across the room. They're tired. Both from lack of sleep and…me.

I smile. It feels hollow and the corners of my mouth refuse to rise. "I swallow sixty milligrams of *help* every morning when I wake up. It coats my insides with pipedreams of saccharin happiness. I've got *help* covered. *Thanks.*" Sarcasm blends maliciously with melancholy.

"They're not working. Talk to your doctor," he implores.

I look away defiantly. I don't want to talk about medication. I don't want him to look at me like I'm a pile of ragged instability. I want to talk about us. The fact that there isn't, and probably never was, an us. "Do you love me?" When he doesn't answer, I look at him and prod, "Did you ever love me, Loren? Before everything went to hell?"

"Do you want me to lie and make you feel better, or do you want the truth?" he asks. I already know his answer. His words formed a question, but all I heard was no.

I want him to lie to me. "I want the truth." *Please lie to me.*

195

He doesn't miss a beat. "No."

I nod.

He feels sorry. I can see it in the set of his shoulders. They've dropped under the weight of his admission. "Did you ever love me?" he asks.

Years ago I did. I lie, "No," and then I follow it up with the truth, "Yes."

His eyes drop to the floor and he whispers, "What are we doing?" The darkness of the hour and the truth filling the room make his question feel substantial, its veracity smothering me.

Denial is rising in me. It's the gentle boil of failure, bubbling in my stomach, up through my chest, until it clogs my throat and I'm blinking back tears. Fearing what's going to happen next. "I don't know."

"Where do you go every day when you leave for work?"

It's a loaded question, I know that by the way it was posed, but I lie anyway because it's what I do. "I go to work."

He takes a deep breath, both to calm and instill patience, and he continues, "Just be straight with me, Miranda. You haven't worked since I fired you. Why aren't you working? Where do you go?"

"Truth?" I don't know if he really wants to hear or he's just going to use it against me. We play games. This conversation feels different. It feels honest. We don't do honest, so I'm skeptical.

"The truth. Please." He really wants to hear it.

"I have a suite at the Hilton downtown. I don't have a job. No one would hire me," I admit. "It seems your HR department didn't paint me in a flattering light when potential employers called. It was all true, of course, but damning, nonetheless." The time for embarrassment is over. I worked with a headhunter early on but was turned down for VP positions. It felt like a punch to the gut and my confidence, and accepting any title beneath vice president was unacceptable, so I gave up. And lied. Again.

"What do you do all day in a hotel room?" He's a workaholic and looks mystified as if the thought of lounging around all day is inconceivable. I used to be him.

I study his eyes. They're still tired and sympathetic and sad—the kind of eyes that used to make me salivate and pounce on my prey, but now they just make me want to wave the white flag and give up. When my balled up nerves say fuck it and begin to unravel in an unceremonious surrender, I decide to let the truth out. No more lies tonight. "I binge watch bad TV, I order room service, I work out in their gym, I get massages, I fuck lonely businessmen I pick up in the lobby bar." I shrug. "You know, the usual." My recent usual is a usual I never thought I'd submit to. My time in Seattle, depression, failure, and rejection have slowly transformed me into someone unrecognizable to the Miranda of old. My master plan has been trampled to dust. I no longer go out and take what's mine, and what's not mine—I merely survive my self-created hell.

He sighs and runs his hands through his hair. I don't know if it's an act of aggravation or pity. "Really?" It sounds like a little of both.

"*Really?*" I mock his tone. "Fuck you and your judgment, Loren. You're the pot. I'm the kettle. Get over yourself." We both live for bad choices.

He shakes his head. "Your moral compass is bent. Holy shit bent," he mutters. "But you have a mind for business like no one else I've ever known. You're wasting it. That's all I'm saying."

I want to fight. I want this to escalate. But because I'm done lying tonight, I answer, "I know."

"I know the paperwork you presented me with that indicated illegal activity was fabricated. I know they were all lies. Lies you created to trap me. Deceit only on paper.

The law wasn't broken, your moral judgment was." He doesn't sound angry.

"It's still broken it would seem." No more lies.

"We're not married, Miranda. The wedding wasn't official. I paid someone to create the marriage license and certificate. The ordained minister who came to the house and married us was an actor. Your ring is glass."

I huff out a laugh, surprised that I'm able to see the irony in this clusterfuck, and then I pull my hands out from under the covers and offer him a slow clap. "Touché, Loren. Tou-fucking-ché."

He's watching me carefully now, but he's not weighing his words. His normal precision is gone, replaced by a version of Loren I've never seen, desperate. "It's time for you to leave, Miranda."

And that's when the tears drop, it's the ultimate rejection, but I'm not thinking about Loren. I'm thinking about Seamus. How hurt he was when I filed for divorce and the last words he said to me that night. *He'll never love you like I do*. He was right. Loren never loved me at all. And I know now, after living in his home and being fake married to him for months; that the destiny I chased and thought I deserved, only led me to misery.

"Your kids should be with Seamus, Miranda. You saw what they were like when they left with him last week. You know how sad they'll be when he brings them back in the morning. I don't know them that well, but they're different kids when they're with him. They light up with life and happiness. That's what every kid deserves. They don't have that here. No one loves them like he loves them."

"That's because no one loves like Seamus does. It's tender, and sincere, and intrepid. He's a saint," I say in defeat. And then I look at him asking for more blunt honesty. "The kids like Rosa more than they like me. I'm their mother. Shouldn't they like me better than the goddamn housekeeper?"

He doesn't try to comfort me. "Genetics doesn't ensure love, or even like, time and effort do. You don't give them your time, and you don't show them effort. Rosa does."

That stings. I know it's my fault, but it still stings. "It's her job."

"It's her job to make sure they're fed. It's not her job to read to them at night, or to tell them bedtime stories, or to ask them how school was when they get home every day, or to praise them when they do well. She's a housekeeper, not a parent. Parenting is your job," he says.

This conversation feels like a long, miserable road trip that I just want to be over, but that I know I can't escape because jumping out while it's in motion would hurt more than staying in and enduring it. "I don't like parenting. I'm not good at it. Seamus was always the parent." I'm not looking for sympathy; I'm just talking because I have a captive audience, an ear to bend.

"I'd be a horrible parent. Obviously." His head is hanging low. Shame is a burden.

"We're a fucking match made in heaven, Loren. Why didn't we work?" I'm asking because I already know the answer, but I want his take.

"That's just it, isn't it? We're practically the same person. We don't complement each other. You don't offset my shortcomings, and I don't offset yours because we're both deficient in the same areas. We're immature teenagers emotionally, both bankrupt in the ability to love and care for another. That doesn't bode well for matrimony or even monogamy."

"Will it always be that way?"

He shrugs. "For me? Probably. I'm old and set in my ways. It's how I've always lived my life. For you? I hope not. You're still young. You have your whole life ahead of you, as well of the lives of your children. You should go back to your husband. Appreciate him the next time around. He was your better half. Go try to live up to that for a start."

I would say I concede defeat, but to concede you have to have won in the first place. I'm beginning to think I don't know what winning is and that I've never, in thirty plus years, won, because my rules were always skewed. I was the only one playing by them, which made them null and void. "When do you want me out of the house?"

"Ideally?" I expected to hear hope in his voice, but the tiredness has returned.

"No, realistically. Ideally, would involve me leaving right this minute, I'm sure, and I'm tired, I can't do that." I'm half joking, half serious. I'm sure if he had his way he wouldn't even let me use the bathroom and dress before ushering me out to my car.

"You have a week."

I want to make a smartass remark, but I nod instead to accept the deadline.

He rises and walks to the side of my bed and kisses me on top of my head. "Goodnight, Miranda."

The gesture seems out of place given our history, given that we just parted ways, but I guess that's the reason it's so perfect, so fitting. Despite the lack of love, and the fact that we can dole out mistrust and dishonesty with an earnestness reserved for a minister preaching the gospel, we genuinely like each other, even through the hate, because we understand each other. My ugliness forgives and ignores his ugliness. And vice versa. "Goodnight, Loren."

I wouldn't wipe my ass with your distorted perspective

Seamus

present

Loren opens the door of his home. I wish it was Rosa. I don't want to say goodbye to my kids in front of him. Proximity is a reminder: he's the winner and I'm the loser. And I'm painfully aware of how much I'm losing at the moment. I have to leave my kids and go very far away. Losing should be a term reserved for board games and bets because it doesn't begin to cover how my heart feels regarding the people I love most.

"Please come in," he says politely. Everything about him is polite. That's one thing the rich do well — polite. Even if it's disingenuous, it's present.

"It's okay, I'll say goodbye out here and send the kids in when I'm ready," I respond.

He steps away from the door but leaves it open.

Hugs, kisses, and tears all around. Goodbye is harder this time for all of us.

When I walk back to my car my heart feels so grievous it's slowing mobility. There's a sluggishness that only sorrow can create. I'm lost in thought until I reach for the door handle of my car and hear someone clear their throat.

It's Loren.

This is the first time I've ever been alone with him. A million insults flood my mind, but the one that comes out on top is, "You're an asshole."

He folds his arms over his chest and tilts his head to the left like he's thinking over my accusation. "You're not wrong about that. I am."

201

I didn't expect that, but I continue, "You ruined my family."

It only takes a moment for him to apologize, "I'm sorry, Seamus," which should make it feel rushed and unfeeling, but it doesn't.

His sincerity only proves to fuel the anger in me. I clasp my fingers together and cover my eyes with my hands trying to shield myself from the situation, from him, from Miranda, from my grief. "Do you have any idea what it's like to lose everything you love?!" I shout. When he doesn't answer, I shout again still hiding behind my hands, so I don't use them to assault him, demanding an answer, "Do you?!"

"No," he says it quietly like an apology.

I shake my head and drop my hands. "Of course you don't."

"Perspective. That's what it's all about. Perspective turns many a negative into a positive, and many a positive into a negative." It sounds cryptic.

I don't have the time or patience to sift through his bullshit. I open the door and climb into my car. After I start the engine and slam the door, I roll down the window. "I wouldn't wipe my ass with your distorted perspective."

I drive away, only stopping for gas and food until I reach home.

Baking a new pie

Miranda

present

I traded in my two-seater, *me*, convertible for a massive, *them*, SUV. I got choked up when I handed the keys over to the salesman. If my identity is a pie, it was sliced and a generous portion was served to the smarmy salesman, complete with whipped cream on top. And goddamn sprinkles. I discovered I don't like sharing my pie, especially with whipped cream and sprinkles. Because once it's gone, it's gone. And then I have to bake a new pie. A new me. *Sonofabitch*. Nothing scares me more than change, evolution. I feel it coming. I thought I was somewhat ready. I'm not. It's paralyzing. I've just been placed on a small piece of glass and slid under a microscope for the world, and me, to analyze. I already don't like what I see. I'm looking away.

I packed up the kids and a few suitcases of our clothes, and we said goodbye to Loren's estate this morning. The rest of our things will be shipped when I find someplace permanent to live. Surprisingly, leaving wasn't as traumatic as I thought it would be, given this whole change-is-a-motherfucker thing. Maybe it's the new meds the doctor put me on a few days ago. Loren hugged us all, which was an uncharacteristic, considerate gesture. I think he was so giddy to return to his former state of bachelorhood that the hugs were more celebratory than civil. I was torn seeing his arms wrapped around Kira. Half of my black heart smiled, the other half wept. It's probably the one and only time it will ever happen. Could have been...should have been...right...wrong...it's all goddamn bittersweet.

We've been on the road for three hours. We've stopped twice for emergency bathroom breaks and once for food. This trip is going to be the death of me. I don't do well on road trips. I prefer the seemingly instant gratification of flight over the drudgery of confinement in a car where eighty miles per hour feels like slow motion.

At five o'clock I tap out, exhausted, and exit for the gleaming Marriott sign. I've never been so grateful for a bed and fluffy pillow.

I sleep in one bed, the kids share the other. I ask Kira if she wants to share mine. The offer feels forced and foreign, and I'm sure that's how she deciphers it. They're much more perceptive than I once gave them credit for. She opts to sleep in between her brothers. I don't blame her. They're a little pack of wolves who protect their own. I'm an outsider.

The next morning everyone wakes rested and ready for California. Showers for us all are followed by a big breakfast. It's my attempt to plump them up and keep them satisfied for more than two hours before hunger puts the brakes on geographical progress. We all order pecan pancakes. I'm not one who puts much stock in things happening for a reason, or divine intervention, but I can't help but feel like our eating my favorite food in harmony is a coincidental, symbolic step in the right direction. I feel like one of their pack instead of an outsider.

A few hours into the drive I glance in my rearview mirror. Kira is sitting in the middle. She's sleeping with her head resting on Kai's balled up coat in his lap. Kai and Rory are both awake looking out their respective windows. They're different, these two. So different that arguments are inevitable and frequent, but their love for each other is fierce. It's Seamus's ability to love that was passed down to his kids, and it resonates amongst all of their other personality traits.

As if sensing my eyes on him, Rory locks his gaze with mine in the small rectangle of reflective glass. He's the most headstrong of the three, bold in both word and action, which is unnerving in a nine-year-old. I shouldn't be intimidated by a child, but his stare is truthful and judgmental and searing. It's the same look I wear most of the time, minus the truthful part. Seeing myself mirrored isn't flattering, it's unsettling.

"Are you taking us to Dad's, Miranda?" Rory started calling me by my first name when I filed for divorce and moved to Seattle. It's said with such disdain that all I hear is *bitch* instead.

My immediate reaction is to say no, to establish dominance, but then I remember that my life is a big pile of steaming shit, and I pause and answer his question with a question. Because the honest to God truth is, I've never had a conversation with my kids about anything. I don't know them. I just live on the periphery, while others engage them. I think of the conversation as a game, I'm good at games, and we have hours to burn on this hell-forsaken highway. "Would you rather live with Seamus?"

"Yes," the boys answer in unison. Kai's yes is sad, like he knows his answer is vulnerable and unattainable. Rory's yes sounds like *fuck you* and *hell yes* all rolled up into one.

"Why?" I ask. Three letters I know will prompt a verbal execution. They'll skewer and roast me over an open pit. I never provoke criticism. I'm holding my breath. Waiting.

Kai answers first, "Because we miss him. And we love him." It's a gentle admission, his nature seeping out.

I look at him in the mirror. His head is dropped like he doesn't want to hurt my feelings. He's absently running his fingers through his sleeping sister's hair. The words *You don't love me?* are on the tip of my tongue, but I

205

can't force them out. I already know he doesn't. It's not fair to ask and put him in the position to tell the truth...or lie. Both would make him feel awful because his tender heart rules him. I usually prey on vulnerability, but looking at my little Seamus, I can't. Instead, I shift to Rory and ask again, "What about you, Rory? Why?"

The icy glare fixes on me again. And for a moment, I take pride in the fact that I already know he's going to grow into a man that people back down from. "What Kai said. And we don't like you." Blunt, assertive, to the point. I want to turn around and high five him.

Until I remember, he's talking about me.

Ouch. Forever I've been indifferent to these kids. They're part of my life by lineage, a part that others manage for me. A part I keep at arm's length and monitor progress like a long-term development project. At the end of which, adulthood, I can either claim my part in if the project is successful, or deny my part away if the project is a failure. Choosy, outcome-based responsibility...or lack thereof. It's the way I conveniently monitor things in my life I'm not passionate about. Things I don't have vested interest in. If I only dabble, it's easier to wash my hands of it if the need arises, or take credit for it if that suits me better. Image is cultivated at a get-your-hands-dirty, do-the-work level, but it can also be enhanced by selective enrichment. It's all about finesse. Rory doesn't give a shit about finesse. I kind of like him and hate him for it right now. "What do you like?" I counter. I don't want to talk about me anymore.

He shakes his head. "What do you care?" he grumbles.

"I like basketball," Kai answers.

"You do?" I question. And then it dawns on me. "Seamus used to play basketball."

"Dad used to take me to the park to play when we lived in our house. And at the apartment, there was a hoop outside where we played."

"Huh," is all I can say. I never knew.

Rory decides to join in. "I like Harry Potter."

"The books or the movies?" I haven't read or seen them, but no one in the free world escapes notice of them.

"Both." His answer is short and clipped, but I can hear enthusiasm beneath his angry armor.

This seems to be passing the time, and I have to admit I like them both talking to me, so I continue with the questions, "What's your favorite color?"

"Blue," Kai answers. God, he is a mini-Seamus, that was always his favorite color too.

"Red," Rory answers. Fiery, just like him, that fits. I like red too.

"What's yours?" Kai's question catches me off guard. Something as simple as a child showing interest in me brings a lump to my throat. Not many people I've ever encountered in my life have shown genuine interest in me, except my grandmother and Seamus. People in the corporate world did, but it was either subordinates kissing ass to get ahead or superiors expecting performance. Neither of those were personal. This is. My first inclination is to say red like Rory, but I stumble on the thought. "I don't know. It depends, I guess."

"Why would it depend? You should just have one. When you close your eyes and think about your favorite color, what do you see?"

I can't close my eyes, of course, because I'm driving, but I stop thinking about everything else and I focus on the question, and the color that comes to mind first is the shade of the hydrangea bushes my grandmother planted on either side of her porch steps. She tended to those plants with such care and devotion. "Periwinkle."

"You just made that up," Rory challenges. "I've never even heard of periwinkle."

"It's a light shade of purplish blue. My grandmother had hydrangea plants that color." Sharing this information with them just turned scary. I don't talk about her out loud. Ever.

"Where does she live?" Kai asks. "Can we meet her?"

The words threaten to pummel me. I don't want to answer. I suddenly feel like I'm not the one in charge of the conversation. I'm always the one in charge of every conversation. That's how it's supposed to be.

Rory doesn't wait for me to answer his brother's questions before he fires one of his own. "What's her name, Miranda?" He can sense my unease, and he's just poked it with a stick to see what it riles up.

I want my words to sound authoritative and threatening to put him in his place. "Kira. Her name was Kira." They don't. They sound sentimental. So sentimental that I may as well just roll over, admit defeat, and let him beat me with the stick he was poking me with seconds ago.

"I'm sorry," Kai says in a comforting manner.

And confusion sets in because A) I don't know why he's apologizing, and B) I hear all of the times Seamus needlessly apologized to me while we were together in an attempt to smooth things over. He wasn't a pushover; he was the bigger person.

"What are you sorry for?" I should let it go, but it seems that pushing my boundaries is what today is made of.

"That she died." It's the same comforting voice.

Followed by the same confusion. "How did you know that?" I ask softly. I don't want him to answer.

"Because you said, 'Her name *was* Kira.' If she was alive, you would've said, 'Her name *is* Kira.'" His explanation is soft, like he's sad to have to say it. Sad it will make me sad. And for the first time I'm ashamed that I'm his mother, that he's related to me. Not from my standpoint, but from his. He deserves better.

208

The tears begin to trail down my cheeks for so many different reasons. I wipe them away. More replace them.

"I'm sorry," he echoes, but this time, he caps it off with, "Mom." And my heart blows apart. He hasn't called me Mom since before they moved to Seattle. And before that, Mom was just a compulsory title that lacked conviction. Maybe I'm hearing things that aren't there, but what I heard just now was acceptance. A sweet, little boy accepting a mean, evil woman.

For the next few hours I tell Kai, Rory, and a freshly awake Kira about my grandmother and me: how she raised me after my mom died, where we lived, about our dog, and our house, and my school, and our neighbors. I share it all. They're good listeners. They ask lots of questions. And with each question my memory expands and my filter shrinks and by the time we approach Seamus's neighborhood I feel different. Lighter, like I've unburdened myself and given a little piece of me to my kids. The good pieces that existed before my grandmother was stolen from me and the world went dark. The part that astonishes me is that they wanted it and didn't throw it back in my face.

My kids are much better at being human than I am.

I planned on driving to the hotel we stayed at prior. I already made a reservation, but for some reason, my car drives to Seamus's apartment instead. I feel like I owe it to the kids to let them see him tonight. Sonofabitch, I don't know what's gotten into me. I'm thinking these meds are some serious mind-altering shit. Or maybe it's the kids. Or sharing my grandmother freely with them, unencumbered by the crushing guilt that's usually anchored to her memory.

Seamus doesn't know we're coming. He doesn't know I'm moving back. He doesn't know his life is about to change for the better.

When we knock on the door of his apartment at nine o'clock, Seamus answers. I didn't know shock was an emotion capable of looking so happy, but it does on him. His eyes go directly to the kids, and he gathers them up in a hug they've already initiated. They're clinging to him before his arms make contact.

I can't take my eyes off his face. Maybe it's because I've spent the past few hours immersed in nostalgia and sentimentality, but it's as though I've gone back in time. Way back. I'm waiting for his eyes to meet mine. I'm waiting for him to say something sweet. I'm waiting for him to kiss me.

I would give anything to kiss him.

Anything.

But that can't happen because he's a saint.

And I'm a bitch.

And everyone knows it.

Including me.

Seamus

"What are you doing here?" My voice sounds hopeful, something I learned a long time ago not to give Miranda because she uses it like a weapon. She can impale me with my own hope.

No one answers. Instead, the kids all look at Miranda like she alone holds the magical answer, which makes sense because she always wields the power.

"I moved back to California." The words make sense, but they don't give anything away.

Hope surges again. "What does that mean?" I want to yell, *Just tell me I get my kids back!* But I wait.

"Loren and I split up." She would've said, *I left Loren*, if that were the case because she loves to gloat, which means he kicked her out.

I want to point my finger and laugh so fucking loud in her face, but I don't want my kids to see that sort vengeful display. I need to talk to her alone, because if she's teasing me with my kids and doesn't intend to share custody, or preferably give me full custody, I'm going to go mental on her. "Hey, why don't you guys grab your bags from the car and you can spend tonight in your room," I tell my kids. I don't give a shit if she had other plans tonight. You don't dangle the carrot and expect me not to grab it with both hands.

My kids are out the door and down the stairs before she has a chance to revoke my offer.

I don't have much time before they come back up, so I go back to what I originally wanted to shout, but I ask it quietly instead, "Just tell me I get my kids back?" A lack of volume doesn't downgrade ferocity. I'm showing all my cards. I don't have one up my sleeve, which is how you should always play with Miranda, but I don't have time for a test of wills or a pissing contest. *I want my kids back!*

I hear a car door slam, and she looks back out into the parking lot and then back to me. "Can we talk after they go to bed?"

Talking after they go to bed would require Miranda staying here, which I am not all right with, but if it means there's a chance I get my kids back I'll do anything. I step back from the doorway so she can step in. "Fine. We'll talk after they go to bed."

When she sits down on the old couch, she looks out of place. She's shiny and fake perched atop comfy and real.

The kids lug up their suitcases, and I help them get to their room. We talk for a while, and even though I saw them only a week ago, there's no shortage of conversation. When Rory and Kira both start yawning we hunt for their pajamas and toothbrushes, and they all get ready for bed. After I hug and kiss them goodnight and close the door behind me, I step out into the hallway and my happiness is put in a chokehold. Miranda is still sitting on the couch

211

just where she was almost two hours ago. There's a bottle of wine in her hand. She must've brought it with her or went to the liquor store while I was with my kids. It's half full. And there's no glass in sight, she's drinking straight from the bottle. She watches me walk into the room and pats the cushion next to her. "Sit." She's not drunk. She could always hold her alcohol better than me.

I sit on the other end of the couch leaving maximum space between us.

"You're not using your cane," she says it like she's surprised.

I nod. "I'm having a good day. When I'm having a good day, sometimes I don't always use it when I'm home. It makes me feel free. The numbness is gone for now, and the pain only amps up when I overdo it." And then I shut up because I'm oversharing. She doesn't care, oversharing only gives her ammunition that she'll stockpile until she needs it.

She extends the bottle toward me. "Have some, Seamus."

"No." Denying her feels so damn good, even something small and inconsequential.

She retracts it and takes a long swig, unoffended. "More for me."

Bitterness floods in when I realize I'm sitting here forced to engage her. That's when I rise and walk to the kitchen where I take a shot of tequila, followed by another, and I return after I pluck two beers from the fridge—both for me.

"Remember when we first started dating, how you used to write me love letters?" She's talking to me, but she's not looking at me. Her eyes stare out across the room, glazed with the image of her memories.

I'm not going to talk about that. My mind says it before my mouth does, "I'm not going to talk about that."

She drops her head back against the couch cushion and rolls it until she's looking at me. The alcohol is starting

212

to soften her purpose, and when I look closer, I see age encroaching on her features. Lines on her forehead and at the corners of her eyes that I'd never seen before. "Why not?"

I down several big gulps of beer before I answer, "There's no point. We need to talk about my kids."

She shifts in her spot and sits sideways bending her knees and pulling her feet up next to her. "I was leading to *our* kids. It all began with a love letter." She's not being snotty like I would expect, she's talking reasonably, truthfully, which scares me a little.

"And it all ended with a hate letter, divorce papers." I take another drink and then tip the neck of my bottle in her direction. "Oh, and you fucking someone else because he wasn't broken. Let's not forget that."

She swallows back some more red. It seems we're trading drinks and words. "I was wrong. I've made a lot of mistakes." She's still scaring me with her levelheadedness.

"You sure as hell have." I can feel the muscles in my neck tighten when I say it. I want to hurl the word abortion at her. My insides are shaking with rage. I'll save it for a time after we negotiate custody.

She blinks a few times, probably trying to ward off shock, but doesn't respond.

I turn my head and look at her, really look at her, and I'm disgusted. How can a woman be so ugly on the inside? I don't know what else to say because everything running through my mind are curse words and insults and condemnation, none of which will change anything. I shake my head, and my lips move without my command. "What the fuck, Miranda?"

The tears start rolling; it's a silent, unnerving, trail of emotion. She never cries. Miranda's always been stoic and unfeeling. "I'm sorry."

I blast her with my anger. It's a biting whisper, "Sorry doesn't change anything." I hate arguing quietly, not that I'm a yeller, but it would give me an outlet for this

213

fury. Subduing this exchange downgrades its intensity and feels like it skews things in her favor.

She shakes her head. "Don't you think I fucking know that, Seamus?"

I'm stunned. I don't believe her, and I have to laugh. "No. No, I don't think you do."

"I'm taking depression medication," she says to illustrate her point.

I shrug. "You fucking devastated me, Miranda. Annihilated me. You don't get my sympathy." I pause. "And you sure as hell don't deserve my empathy." I pause again and then continue with the verbal blitzkrieg, because I can't hold this in any longer, "Fuck you and every single one of your piss poor choices."

She's still crying and was taking the assault on the chin until that last insult. She sniffs and wipes her running nose with the back of her hand. "You wouldn't say that if you knew."

I can't listen to her for one more second. I stand. "You need to get out. Go home. Wherever that is."

"I can't drive," she counters.

I know that. "Call a cab. My kids stay here where they belong." I don't wait for her to argue. I walk to my room, and I grab my pillow and blanket, and I lie down on the floor in front of the kids' room and sleep just in case she tries to get crafty and sneak them out before I wake up. I know I'm paranoid, but I just got them back. There's no way in hell I'm losing them again.

Sick and tired of feeling the ugliness

Seamus

present

"Sorry, Daddy." Wakefulness is instigated by these words coupled with a little girl's socked foot stepping on my cheek.

I open my eyes to a fuzzy image of Kira's sweet face inches from mine. "Are you okay, Daddy?"

I smile at the concern in her wrinkled forehead and drawn eyebrows. "I'm okay, darlin'."

She wraps her arms around my neck and squeezes. "You shouldn't sleep on the floor in the hall."

I wrap my arms around her, and my body seconds her words. "I know, I shouldn't." I'm too old to sleep on the floor, and my body aches.

"It's dangerous." And then she releases me. "I gotta pee. I'll be back. We can watch cartoons."

"Sounds like a plan." And just like that, everything's back to the way it used to be. To the way it should be.

Until I put the blanket and pillow back in my room and walk to the kitchen.

And Miranda is sitting at the table drinking a Starbucks coffee, eating a bagel, and reading a newspaper. Like she belongs here. She's wearing different clothes than she was last night and she looks wide awake. Sleep was always something she could do without; she thrived on four or five hours a night. I always envied that. "What are you doing here?" I feel like I need to walk back out into the hall and walk back in and hope this is all an illusion.

She takes a bite of her bagel and talks tightlipped through it, pointing to the counter behind me. "Breakfast."

There's an Einstein Brothers Bagel box with enough food in it to feed an army, three tubs of flavored cream cheese, six bottles of fruit juice, and a large Starbucks cup. I can't remember her ever buying food for anyone but herself. As I pour the contents of the lukewarm Starbucks cup into a mug from the cupboard and walk it to the microwave, I say, "I thought I told you to leave last night."

She shrugs as she swallows another bite. "I fell asleep. Then I left. Then I came back. With food. Your food selection is pathetic."

Punching buttons on the microwave, I defend, "Oatmeal is good for lowering cholesterol."

"I hate oatmeal. It tastes like wet sawdust."

I know she doesn't like oatmeal. I know she thinks it tastes like wet sawdust. And I don't care. I shake my head. "Why are we talking about oatmeal, Miranda? What are you doing here?" I ask again.

She's picking at her bagel. Stalling.

"Daddy, what's for—? Mommy, what are you doing here?" Kira asks. She looks confused.

I jump in before confusion takes over, and Miranda says something to make this worse. I want the answer to that question. Kira doesn't need to be encumbered with it. "Bagels, darlin'. Pick one out and we'll put some cream cheese on it, and eat in the living room while we watch cartoons."

She does as I ask and we take our breakfast to the living room to sit in front of the TV and go through our early Saturday morning ritual that I've missed so much.

Fifteen or twenty minutes into "Adventure Time" Miranda joins us. She walks in quietly, which is unlike her, usually she's showy and has to be the center of attention. She sits on the floor cross-legged. Kira tracks her but doesn't say anything, and when Miranda settles, she rests her cheek back against my arm and loses herself in Finn and Jake on the screen.

216

All's quiet, uncomfortably so, but still quiet until Kai and Rory join us. They're both eating bagels, and Rory has cream cheese smeared on his lips and cheeks in the shape of a smile, the residue left after the huge bite he's just taken. "What are you doing here?" the boys ask together. I almost laugh, because we've all asked her, verbatim, that same question now within the span of an hour.

We're all staring at Miranda waiting for an answer. Her cheeks are reddening and her eyes look glassy when she whispers, "Breakfast," and then stands and walks to the bathroom.

Rory shrugs, unconcerned, and continues to devour his bagel as he sits next to Kira on the couch.

Kai, on the other hand, looks saddened when he sits down next to me. I put my arm around him, and he rests his head against my shoulder while he finishes his bagel.

Miranda returns five minutes later. Her eyes are red.

"Thanks for the bagel, Mom."

Kai just schooled me.

On compassion.

And forgiveness.

I'm not ready for forgiveness; the wounds are too fresh. For all I know forgiveness may never come. But compassion is something we should all be willing to show. Treating people badly in reaction to how they treat us plays into the ugliness in the world and perpetuates it. Treating people well, not in the hopes that they'll change, because sometimes people never change, keeps our hearts and minds free from the ugliness. I'm so fucking sick and tired of feeling the ugliness.

Sometimes it takes the purity of a child to remind us what's important.

Miranda sniffs and answers, "You're welcome, Kai."

So, I vow, at least for now, to deal with Miranda with caution instead of hatred. I don't have to like her to do that.

"Miranda, can you help me take the trash out?" I need to talk to her and find out why she's here and, most importantly, where my kids fall into her plans, because on paper, she still has full custody.

I grab the bag out of the kitchen trashcan — it's only half full — and walk outside. She follows me down the stairs. At the big dumpster at the back of the building, I ask again, "What are you doing here?"

She finally answers. Sort of. "In California? Or here at your place?"

I lift the lid on the dumpster and toss the trash bag in. "Both."

"In California? Looking for a job and trying to find a house. And here? Hoping I can stay until I find both of those." She doesn't even blink when she runs through her list. She doesn't sound confident. She's unsure, not at all hopeful, pessimistic. She says it like she may as well because she doesn't have anything to lose.

I'm dumbfounded by almost every answer. I can understand the looking for a place to live part, but the rest makes no sense. "You don't have a job? Why can't you transfer back to the Marshall Industries office here?"

She raises her eyebrows, and there's no pride in her answer. "Because I was fired months ago." And before I can say anything she adds, "I lied. Blackmailed Loren. He didn't trust me with his business after that."

I close my eyes and shake my head. She's like bad reality TV. "Was this before or after you married?"

"Before."

I know I'm looking at her like I don't understand what she's saying because I'm having trouble wrapping my head around it. "And he still married you?"

She nods and then stops and tilts her head almost like she's going to change her mind and shake it side to

218

side. "Yes. And no. I thought we were married. We never were, the license and certificate were fakes."

"Jesus Christ, you two were perfect for each other." I probably shouldn't have said that, but it's true. It's so goddamn true.

"We were a fucking disaster." She shrugs because there's nothing more to say on the subject, I'm sure. Fucking disaster sums it up.

I don't want to talk about her dismal love life. "I want my kids here. Winter break ends, and school starts up again Monday. I'll go in late to work and re-enroll them."

"I can do it," she offers.

"Really?" I sound doubtful and mocking.

She sighs and a little bit of the old defiant Miranda peeks through because that comment pissed her off. "I ran a goddamn Fortune 500 company, Seamus, give me some credit. I can fill out a few mundane forms."

"Are you trying, Miranda? Is this you trying to be a parent? I want so fucking badly to believe you're being real with me and that you've finally come to the realization that you have the most amazing children on the planet, and that it's a privilege to be their mom." I know I'm begging, but I want this for my kids. I want them to have a mom who loves them. I don't care if she's in my life, but I want her to be in theirs if she's going to try.

"I'm trying, Seamus. I'm not perfect, and I don't know how to do this, but I'm trying."

"I'm only going to say this once, Miranda. Go all in or go away. This isn't something you try and then get bored with like yoga and give it up. These are children who've been waiting their whole lives for a mom. Think about them. For once. You're a mother, not a martyr."

"I'm all in," she says.

I hesitate because our past is screaming at me, *Don't believe her! She's a liar!* But then I remember Kai…and compassion…and shit, before I can talk myself out of it my mouth is sounding offers, "You can stay here for a month while you look for a job and a place to live. You're sleeping on the couch, no one's giving up a bed for you. If you don't find anything in four weeks, you're out. You can go stay in a hotel or sleep on the corner, I don't care. My kids stay here during the week to go to school. We can discuss joint custody on the weekends. I'll have my lawyer outline the new arrangement. And you're paying the lawyer fees to straighten it all out because you fucked it up. And every goddamn day you better make an effort to be part of their lives. Do you hear me? Real, no pretending. You wake up and take them to school, and I'll pick them up. You help them with homework a few nights a week. You play with them. You talk to them. And you can make dinner a few nights a week too."

"Can I order takeout? I don't cook."

Nothing's ever easy with her. I shake my head. "I don't fucking care. Put some goddamn food on the table. This is about responsibility. You're not going to be judged on your cooking abilities."

She nods her head.

I feel like I'm talking to a child instead of an adult. "Can you do that?"

"Yes, I can do that," she answers.

I reword for clarification. "Do you *want* to do that?"

She nods.

Shit.

I can't believe I just agreed to this.

I hope she can.

Where's the fucking butter?

Miranda

I'm trying.

I'm really trying.

But this domestic shit is for the birds.

Cooking and baking should be easy. I have an IQ of 155. It's just reading a recipe and following directions.

Apparently I'm awful at following directions because almost everything I've attempted this week has been inedible. I do it while Seamus and the kids are gone because I don't want them to know I failed. I hide the evidence in the dumpster out back and order take out instead.

Today, I'm trying again. Because Betty Crocker can kiss my motherfucking ass if she thinks I'm giving up. I'm going to make monkey bread. I saw it on Pinterest. Yeah, yeah, I know...*Pinterest*. The porn of housewives everywhere. I'm ashamed to admit I like it. I feel like I need to turn in my Gucci suits and Jimmy Choo peep-toe pumps for ill-fitting Target yoga pants and baby puke stained tank tops for the betrayal of good taste. But these damn recipes, they look so good. And they're photographed and presented with the skill of Ansel Adams. The monkey bread is a work of art in a magnificent Bundt pan. Not to mention, just the thought of all that gooey goodness makes me feel gooey. I practically spontaneously orgasmed reading the recipe. Fuck me, I'm being warped by social media and stereotypical America. I need a job.

Back to the monkey bread. I went to the store earlier and bought the ingredients, a Bundt pan, and an apron because I figure maybe that's where I've been going

221

wrong. Maybe you have to look the part to play the role. The apron should help. It does on Pinterest anyway.

Everything is going smoothly. Success will be mine. Finally.

Until I figure out there's no butter in the fridge.

Sonofabitch, butter is going to be my downfall!

Think. Think fast. What would Rachael Ray do? Would she give up on her monkey bread? Hell no!

I'm out the door and down the stairs in five seconds flat banging on the door of the apartment under Seamus's. I'm looking at the number one on the door while I'm whispering under my breath, "Hurry up, this monkey bread is not going to make me its bitch." When the door opens, I don't wait for an introduction or to be invited in. "I need butter," I announce as I speed walk toward the kitchen. When I open the fridge, I go straight for the little plastic door that always houses sticks of butter and pop it open. It's empty. "Where's the butter?" I ask exasperatedly. The owner of the fridge is standing on the other side of the open door. She looks a little sketchy, and she's not answering my urgent plea quickly enough, so I ask again, *"Where's the fucking butter?"*

"You shouldn't swear. It's a sin." It sounds like a recording when she says it, a droning sound bite.

"Not having butter is the only sin here, missy." I slam the miniature door shut before I slam the fridge door and put my hands on my hips. I'm frantic. This goddamn monkey bread has me worked up into a frenzy. "Where can you get your hands on some? Quick?" I rephrase, "I need it now." It sounds like I'm trying to score illegal drugs instead of a simple dairy product.

She looks a little rattled, calmer than I would expect for a stranger bum rushing her home, but still a touch rattled. "Maybe Mrs. Lipokowski has butter."

I pat her on the arm as I walk quickly past her to the front door. I don't know who Mrs. Lipokowski is, but I need this woman to come through for me, so I'm talking to

222

her like I'd talk to someone who works for me. It's a flurry of pep talk mixed with get your ass in gear. You don't give people time to think when you need something, you just tell them what they're going to do. They usually never question it. Couple that assertiveness with my desperation and it's a volatile mix that anyone would be crazy to challenge. "Good thinking. You run and get a stick of butter from Mrs. Lipokowski right now and bring it up to apartment three." I'm talking fast, but watching her eyes to make sure she understands the importance of this mission.

"Okay?" she says it like a question.

I clap my hands, and she startles at the sound. "Come on. Chop chop. I need your head in the game. Mrs. Lipokowski. Butter. Now. *Go.*" I'm a coach barking out orders.

She walks out the door and I pull it closed behind me.

"Apartment three!" I yell at her retreating figure.

I race back up the stairs and leave the front door open so the butter can easily find its way in.

A few minutes later, the neighbor appears in the kitchen with a stick of butter. She's out of breath and hands it off like a baton in a relay race before she drops into a chair at the table.

I accept it like a baton in a relay race, remove it from its wrapper, drop it in a mixing bowl, and stick it in the microwave. I look at her, because if she didn't fail me with the butter, maybe... "Do you know how to bake?"

"I bake pizza sometimes."

"Frozen?" I question. Warming a frozen pizza isn't baking. Because frozen pizza isn't really food.

She nods.

Damn.

I pick up my phone off the counter and tap the screen to bring up the recipe and hand it to her. "Do you think you can make this?"

She accepts the phone, and it takes longer than I'd like for her to read the recipe, but when she stands and starts opening the tubes of Pillsbury biscuits on the counter, hope erupts within me like Mount Vesuvius.

We take our time and when the Bundt pan is in the oven, I look at the woman I've been working with for the past thirty minutes and I extend my hand in celebration. "I'm Miranda." I don't say thank you because those are words I use sparingly. Most things we do during the course of a day are trivial, or are meant to propel our existence forward, they don't require thanks. People *do* — it's how we get through the day. It's how we persevere. No thanks are needed for doing.

"I'm Hope," she responds. She's awkward now that we don't have a task to focus on. Or maybe she was always awkward, and I didn't notice because I was all hopped up on daydreams of monkey bread. She won't look me in the eye.

"Do you want something to drink, Hope?" The monkey bread has to bake for thirty minutes, and I don't want her to leave until I know if an emotional meltdown over dough is needed.

"You got any iced tea?"

Her incorrect grammar makes me my teeth grit and my eyes squint. "Do I *have* any iced tea?" I correct.

"Yeah, you got any iced tea?" She missed the correction.

"No. I have orange juice, Pellegrino, milk, or Coors Light." I don't care if she did just potentially save my ass, I'm not offering her my wine.

"Orange juice."

I pour her a glass and then sit at the table with her. She fidgets like a child. Her mannerisms are all childlike. I wonder what her story is. I'm usually not interested in people personally, but she's odd and it's intriguing. "How long have you lived here, in your apartment?"

She thinks it over and then answers, "A long time."

224

"One year? Five years? How long is a long time?" I press.

"I came when I was eighteen."

"How old are you now?"

"Forty."

Shocker. I would've guessed her ten years older. I want to tell her about dermabrasion, and chemical peels, and Botox, but I don't think those words are in her vocabulary. And then I have an idea and run to the bathroom to retrieve my bag of tricks.

When I return, I hand her a hair elastic. "Put your hair up."

She's good with commands. I like that. She gathers back her long, tangled blond hair into a ponytail.

I do the same with mine.

Then I turn on the hot water in the sink until it's steaming and wet two washcloths and wring them out. "Now tip your head back. I'm going to put this on your face. It's hot, it will open up your pores."

"Pores?" she questions.

"Just do it. Your skin is screaming for attention like a middle-aged woman in the front row at a Bon Jovi concert." After I put the washcloth on her face, I do the same with mine. When it starts to noticeably cool, I remove them and set them on the counter. Hope flinches when I smear the mask on her face. "Sorry, I know it's cold."

"What is it?" she asks.

"It's a mask. It contains lactic acid and beta glucan."

"Huh?" I've lost her.

"It's going to make your skin feel and look younger. You haven't been good to your skin. It shows. You have to be friends with it if you want it to treat you well in the long run. Skin care is a marathon, not a sprint." I'm not putting her down, I'm being honest. And I think she's the type of person who can take it.

225

"Oh. It will make me pretty. When do we take it off?" See? She can take it.

"Twenty minutes," I say as I slather a coat on my face.

Seamus

I walk in on the most bizarre sight I think I've ever seen. Miranda and Hope are sitting at the kitchen table with green shit all over their faces, drinking orange juice, amongst a plethora of dirty baking utensils filling the sink and counter. Never mind that the entire apartment smells like heaven. When I reach for the oven handle, Miranda swats my hand away in a protective gesture that would put a riled up tomcat to shame. "It's not done yet. Leave it alone."

"What is it?" I ask.

No answer.

The kids all walk in behind me. "Hi, Hope," Kira says.

"Hi, Kira," Hope says.

"Hi, Hope," Kai says.

"Hi, Kai," Hope says.

The kids and Hope only met each other once and that was months ago, I'm surprised they remember each other's names. It's like a sitcom where everyone is oblivious to, or is choosing to ignore the weirdness.

Until Rory enters and keeps it real. "What smells so good? And why do you have that crap all over your faces? You look like freaks."

I'm about to tone him down when Hope answers, "It's a mask. It's gonna make me look pretty. Me and my skin are gonna be friends."

He lifts his eyebrows. "O-kay." And he leaves.

226

Just then, the timer sounds on the oven and Miranda jumps out of her chair like she's been stung on the ass and she shoos us away. "Everyone out."

Ten minutes later Miranda and Hope enter the living room with clean faces and a plate piled with something sticky and doughy and sweet. Miranda is beaming. I don't think I've ever seen her smile so wide. A toothy grin happens when joy can't be contained.

And the monkey bread is the best thing I've ever eaten.

You used to be nice

Seamus

present

You know those stories of demonic possession? The movies or books that depict a human taken over by an evil spirit?

Can they happen the other way around? An evil person gets possessed by a good spirit?

Because what's happening with Miranda lately defies logic.

She gets up early and makes breakfast for the kids. She packs their lunches. She takes them to school. She cleans the apartment. She tries to cook dinner, which she usually fails at but I give her credit for trying. She's friends with Hope and even gets her out of her apartment during the day. She talks to the kids and listens to their answers.

And even though I know I should just be thankful for the effort she's making, it all makes me suspicious instead. I lived with my head in the sand for years overlooking. They say love is blind—it sure as hell is, either that or I had embarrassingly low expectations, because I loved her through the worst.

Being a good person is partially subjective, beauty lies in the eyes of the beholder. It's whatever we deem acceptable, whatever we find ourselves worthy of. I always held myself to one set of criteria—being kind and supportive was the man I always wanted to be. Because my father wasn't. He was in my life, in our home, but never present, and always, without fail, oppressive. His sentences, when he chose to speak to me, usually began with *you can't, you don't, or you won't*. I know human beings are made up of cells, but I'm convinced my father

228

was made up of negativity. It festered within him like a poison and made him incapable of love.

I vowed to never be like him. I married someone like him, instead. Granted, Miranda was more refined than my father. She played games with lies and manipulation, while he favored spewing blunt hatred. And the difference between the two is stark; I blindly loved one and with eyes open resented the other.

The root deep maliciousness is what keeps me from believing Miranda. It's that little wounded voice in the back of my head warning me that people don't change. Which is strange, because I'm a counselor, I've always had faith that people can change for the better. That sometimes all they need is someone who cares and some resources to aid them. I thought my father was the only person who would ever dodge that feeling of optimism in me. It seems Miranda is the second. My heart can only endure so much brutality before it shuts off and starts to hold a grudge. A lifelong grudge.

I think that's why I'm so pissed. She's stifled optimism in me. I have to work at it harder than ever.

Never was that more apparent than today when she walked into my office at lunch. She's never, in all the years I've worked here, stepped foot inside this school. So, hearing the knock on my open office door accompanied by Miranda, momentarily puts me into self-preservation mode.

Instead of saying hello, I say, "What are you doing here?" God, I ask that question of her a lot lately.

My desk phone rings before she can answer. I lift the receiver, and Janet is whispering in my ear, "Seamus, your ex-wife is headed your way. Do I need to call someone to remove her from the premises?"

I look at Miranda and the brown, deli lunch sack in her hand, and answer, "Yup, she's here. And no. Thank you, Janet."

"Okay. Call me if you need anything," she replies.

"Will do. Thanks."

When I hang up, Miranda is settling in the chair across the desk from me, and she's amused. "The office secretary hates me, Seamus. She's a pit bull."

I plan on commenting, but I'm speechless as I watch her take two sandwiches and napkins out of the bag and then she hands me one. She does it like it's natural and has been done a million times before. It hasn't. I search my memory, and I never remember her doing anything like this. I'm more convinced now than ever she's possessed. I unwrap my sandwich and lift the top roll to peek inside, it's roast beef with spicy mustard and banana peppers. "How did you know I like this? This is my favorite." It sounds accusatory instead of grateful.

She shrugs, untouched by my cynicism, as she takes a bite of her sandwich. "I asked Mrs. Lipokowski. Weird woman, but nice enough I suppose. And she loves you, Seamus. You should've seen the sparkle in her eye when I mentioned your name, it was like some sort of magical Peter Pan pixie dust shit."

"She is nice," I defend. Not that Miranda was degrading her, but I still feel like I need to say something. I look at her, basking in nonchalance like she was born that way—which I damn well know she wasn't—eating her sandwich I'm more dumbfounded than ever. "Why are you here? Am I about to be poisoned? Did you put something in this sandwich?"

"Can't I just do something nice for you?" she says offhandedly like nice is all she's ever been to me.

I shake my head. "No. You never have before."

She huffs, but it sounds more like a slightly amused laugh. "I deserved that." Then she's serious and whispers, "I'm trying, Seamus."

I give in to the mouthwatering aroma of the sandwich under my nose and take a bite. "Thank you." Giving thanks should never feel forced. These past two weeks with her, it has. The words feel disloyal somehow and get stuck in my throat. "For the sandwich," I clarify. "Now, tell me what it is you want." I know she wants something. She wouldn't be here otherwise.

"You used to be nice, Seamus."

"I used to be blissfully unaware. That played well into being nice. There's a difference. You fucked me over, that changed me."

"Time changed you. MS changed you. It wasn't just me."

She's right. But I won't let on. "What do you want?" I repeat the question.

"Fine," she says. "I need to use you as a reference."

My mind is confounded by her, and partially by the magnificence of my sandwich because it's so damn good. I consider her request and find that an explanation is needed. "A reference for what?"

She looks down at the empty sandwich wrapper in front of her on my desk. It's the first time she's looked away the whole time she's been sitting here. It screams mortification. "A job."

I laugh. It's not humorous, and it's not degrading, I don't know what it is, but I don't know what else to do. "You want to use *me* as a reference?"

She nods, eyes still downcast.

"Why don't use past employers or colleagues?"

Her eyes draw up to mine, and she smirks. "Does the term 'burned bridges' mean anything?"

The same laugh escapes my lips for the second time in twenty seconds. "Are you seriously asking me that, Miranda?"

She just stares at me. *She's seriously asking me that.* Sometimes I think she assumes that because I loved her once, she can do whatever she wants to me and there are no consequences. Love negates or counteracts bad behavior, it's a screwed up scale. She piles up shit on one side, and I'm supposed to balance it with unconditional love on the other. It doesn't work that way. Not anymore.

231

"So, burning bridges professionally means you have the dignity to acknowledge wrongdoing on your part and not ask them for favors because that would be in poor taste?"

She shrugs. "Pretty much. I overstepped my bounds. The business world is cutthroat. They take pleasure in exacting revenge."

"What makes you think I wouldn't?" As I ask it, I realize I wouldn't do it. As much as I don't like her, I wouldn't sabotage her. I couldn't live with that on my conscience.

She looks me in the eye and doesn't hesitate. "Because, you're a saint, Seamus."

I shake my head to disagree. "Saints don't have hateful thoughts like I do."

"Will you do it? Be my reference?" She's all but begging.

"Yes. But only because you need a job, and I need you out of my apartment," I add.

She stands to leave and gathers her trash, satisfied that she got what she came here for.

"What's the job you're applying for?"

"It's a director position." Her answer is vague.

"What's the company?"

She sighs. "It's not important." The sigh tells me it is important.

"Why won't you tell me?" I press.

She turns at the door and says, "Because you'll judge me."

"Since when have you ever been worried about that?" This conversation is almost comical.

"Since now." She sighs again and closes her eyes. "It's a non-profit, a homeless shelter."

Stunned. I'm stunned. So stunned that a chuckle escapes me. A stunned chuckle.

She opens her eyes and raises her eyebrows as if she's calling me out.

"What? You can't expect me to not be surprised?" I ask.

"Surprised is judging, Seamus." She sounds hurt and leaves.

She's right.

How is she right?

How did this get turned around on me?

I always have a choice

Faith
present

There have been times in my life I prayed for change.

For rescue.

For strength.

For answers.

There have been times in my life I blamed others for everything that went wrong, bypassing accepting responsibility, because it was easier.

And didn't require self-analysis.

Or growth.

Or maturity.

And there was a time in my life I hit rock bottom, like a boulder dropped from the top of the Empire State Building. It was ugly.

And soul-splintering.

Like the darkest death.

Death that I survived.

Even though I shouldn't have.

It shed perspective.

And in time, it led to research because, at that point, I had nothing to lose.

Everything, and anything, to gain.

Going to Kansas City again felt like a necessity, like picking a scab or scratching a mosquito bite, because in the end I knew it would only serve as an antagonist. An aggressive antagonist that's selfish and unconcerned about others. When I arrived I intended to stay, not because I wanted to, but because I didn't think I had a choice.

Claudette reminded me I always have a choice.

And she bought me a bus ticket.

Back home to the only place that's ever felt like it accepted me — imperfections and all.

The air, when I step off the bus, is warm. The warmth of an old friend I've missed, even though I've only been gone for a few weeks. I can't resist taking deep breaths, filling my lungs with California, someplace I thought would always remain a memory.

The month is almost up, Mrs. Lipokowski will be renting my apartment to a new tenant. I don't have the money to pay next month's rent and renew the lease, but at least I'll have a roof over my head for a few days. My heart explodes into a riot thinking about Seamus. I think about him every day, but knowing he's just miles away is so tempting.

I'm good about not giving into temptation. It's not an option. Temptation leads down a path of destruction.

But Seamus is so damn hard to resist.

It's late when I reach the apartment on foot. I only have fifty dollars to my name, and I wasn't about to spend any of that on a cab, so I walked the eight miles to my apartment.

My scooter is sitting in front of Hope's apartment where I left it. I gave it to her though I doubt she'll ever learn how to ride it. I hope she does. It would make life easier for her and might encourage her to get out.

The lights are out in all of the apartments. The neighborhood is sleeping.

When I unlock the door of apartment two, it smells musty, like it's been locked up for eternity and not allowed to breathe. I open the windows, change into my nightshirt, and sleep comes for me when my head lands on the pillow.

I wake to the sound of children talking. Even freshly roused from deep sleep I know those voices,

235

Seamus's kids. Kira is singing, and Rory is complaining about not liking celery packed in his lunch—it doesn't sound right in an American accent. I lay there a few seconds and listen because it makes me smile—Seamus got his kids back. And then I crawl to the window and peek between the curtains hoping to catch a glimpse of Seamus and his kids leaving for school.

It's not Seamus. It's his ex-wife.

My heart drops initially, but then it backpedals because partial custody is better than visitation out of state any day of the week. They're obviously going to school—the kids all have on their backpacks and are carrying lunch sacks. Maybe she moved back to California with them. Or maybe she's visiting during the week, rather than the weekend. So many possibilities, but all of them work in Seamus's favor. I'm happy for him. I'm happy for his kids.

Before I tuck away back under the blanket, I see movement on the stairs. Cautious movement. A cane and a beat up pair of Doc Martens. Then dark denim. Followed by a navy blue sweater. And finally the back of a head covered in hair so dark and so soft. Seamus. *Goddamn.* How is it possible that he looks better than I remember?

And what I remember was breathtaking.

I want to open the door.

I want to invite him in.

I want to take off his clothes.

I want him to take off mine.

And I want to feel us again.

So badly.

But I can't.

He's headed to work. I don't know the whole story yet on his kids and their custody, and I would never jeopardize any of that.

So I stay hidden away.

At lunchtime, I venture over to Hope's.

236

"You're back." She sounds surprised. Happy surprised, which isn't like her.

"For a few days, yeah. How've you been?" I don't know how to describe it, but she looks different, healthier. She was always so pale before, but she's has some color like her skin's seen the sun. Her hair has been washed and is pulled back in a ponytail.

"I been good," she says, and I know she means it.

She asks me to stay and watch her favorite movie. I do. Just like we've done dozens of times before. We eat toast and applesauce and play a board game afterward.

But at four o'clock she announces, "I gotta go. You wanna come with me?" and walks to the door and slips on her flip-flops.

I'm puzzled because she never leaves during the day. "Where are you going?"

"Upstairs to help my friend, Miranda, cook dinner," she says it like it shouldn't be news to me, like I haven't been gone for weeks.

"Miranda?" I question. Seamus's ex-wife? My stomach turns, and I wish I could take back the question. I wish I could take back being here right now. I wish I could take back seeing her this morning. I wish I could take back a lot of things, because the next thing Hope says, stomps all over my heart.

"Miranda lives with Seamus. They're a family."

I want to look brave and take the news stoically. He's not mine. He was never mine. He belonged to her for years. They share a connected past. And children. I should be happy for him.

But, I'm not. I feel like I want to beat my head against the wall, throw up, and scream all at once.

I walk out of Hope's to my apartment without saying a word. She didn't notice. She was already walking upstairs when I shut her door behind me. I saw the envelope with Seamus's name written on it that I left with Hope still sitting on her floor, unopened, half buried under a pile of junk mail. I guess she didn't get around to giving it to him. Which, is for the best, given the news I just received.

The minute I'm inside my apartment, I'm sitting on the floor crying. I'm grieving a man I have no right to. I'm grieving birth parents I'll never find. I'm grieving this apartment I'll have to leave in a few days. I haven't been this down in years. It's all mounting. And suddenly ugliness is rearing its head. The demon I slayed years ago is back clawing its way from the inside out. Breathing down my neck, leaving a trail of sweat covered goosebumps.

I'm shaking my head, chanting, "No, no, no, no, no. I won. You don't own me. I'm stronger than you are."

I want to use.

I want to use so fucking bad.

I can't see through my tears.

I can't hear through the voices in my head.

I need to get out of here.

Now.

Packing up my bag takes minutes.

I set out on foot.

And I pray like hell that I find strength.

I don't know who to call. The last thing I want to be is a burden. But I also don't want to be a statistic. I fought too damn hard to get clean. And I promised myself I'd never go back. I take my cell phone — which will be canceled in a few days — out of my bag and call Claudette. She's the only person I can confess this to. She helped me fight this monster once before.

"Hello," she answers.

I take a deep breath and jump in. "I need to get high. Right now." As soon as I say the words out loud I'm crying again. "I need help. I can't do this, Claudette. I'm not strong enough."

238

"Honey, Faith, listen to me. You are strong enough. You don't need to use." Her voice is calm, but I can hear the subtle vibration that worry adds. "Where are you?"

"I'm walking to the beach," I answer. I don't know where else to go.

"Whatever you do, do not hang up the phone. Do you hear me?"

I sniff. "I hear you."

An hour later I'm walking in the door of Good Samaritan House. It's a homeless shelter that Claudette tells me offers counseling and other services.

I'm met at the door by a gentleman in his late forties or early fifties, who introduces himself as Benito. His hair is graying and his eyes are thoughtful and wise, like thousands of stories and lessons are housed behind them. He's the shelter's crisis manager. After a brief, no holds barred, verbal retching of my guilt and doubt, he asks me to leave my bag in his office and follow him. "Before we do anything, you need to eat. It's dinnertime."

The tables are all full of men and women in various stages of neglect and vagrancy. I try to turn down the food because I ate a few hours ago with Hope, but he won't hear of it. "Eat. We'll talk after you eat."

I give in and eat.

And afterward, he talks, addressing our earlier discussion and my confessions. "Since you were brave enough to share your story with me earlier, please allow me to share mine with you because I think you need to hear it. I was a heroin addict for fifteen years. I lived on the streets for many of those years. My family disowned me because I lied to them, I stole from them, I disrespected them. I chose getting high over them. I chose getting high over everything. Until I overdosed and woke up in a hospital bed, being told that not only had I almost lost my life, but that I was HIV positive. HIV positive. There aren't many other words that will get your attention like those

239

will. Every drug addict gets a wake-up call, and if we're lucky, the wake-up call isn't death. That was my call. It was also, coincidentally, the moment my little brother, who I hadn't seen in five years, reentered my life. When I was released from the hospital, he took me directly to an inpatient rehabilitation facility. My little brother saved my life. I haven't used since. That was twelve years ago. I don't let my past define me. For a long time, I did. I carried a lot of guilt. Then I realized that I had potential and something to offer the world, everyone does. So, long story short, I see myself in you. I like your spirit. You overcame. You have so much potential, Faith. You just need a little help."

"But, I almost threw away four years of being clean tonight," I say. I don't feel worthy of the help he's trying to give.

"The important thing is you didn't. You had an urge, and you managed it. That's what sobriety is. And I believe deep down that if you had access to drugs, you wouldn't have given in. You would've fought for yourself. Because the young lady who walked in here looking for help is a fighter. A fighter with a gentle heart. That's the best possible combination." He sounds convinced.

By the time I lie down on a cot in the women's room, I'm convinced. The demon is gone. Chased away. The fact that I'm unemployed and homeless remains. I'll take that trade any day.

Pine-Sol gives me a headache

Miranda

Present

If you would've told me I'd be running a homeless shelter a year ago, I would've brazenly, and unapologetically, laughed in your face. There's no reward, and the pay is shit. There's no prestige. The building is in shambles. But, the hardest part is, this job requires compassion.

Compassion is a language I don't speak.

I remind myself I'm trying as I walk in the door my first day on the job. The first thing that assaults me is the smell. It's a mixture of the state of decay of the building itself and the people housed inside. The second thing that assaults me is the voice inside my head shrieking at me to turn around and go home.

I'm questioning everything at this point. But, the biggest question is, why am I trying?

I could lie and say it's for me. That I want to be a better person and grow, but that's unrealistic. The depression is lifting, that's a positive. But actual transformation into a do-gooder isn't possible with my past.

I could lie and say I'm trying for my kids. Though I do feel like we've bonded now, and I enjoy spending time with them, but that's not it either.

Deep down, I know I'm trying for him. For Seamus. I don't need a get out of hell free card, my fate is sealed in that department, not even Seamus could help me avoid it...but I love him. I know I don't love like other people do. My version of love is driven by selfish need, a little self-loathing, and some jealousy. But it feels so damn real when it beats inside my chest, and it's starved for his

241

touch, and his adoring stare, and his loving words, and his complete devotion. God, I miss that. I know games don't work. I wasted years on games. I thought I was winning, most of the time I was losing. Losing him.

So, I'm here. In a job rooted, like Seamus's, in humanitarian effort. Trying. Trying out a job that already doesn't feel like it fits, for a second chance with him. Struggling to open up my mind to the idea of service to others to connect with him. It's a long shot, I know.

The saving grace in all of this, is that this establishment and the non-profit itself, are on the brink of disaster. That's where I come in. It's a business that needs to find funding and efficiencies to ensure its survival and prosperity. I'm looking at it as a chance to push myself creatively and think outside the box. It's about developing a plan to make this company run like a well-oiled machine. It's a challenge. A numbers and strategy challenge, I'm good at those.

I'm introduced to the staff, the vast majority of which are volunteer residents. They cook, they clean, they do maintenance, they act as security, and they manage tangible donations like clothing, food, and hygienic items. They're the engine that powers this train. By the time I make the rounds, I've learned a few things. One: I need to buy some different clothes for work. A five thousand dollar pantsuit doesn't earn me respect from someone in secondhand, ten-year-old, stained, frayed denim. Two: The smell of Pine-Sol gives me a headache. I've never set foot inside a Costco, but I'm stopping at one on my way home and filling the back of my SUV up with cleaning supplies that don't smell like a lemony, antiseptic, artificial, mountain forest. Third: Benito, the shelter's crisis manager, is a good person. I hope he hasn't already figured out I'm a bitch because I need him to stay and help me turn this place around.

You don't get a medal for trying

Seamus

present

My body is being a bastard today. My legs are killing me and my head is thumping like a bass drum, that's been the norm for a week now. But today I feel dizzy, like I'm walking the deck of a ship on rocky waters. I'm leaning into my cane fighting the urge to topple over. Things could be worse, things could always be worse, but I'm in a bad mood, and irritation has put an end to my ability to parley with Miranda.

My kids are in bed. I need to be in bed myself, but I need to have this conversation before I do.

Miranda is sitting on the couch drinking a glass of wine, when I approach and sit on the other end. I lead in with, "How's the new job?"

She nods slowly, I don't know whether she's gearing up for a negative response or if she's just tired. "It's going well."

Good. "Good." Now that I know she's employed, I don't feel bad following it up with, "Your time is almost up here, Miranda. I need you to move out this weekend."

More slow head nodding, but it's different this time, she's thinking, scheming. I know that look. "I'm going to buy a house. I want you and the kids to move in with me."

A sigh whooshes out of me like an angry gust of wind. Maybe I don't have the patience to have this conversation after all and should've gone to bed. I close my eyes to ward off the beginnings of an argument and simply say, "No."

"But, it would make life easier for everyone. You could get rid of your rent payment and save some money. And we could all be together."

For a split second she makes sense: convenience, save money. But then I come to my senses, and *we could all be together* rings like an alarm. "No, Miranda. You need to get your own place. And I need to stay here."

"I'm trying, Seamus," she says softly.

"I know you are." It doesn't sound convincing. I don't have it in me tonight to sound convincing.

"Why aren't you?" she asks.

I'm too tired to decode. "Why am I not what?"

"Trying," she says it as if she's justified in asking. She's pointing a self-righteous finger at me with that one little word.

"That's my goddamn life, Miranda. *Trying*," I say it louder than I should. "Trying to be a good dad. Trying to be a good counselor. Trying to be a good person. Trying to be patient and accepting of my body, and this disease." I could go on and on. "That's what life is, *it's fucking trying*. You don't get a medal for it. It's expected, as a member of the human race, *that you try*."

She's good at keeping her mask on, but I know that's not what she wanted to hear. "Think about the kids. They're thriving with all of us under one roof again."

I shake my head. "They're thriving because they're happy to have two parents who are engaged in their lives. It's all they've ever wanted. Hell, it's all I've ever wanted. Propinquity isn't driving the parent-child relationship, effort is. Effort can be made successfully from two houses divided by miles, especially if it's a handful of miles instead of hundreds."

She's thinking, not about what I just said, but about what she's going to say next.

I stand before she decides to continue the debate. "I need you out this weekend. Goodnight."

I know this will turn into a fight, not an arguing match, but quiet evasion. She'll stay, hoping I'll cave to avoid confrontation—the passive aggressive approach. I mastered passive aggressive for years, so I know it when I see it. I'm prepared to put her shit in my car and drive her to a hotel myself. I'll show her how aggressive this pacifist can get.

I see myself in you

Faith

present

"Faith, can I speak to you for a minute?" Benito asks as I'm mopping the floor of the dining hall.

"Of course. What's up?" I'm worried that because I got a job yesterday, they're going to ask me to leave. But I can't find a place to live until I save up some money.

"I hear you got a job yesterday?" he asks.

"I did. Waitressing evenings at a diner. I start at five tomorrow." *Please don't ask me to leave. Please don't ask me to leave.*

He smiles his big, gentle grin and I relax into it. "Congratulations."

"Thank you."

"And because you're already working, I understand if you decline my offer. I'm opening up a bakery with my brother in a few weeks. It's always been a dream of his." He smiles as if the thought makes him happy. "I would like to hire you."

"Pardon me?" I only ask because I need time to calm my excitement.

His smile grows as I'm unable to contain mine. "I want to hire you."

"I would love to, but I don't know how to bake. Except bread pudding. Oh, and chocolate dump cake, I can make a mean chocolate dump cake." I'm rambling, so I stop.

He's laughing quietly. "My brother is the baker, he'll stay back in the kitchen. He needs someone friendly and competent to run the front end, selling goods to customers, both walk-in and phone orders. His wife will

246

work Monday through Wednesday. Your schedule would be Thursday through Sunday from five in the morning until two in the afternoon. Does that sound like something you'd like to do?"

My head is nodding very fast. "Yes. Yes! Yes, please. Thank you. Thank you so much." And before I know it I'm hugging him, which makes him laugh harder.

"No. Thank you, Faith. One more thing, I live with my brother. He and his wife rent out a few rooms in their home. They set up the basement like a co-op. There are three small bedrooms, so you would have your privacy; and a community living room, kitchen, and bathroom that you would share with two other tenants. They charge four hundred dollars a month, but that includes utilities. They have a room opening up this weekend. If you'd like to check it out, I can give you the address. No pressure, but if you like it, it's yours."

I'm waiting for the punchline. I'm waiting for him to tell me this is a joke. But I guess the joke is I don't have four hundred dollars. I shrug. "That's so kind of you, but I don't have the money. It will take me a week or two to earn that much."

His face softens at my admission. "I know you don't. My brother is aware of your current living situation and is willing to let you move in and pay him when you're able."

Being genuinely stunned by overwhelming kindness is one of my favorite occurrences in life. Maybe because it happens so rarely on a grand scale like this. Or maybe because it comes out of the blue and you're not prepared for it. But it threatens to knock me off balance and bring me to my knees every time. There are tears in my eyes when I hug him again. I hug him hard and long, and I cry into his shoulder. When I release him, I look him in the eye. "Why? Why me?"

"Remember the first night we met? After dinner, we talked, and I shared my story?" he asks thoughtfully.

247

I nod. I'll never forget that night.

"Like I said, I see myself in you. That and I've watched you working hard at the shelter this week; any task you're given you do it without complaint, and you do it well. All with a smile on your face and a grateful heart. You show kindness toward others, never judging circumstance. That's refreshing. As I said earlier, you have so much potential. You just need a little help."

Claudette's words spring to mind, something she told me on my recent visit about superheroes walking amongst us, and that they have the ability to make someone who felt unseen, unwanted, and unloved feel special. I'm convinced Benito is a Batman angel like Claudette, and that's all it takes for me to accept his help and stop questioning myself. "I'll take the room. Thank you."

He writes down the address for the bakery and the home, they're only blocks apart, and hands it to me. The paper feels heavy in my hand, heavy with hope and promise and new beginnings.

"Thank you," I tell him again. I have a feeling I'll tell him that a lot.

Nobody pisses on my rainbow

Miranda

present

I'm a jealous person. I think most people are if they're honest with themselves. I feel a small degree of jealousy most of the time. Whether it's directed at the person in front of me in line at Starbucks who the handsome barista flirts with, or the twenty-year-old running on the beach with the perfect body who reminds me those days are gone, and it's all about maintenance from here on out, or that goddamn Bobby Flay because he can cook his ass off. I'm jealous.

But, what I feel when I look at this woman is a raging variety, so rare that its presence is manic, and I'm unable to function normally when I'm bound by it.

It's her. Faith. God, even her name makes my insides tighten up into a fist. An MMA fist. The kind of fist that can pummel another human being into unconsciousness. Seeing photos of Seamus's hands on her, his mouth on her, are burned into my brain. And meeting her face to face was sickening: skin so flawless it glowed, eyes so blue they look Photoshopped, hair so edgy it only adds to her sex appeal, a body so perfectly youthful that any man would beg to give it a ride, and her goddamn sweet disposition. Beautiful and nice; fuck the creators of that little angel. She makes me feel like hell.

I pried her and Seamus apart with lies. She didn't make it hard, she was a stripper for Christ's sake. Not that I blame her, with a body like that I'd show my tits to the free world too. But she wasn't a prostitute. I paid men to approach her with outrageous amounts of money, so I could get the proof I needed. She always denied them. In the end, I lied instead.

249

Why is she here at the shelter? Hope said she moved. I thought she was long gone. How am I supposed to get Seamus back if she starts poking around again?

Fuck.

The longer I stand here and look at her the more deranged I feel. It would be wrong as the director of this facility to punch her in the throat, right? But she's ruining my mojo. I was having a good day. My lunch meeting with a key contributor resulted in a six-figure donation. We fed fifty additional people this morning. And it turns out my ass looks fantastic in utilitarian denim, who knew?

I march to my office and call in Benito.

"What's Rainbow Bright up to?" I ask before his ass hits the chair.

"Excuse me?" I know political correctness has its place in the corporate world, but anyone who's ever worked directly under me knows I leave that shit at the door. I guess Benito is about to get an introduction.

"The girl with the dreadlocks." They're fading from what they were months ago when I met her, muted pastels and blond now.

"Oh, Faith?" he questions.

I nod. "Faith."

"She's a resident. She's been here for a few days now. She's in transition between jobs and homes." He always sounds so damn considerate when he talks, respectful and professional.

Which makes me sound like a miscreant when I ask, "You're shitting me?"

His forehead pulls up in mild confusion. "No. Is there a problem?"

"She slept with my husband." I'm talking to myself more than I'm talking to him, but he responds anyway.

"I didn't know you were married?" he asks. He's uncomfortable talking about all of this I can tell. Clearly political correctness is an adage he subscribes to.

250

"I'm not. He's my ex-husband. She slept with him while I thought I was married to someone else." I shake my head because that sounded ludicrous. "It's a long story we don't have time for."

He nods slowly. He's confused.

I wave him off. "Thanks for the information, Benito. You can get back to work."

My mind is reeling, I haven't been this angry in months. Depression dulled everything. Now that that's lifted, and I'm working again and working on Seamus again, I was flying high. I was making plans. She's just pissed on my rainbow. Nobody pisses on my rainbow. Especially not beautiful, young women who've fucked my ex-husband. Sonofabitch, I hate that word...ex-husband. Because in the pit of my stomach, where I try to deny it away but can't, it feels final, rigid, and irredeemable.

I need to dream to sleep

Seamus

Present

The kids and I walked to the beach this afternoon after school. I always find myself searching the crowds for Faith. Hoping I'll see her standing on her milk crate with her *free hugs* sign. She's never there, and every time I kick myself for not fighting for her. I didn't have a choice, though, did I? It was my kids or her. So, I dream about her instead. Every night. I don't have to sleep to dream, but I've found lately that I do need to dream to sleep. I dream about her until I drift off…and then I dream about her some more.

It's Friday night. Miranda moves out this weekend. We all watched a movie together at home. The kids ate popcorn. Miranda had a glass of wine. And I had a few beers in quiet celebration because shouting, "Yay, you're finally leaving!" would be a dick move. Getting buzzed and thinking, *Yay, you're finally leaving!* was much more discreet.

After I put the kids to bed, I'm already dreaming of Faith, but I don't want to go to bed yet. I'm restless and missing her. Most days I think about her smile, or those eyes, or how she made me laugh, or how she accepted me exactly the way I am, flaws and all; but tonight I'm thinking about our last night together. The way she looked, how she tasted, the sounds she made. It was perfect. I need some fresh air, I feel claustrophobic. Maybe I had too much to drink.

Maybe I didn't have enough to drink.

As if she heard that last thought, Miranda joins me outside. "You look like you can use this." She's holding a bottle of tequila and two shot glasses.

I almost hesitate because I don't want to get drunk. But then I figure what the hell, *Yay, you're finally leaving!* "Sure, why not."

She pours two and I throw it back before she toasts. She pours two more and says, "To the future."

I was trying to ignore her, but I mutter, "To the future," before I toss it back and finish the thought, *and you leaving*, in my mind. I'm leaning against the railing looking down below at Faith's scooter, that's no longer Faith's scooter. The tequila is mixing with the beer in my system. And slowly everything starts blurring and there's a whooshing sound in my ears.

"One more," Miranda offers.

I shake my head. I don't want it. I want to go inside, take off my clothes, crawl into bed, and dream about Faith.

She pours anyway and hands it to me. "I don't want it," I say immediately after I drink it. Then I hand her the empty shot glass and stagger inside. I shut my bedroom door behind me, and as I take off my clothes, all I see is Faith. Naked. And so fucking beautiful. And before I know it I'm naked in my bed, taking care of business, and pretending it's her. The big finish comes quickly, but it doesn't stop me from continuing the dream while I drift off to sleep.

Her weight on top of me is welcome, her presence foreplay in itself. It's dark, I can't see her, but her lips are working their way across my chest, up my neck, across my jawline.

"Kiss me," I beg.

She does. Lips, tongue, teeth, they're all in play. Slow, languid sweeps of her tongue. Teeth pulling playfully at my bottom lip. Lips so soft.

253

"I've missed you," I whisper between kisses. "I've missed you so much." I'm talking to her, and to me, and to us.

The rest of my body awakens as her nakedness grinds purposefully against mine. Legs draped on either side of my hips. Flesh on flesh creating friction that speaks to nerve endings and sends jolts of pleasure through both of us.

"I've missed you, too."

I freeze. I've dreamt about those words coming out of Faith's mouth.

But that wasn't Faith.

And this isn't a dream.

It's a goddamn nightmare.

I push her off me, climb out of bed and turn on the light.

Miranda is lying naked in my bed.

"Jesus Christ," I mutter, as I search for my boxers on the floor and slip into them. This can't be happening. "Get out."

She grins, but it's complete humiliation as she covers herself with the sheet. "You thought I was someone else." It's not a question, it's a statement saturated with embarrassment and regret. Uncharacteristic.

I look her in the eye and nod. "I'm drunk. I was dreaming. In the privacy of my own bed," I add to remind her how warped this whole scene is. "Yes, I thought you were someone else."

"Faith?" she questions.

I nod again.

"What is it about her, Seamus? Why is she so special?" I would expect this to sound whiney or pouty, but she sounds sad like she's finally come to the realization that we're over and there will never be a second chance.

I don't want to have this conversation, especially in my current state and hers, but I also fear that if I don't air this, we'll revisit it again because Miranda is nothing, if not

254

persistent. "Her heart. It rules her. Every action, every smile, every word, every touch, is driven by it. Do you have any idea what it's like to be on the receiving end of that?"

She pulls back the sheet and climbs out of bed, immediately pulling on her nightgown. "I do." She shrugs. "She's you." She walks out without another word. Understanding firmly in place.

Maybe it's the alcohol in my system muddying it up, but I feel bad for her. It's overwhelming pity; that downgrades hate to dislike, with disclaimers that ward off lifting the veil to allow forgiveness in. Damn her; hate is preferable where Miranda's concerned.

Parenthood isn't genetic

Seamus

present

Miranda is out with her realtor looking at a house. She took the kids with her, which was considerate given they'll live with her half the time according to the new custody arrangement my lawyer is working on. Miranda's committed to staying in this neighborhood to make things easier for everyone, which shocked the hell out of me, but I'm thankful. So thankful. My lawyer wants to make sure that happens before we finalize the paperwork. We already have Miranda's written agreement to modify custody to joint. It's just the details we're waiting on now.

It's Saturday morning, and I'm not quite sure what to do with myself. The apartment is too quiet. I don't like being here alone without the kids, it's almost terror inducing because my mind reverts to the months they were gone. I don't ever want to go through that again.

A knock on the door saves me from myself.

When I open the door, I want to close it immediately.

"Seamus." There's an odd combination of formality and friendliness in his voice. The friendliness seems out of place.

I meet it with formality. "Loren."

"I know this is unexpected." He looks pale, thinner than he was weeks ago.

I nod. "I assume you're looking for Miranda. She's not here. She'll be back later this afternoon."

"Actually, I'm here to talk to you." I can't read his voice, but the look in his eyes is regret.

256

"Okay." I sound confused. I am confused. Very confused. "Come in."

He sits down on the couch and sets his leather briefcase on the floor next to him. He looks out of place. His eyes are darting around the room taking in everything. He's judging me, I can feel it. Fuck him and his superior attitude.

"Seamus, I'm going to get right to the point." I feel like I'm being talked to by administration at work. It's the tone taken by those in a position of authority when they have to deliver bad news, and they've already divided themselves from the emotional aspect of it and are going in as a spokesperson only, not a supporter.

"I'd appreciate that," I offer. I wish he would just spit it out. He's making me nervous now.

He clears his throat and sets his briefcase on the coffee table, unlatching the lid while he says, "Please sit down." He looks at me and his eyes tell me he's not messing around, that this is serious.

"I'll stand," I counter. I want to sit now, but my stubborn streak has just been issued a formal challenge.

He looks down like he's displeased with my decision. "Very well. I'll begin. I had a massive heart attack days after Miranda left. Triple bypass surgery to put the pieces back together immediately followed. They tell me I'm extremely lucky to be alive."

"I'm sorry." I don't know why I said it, he didn't pause his story looking for a reaction; I guess I just felt it needed to be said.

He nods. "Thank you. Coming that close to death led me to a re-evaluate my life and my priorities. I'm selling my business and retiring. I'm selling my home to travel the world to see all of the places I never allowed myself time to visit. Hopefully, I'll find somewhere that suits me, and I'll settle down there."

"Okay. No offense, but I don't understand why you came all the way to California to tell me this." I'm not trying to be rude, but this doesn't make any sense. This is a conversation you have with friends or family, I'm neither.

"I have something that's yours, and I need to make that right before I leave." There's compassion in his eyes.

Now I'm nervous again. "What?" It's the only thing I can say. My brain won't come up with anything else.

He looks me in the eye, and I'm in no way prepared to hear what comes out of his mouth. "I'm Kira's father."

What? I don't know if I'm thinking the word, or if I said it out loud, but it's echoing inside my skull. He was right, I need to sit down. I take a seat on the couch next to him, and my head drops into my hands. This cannot be happening. "Please tell me this is a cruel joke," I say from behind my hands.

"I'm sorry, Seamus. I knew Miranda would never tell you, but I felt you had the right to know. And as I said before, I need to make this right."

I huff out a disgusted laugh. "Right? *Right?* How in the hell are you going to make this right? Kira is my daughter. I love that little girl with everything in me." Tears are blotting my eyes as my thoughts race, and this conversation takes a nosedive into an abyss.

"I know you do. And you're correct, she is your daughter. I may be responsible for half of her genetic make-up, but you are her father and always have been." He reaches into his briefcase and pulls out a stack of papers. "I know that your name is already on her birth certificate, but there was a test done that established paternity. I would like to complete this official adoption paperwork, just in case Miranda ever tries to take her away from you. Miranda can be quite conniving, and I couldn't live with myself knowing I could've done something to protect Kira and didn't. I want to leave knowing she's yours, once and for all."

I don't know whether that was a callous or a considerate thing for him to do. I'm still talking into my hands. "How long have you known? How long has Miranda known?"

"We've both known since she discovered she was pregnant. The paternity test was done at birth." He sounds truly apologetic.

"What the fuck?" I'm whispering. I'm talking to me. I'm talking to him. I'm talking to Miranda, even though she's not here. I'm talking to a God I'm not sure I believe in because he wouldn't let shit like this happen. Loren leaves me to wallow in my shock induced silence for several minutes. When I finally look at him, I ask him point blank, "What do you want? You must want something, what is it?"

"I want to die with a clear conscience. I've done so many things I regret. So many things I can't change. So many things I can't make right. This is one that I can. Kira deserves to be yours in every way possible. You are her father and a far better man than I. I never intended to bring a child into this world, Seamus, but she's a beautiful child, and that is solely thanks to your hand in raising her. I want you to finish that job unhindered."

So many questions, I have so many questions, but my mind can't put the words together properly to articulate them. "Do you want Kira to know about you?"

He shakes his head. "No. She loves you. Not that her knowing about me would change that, but I don't want anything to complicate your relationship with her."

I look at the papers on the table. "So, I sign these, and you walk away, and we never hear from you again?" I ask.

He nods and the look in his eyes is sincere, a father talking to a father. "Yes."

"What if Kira finds out someday? Miranda has a big mouth. What if she wants to get to know you? Or what if there's a health issue and we need information from you?"

259

"You or Kira can always contact me if that sort of need arises. But, if the need never arises, I would prefer she never know."

I want to call him a deadbeat father, because who does this? Who lets someone else raise their child and doesn't get involved? But then I think about the kids I've counseled over the years; the kids who had parents who didn't want them or mistreated them; or the kids who were raised by guardians other than their parents who loved them fiercely and guided them into adulthood successfully and gracefully. Parenthood isn't genetic, it's about commitment and love. Period. I look him in the eye before I sign the papers. "Kira's always been mine in my heart. This paperwork doesn't change that."

He nods. "I know that, Seamus. And thank you."

"I'd like to have my lawyer review these before I sign them." I'm never signing anything again without my lawyer's blessing.

"I expected that you would. Overnight them to my office when the review is complete."

"I'll have them back to you in a few days if he's satisfied, or call with questions if he's not."

"Of course, I'm always available by cell phone. My number is in the documents."

"Thank you."

We shake hands.

And he leaves.

My mind is full of questions. How did I not know? Why did Miranda hide this? What would Kira think if she knew? But the one thing that rises above it all isn't a question at all, it's an absolute: I love Kira. Because more than anything else that's what matters. Am I angry? Hell yes. Do I feel betrayed? Beyond belief. But, more than that I love my little girl.

The wait for them to return is long, not in a matter of minutes, but in heartbeats. Because each one reminds me of my anger. I feel it pulsing along in my bloodstream.

Each time it constricts I tick off another thing about Miranda that disgusts me. It's a cause and effect. One leads to the next, leads to the next, and before I know it I'm thinking about things I haven't thought of in years. Things I'd put behind me are heat in my veins again.

When the door finally opens, I hug each of my kids to absorb some calm. And I vow someday very soon to get answers from Miranda, someday after the adoption is finalized and she can't meddle.

That's a stunner to open with

Faith
present

"Faith?" It's accompanied by knocking on my bedroom door. It's Benito's voice.

I open the door to his smiling face. "I brought you a cup of coffee."

I perk up at the sight of it. It's become a ritual at my new home to have coffee with him on the nights I don't work at the diner. I look forward to it. Our chats are short, but they always cover a wide range of topics. Benito knows a little bit about everything because he reads so much, but he's not a know-it-all. He usually delves into something further only when I've prompted him or asked questions. And he's always curious to hear what I have to say; I like that. Good listeners are rare. He's like the dad I always wanted.

"What are your dreams, Faith?" Our conversations begin with a question like this, because we need a starting point. Usually, they go down bunny trails, in two minutes we could be talking about the relevance of hip-hop in modern culture or if the Dodgers are going to make the playoffs this year, you just never know.

"That's a stunner to open with, Benito." I'm thinking. Dreams are hard to put into words.

"I like to keep you on your toes, young lady." His grin tells me that's true.

"That shouldn't be a hard question, should it? I mean, most people grow up with dreams. They're defined and vivid and can be measured. My dreams growing up were survival based for the most part. I dreamed of a nice family to live with. I dreamed of my favorite meals. I

262

dreamed of having a new pair of shoes. The older I get I dream about going to college someday. I dream about finding my birth mother. I dream about figuring out who I am...so I can just be her, you know?"

Benito nods at my words. "I believe you do know...*you are her*. You're just too scared to go after the things you really want because you don't think you deserve them. I'm here to tell you that you do."

"Addiction is a hard thing to get out from under. It's shameful. It's polarizing. It's defining. Even when it's behind you, it's never really behind you. I still feel like my past will always dictate my future. That's a tough hurdle." It's nice to talk to someone I can be this candid with.

"Every day is a new day. It took me years to believe that, Faith, but it's true. Every day is a new opportunity to be the person you've always wanted to be. Some days your heart will be in it, and some days you'll fake it, but eventually it will become a habit and without thinking about it, you will be changed anew. A new attitude. A new outlook. A new perspective. The human mind is a wonderful thing to grant us that kind of change." He pauses and smiles. "What else do you dream of, Faith?"

I sip my coffee before I answer because this one is harder to explain. "Love."

He's leaned back in his seat. His posture is never lazy, but it's always relaxed. I think that's one of the reasons he's so easy to talk to. "Love. That's very general. Do you care to expound on that?"

"When I was growing up I just wanted someone to love me." I shrug. "That's what every kid wants, right? The past few years that's changed. I mean, I still want someone to love me, but more than that I want someone to love. I want reciprocation. I want connection. I want to wake up in the morning thinking about him and go to sleep at night doing the same. Not in an obsessive, unhealthy way, but I want to know what it's like to have

263

so much emotion inside for another person that it manifests itself in selfless, kind, random acts. I want their well-being and happiness to be taken into consideration unconsciously, because it's second nature. I want attraction, not just physically, but emotionally and mentally, I want to be inexplicably pulled to someone. And for them to feel the same. What an unbelievably beautiful circumstance that would be to be in..." I trail off, because all I can think about is Seamus.

His eyes are thoughtful. He can read between the lines. "What an unbelievably beautiful circumstance to be in indeed. Well put, my dear."

He stands, which means it's time for him to leave. Sometimes our time together only lasts minutes. "Thank you, Benito."

"You're welcome." He walks toward the stairs, but stops just short. "Faith?"

I'm still sitting on the couch. "Yeah."

"I hope he knows what an unbelievably beautiful circumstance he could be in with you."

I smile, this is Benito giving fatherly advice. "Sometimes life isn't that easy, Benito."

"And sometimes, it isn't that hard." He disappears with a wink.

Were you sent straight from hell to destroy my life?

Miranda

present

I'm worshipping at the altar of Pinterest again. Lasagna is the target of my affection. I've been stalking it like a sociopath, a carb-loving sociopath, for the past thirty minutes.

I check my watch. Seven o'clock. In the morning. It's Saturday, and I'm picking up the kids from Seamus's at eight. Now that I'm in my new house we've agreed they'll spend weekends with me.

I clap my hands. "Hell yes, we're having homemade lasagna for dinner." It's positive reinforcement, mental preparation for the culinary challenge ahead. I grab my keys and purse and march out the door on a mission. The mission includes the grocery store, Seamus's, and while I'm at it I hijack my cooking talisman, Hope — a little insurance that dinner will be palatable. Hope is a goddamn genius in the kitchen. Everyone has a hidden talent — Hope's, it turns out, is food.

Everyone and everything gathered, we assemble back at my house for Operation Lasagna.

Rory, Kira, Hope, and I are knee-deep in making noodles using the fancy contraption I bought, when Kai bows out to go outside and ride his bike. "Stay close, Kai," I yell when I hear the front door open.

"I will, Mom," he answers.

This is the point at which, in hindsight, I want to stop everything and put it in temporary suspense.

Life.
The Earth spinning on its axis.
Every.
Fucking.
Thing.

I want a do-over.

In my do-over, this is what would've happened:
I tell Kai no, he can't ride his bike. Ever again.
He stays and we all tag team the hell out of building a glorious pan of Italian magnificence.
We eat said Italian magnificence in blissful harmony at my dining room table.
Happily ever after.
The end.

Instead, this happened:
I realized I forgot the damn ricotta cheese, because I'm a forgetful loser.
I asked Hope to watch the kids while I ran to the grocery store, instead of taking them with me like a good mom would.
I hurried out to my car and started it with only conquering lasagna on my mind in true self-absorbed fashion, because I'm a selfish bitch.
And then I backed out with a vengeance, forgetting there are more important things in the world than making lasagna.
I heard the crash.
I felt the impact.
And my heart.
Stopped.
Beating.

They say change comes when you least expect it.
That all transformation needs is a catalyst.

266

I'll take transformation, but I want a different fucking catalyst.

I'm mechanically filling out forms though I can't see the words on the page through the fear blotting my vision and streaming down my face. The words, *You're a horrible monster*, repeat over and over taunting me like the soundtrack of a horror movie. I'm arguing with them, praying, trading promises, *I'm sorry. I'm so sorry. Please let him be okay. I'll do anything. Anything. Take me instead.*

"Daddy," Kira's voice is weak with sadness, and it pulls me out of my trance.

Seamus is standing just inside the automatic doors, scanning the waiting room for us.

Rory charges to him from the seat next to me.

I'm scared to look at his face. Whatever emotion he's wearing will be a variety so raw it will strip me to the bone. And I've got no flesh left. I forgot what I said to him on the phone when I called. *Kai. Bike. Car. Accident. Hospital.* Those are the only words I can recall now.

"Is there any news, Miranda? What are his injuries? What have the doctors said?" The words are shaky with dread, but to the point and protective. He's laser-focused in thought and mission, in problem-solving mode. His posture is stiff and rigid with determination.

But when I meet his eyes, all the fear I feel is reflected back at me tenfold, so I do the only thing I can do. I lie. To put his heart at ease for a bit, I lie. "We don't have details yet, but he's going to be okay, Seamus."

"You're sure he's going to be okay?" he asks, eyes pleading for good news.

I nod, and my stomach turns at the lie.

He releases a wobbly breath. It's relief, and he sits in the chair next to me. Rory crawls into the chair next to him and takes his hand, and Kira climbs into his lap, and he wraps his arm around her. The three of them cluster

267

into a loving, supportive mass because they know how this whole family thing works. They've mastered it.

I'm reminded again that I've failed. Kai. Them. Me. You name it. I've messed it up. I let them find comfort in each other while I finish the paperwork. When I return it to the nurse's station, I ask if there's any news. "They're prepping him for surgery. A doctor will be out to speak to you shortly."

Shortly isn't soon enough when the mortality of my child is in question.

"Lost a lot of blood. Broken femur. Ruptured spleen. Broken ribs. Surgery." He says more, but those are the words I remember.

I'm pleading again. *Please let Kai be okay. I'll do anything. I'll change. I'll be the best mother the world has ever seen if you just let my little boy be okay. Please.*

As if he can read my desperate thoughts, Seamus says, "He's a tough kid, Miranda. He's going to get through this." Even though he just heard the same news I did, it's optimistic Seamus putting positive words into action. Willing it to be true. He won't even allow himself to consider a different outcome.

I felt pain when my grandmother died. It was crushing pain. My world was forever changed, my guiding force was gone. This pain is different. I've never felt anything like it. It's worse, *it's so much worse.* It feels like pain I won't be able to recover from. Pain that's slowly squeezing my heart within a fist, and if this all goes bad it will constrict until it ruptures from the pressure, leaving only mutilated pieces to fall away in an act of defeat.

The pain is also the biggest epiphany I've ever had. I love my kids. Because only love could create this kind of reaction within me. Not guilt, but love.

I stand only to kneel in front of them. I take Kira's hand and rub the side of Rory's calf. "I'm going to find you both something to eat." When I look at Seamus's face

268

it's blank, he's checked out and pulled inside to deal with this. Focusing all of his energy and thoughts on Kai. "Can I get you anything?"

The question doesn't register in his eyes, but he shakes his head.

The wait is hell. I never realized what a formidable opponent time could be. It teams up with my thoughts and drives me to the brink of insanity all within the span of a few hours. It's a constant battle. One minute I have myself convinced Kai is going to be fine. The next minute I'm cursing the universe that the possibility exists that children can be taken before their parents.

By their parent.

The doctor returns with more news. More words. "Critical condition. Sedated. ICU. Monitor closely. No visitors."

Though his body still looks alert and determined, the light is still absent from Seamus's eyes, exhaustion and fear have drained him. "I need to see him," he pleads. "*Please.*"

"I'm sorry, Mr. McIntyre. The situation is too unstable at this time to allow visitors." I can't see through my tears, but the doctor sounds sadly sympathetic.

Seamus was keeping it together. Not anymore. His eyes are glassy. I watch his Adam's apple bob as he swallows, he's struggling to keep his composure. "He's my son. *Please.* He needs to know I'm here. That he's not alone. I need to see him. *I just need to see him to know he's okay.*"

The doctor offers another, "I'm sorry," before he disappears down the hall to our son.

Seamus hesitates for a minute before he rises and marches down the hall leaning heavily on his cane. I know where he's going, but I don't stop him.

The nurses do. "Sir, you can't go back there. Sir, stop."

269

Seamus doesn't stop and disappears behind a door.

Only to reappear moments later escorted by two males in scrubs.

"He's my son! I have a fucking right to see him!" His shouting is pain, nothing more. Sadness and fear have grown so great they've turned into pain.

The men are holding his arms tightly. They look small flanking his tall frame. "He can't be back there," they say to me when I approach. "Get him under control," one of them adds rudely, as if Seamus is the first person to ever act out under stress in this facility.

I nod. "He's upset."

"Upset doesn't mean you don't have to follow the rules, ma'am." He's laying down the law like Seamus was caught trespassing on private property, there's no emotion involved. And then he repeats, "Get him under control or I'll call security and have him removed. Understand?"

I step to him. "Do you have children?"

He shakes his head.

I lower my voice and the barracuda in me comes out. No one is going to fuck with my family today, Seamus included. "Then you have no idea what he's going through. Don't be an asshole. I'm not asking you to break rules, but back off and show some goddamn compassion. His son is fighting for his life back there." I point to the door in a violent manner because punching this guy in the teeth won't help our situation. "There's no need to make threats."

He's unblinking but unhands Seamus. Words are over. My dirty looks aren't, my scowl follows them as they retreat behind the door.

"I need some air, are you good with Rory and Kira?" He's a shattered man and it's killing me knowing I've done this to him. I'm responsible for all of the pain in his life. All of it.

"We'll be fine. They're sleeping. Go outside. Take your time. We're not going anywhere." I wish I could help him. All those years when he needed me and would've accepted and welcomed my help, I ran the other way. Now, when I want nothing more than to be the one he turns to, it's his turn to run. My timing is absolute shit.

Watching him walk away makes me realize that when you love someone, you only want what's best for them. And how much I wish what was best for him was me. It's not. It never was, and it never will be. And then I sit down in a chair next to Rory and Kira, who are both sleeping, and I bawl. It's crying that wets my cheeks and demolishes my soul. The tears are for Kai. And Seamus. And me. And my grandmother. All for different reasons. I can't get the visual of Kai lying crumpled, bleeding, and unmoving on the street out of my head. It was an accident.

Accident.

An innocuous occurrence.

Until it involves my little boy on a bike being hit by my car.

Or my grandmother riding in the seat next to me.

There should be a different word for this type of accident. Accident seems too mild when tragedy is involved. Accident—Kai and my grandmother are meshing together in my mind until they're one bloody heap that I feel wickedly responsible for. For years, I've tried to ignore the guilt that crushes me regarding my grandmother. It has a far weightier companion now.

When Seamus returns, I'm cried out. For now, anyway. I excuse myself to the restroom.

Bladder relieved, face splashed with cold water that does nothing to relieve mental or physical anguish, the waiting room receives me back in like an unwelcome guest. I wonder if Seamus can feel my guilt, it's a larger presence in the room than I am. I need to tell him what happened and face his justified wrath.

Rory and Kira are huddled together, still sleeping in one big chair under Seamus's jacket. Part of me wants to close my eyes too, but even if I did, I know I wouldn't be

271

able to sleep, my waking nightmares are worse than anything my imagination could dream up. I may never close my eyes again and just endure the torture.

I drop into the chair across from Seamus. He's sitting up straight in his chair, but it's contradictory to the exhaustion and sorrow in his eyes.

"You can talk to me, you know?" he says. It's quiet, I'm sure because of the late hour and the kids sleeping next to him, but it's also his concerned voice. A voice I haven't heard in years. A voice that wraps me up like a warm blanket.

"My grandmother died." This is me talking.

He looks at me thoughtfully, he's never heard this story, and I'm sure he wasn't expecting anything remotely close to this. "The one who raised you?"

I nod.

"When did it happen?" he questions. I know he thinks this is strange; I've always refused to talk about her to him.

"I was eighteen. She was sixty-two though I always thought of her as ageless. A woman with the wisdom time affords, but with the vitality and enthusiasm of someone much younger. An enigma. The type of person who should be able to dodge death, outsmart it, forever."

"I'm sorry," he says.

"I killed her. It was my fault." I've thought those words thousands of times. They're loud and condemning in my head, but quiet and wounded when they dribble between my lips. It should worry me that this type of shock-worthy declaration is registering shock-free on his face. But I'm not worried about me for once. I'm purging. Purging all the bad. "We were in a car crash. Hit a tree. I was driving."

"Sounds like an accident. Accidents aren't anyone's fault." It's still his concerned voice. I know that will all soon change.

I take a deep breath and when I do the sob climbs from somewhere deep in the bowels of me where I bury the ugliest of the ugly and erupts in quiet expulsion. "It's my fault. I was in such a fucking hurry. I needed the fucking ricotta cheese, and that's all I was thinking about."

When I look at Seamus, his eyes are wide and disbelief is mounting in them, contorting his face though he's fighting it. I watch it slowly transform into the grimace of hate. He knows I'm not talking about my grandmother. "What exactly are you saying, Miranda?"

I look away and turn my brain off because I can't bear to hear the words, let alone say them. "I hit Kai. It's my fault. It's all my fault. I'm sorry." My body is shaking, not in fear, but self-loathing. I'm preparing myself for the onslaught of rage.

He leans over and presses the heels of his hands into his eyes and I watch his fingers curl into fists that look like they could punch through steel. His right heel is vibrating up and down like a jackhammer, ferocious and destructive. Quicker than I've seen him move in years, he leaps from his seat and strides roughly on a grave limp to the other side of the room. When he stops, his back is to me. He looks larger than his six foot four inches, filling up the other half of the room with his presence. Hands on hips, head dropped back so he's peering at the ceiling, I watch his posture stiffen into something I've never seen before. He's preparing for a fight.

Let me have it, Seamus, I think to myself. *The kids are sleeping; say everything you've kept bottled up for years. It's time. I deserve it.*

He doesn't hesitate and spins on his heel. Eyes blazing, he thrusts an accusatory finger at me. *"You. Fucking. Bitch."* It's a low, growling whisper.

I don't respond. The truth pierces my nonexistent armor, and I let it wound me, breach my skin, muscle, and bone.

273

"Were you sent straight from hell to destroy my life, Miranda? Because that's how it feels. Years upon years of destruction." He's spitting the words at me through barely moving lips and gritted teeth. "Is there anything you'd like to say before I continue because shit's about to get real? Buckle up."

"I love you." It isn't filler, it's the prologue to the horror story that's about to unfold. It's my one ultimate truth.

For a fraction of a second he just stares at me; it's outrage. *"You don't know how to love, Miranda."* His words are biting, bitterness and anger, a vicious pair.

Regret is leaking from my eyes and dripping on my folded hands in my lap. A year ago I called him broken. He's not. I am. Always have been.

He shakes his head and takes a deep breath before he stabs me again. "You killed my baby. Without even telling me, before, during, or after, you killed my baby." His voice cracks. "Why? Why didn't I get a say?" He's trying to hold his outburst to a whisper, but it's strained. The veins in his neck are bulging with effort. "Why?" His lips don't move when he says it. His words pry my ribcage open to get at the heart of me.

"I'm sorry, Seamus." I have no idea how he knows about the abortion, and I don't bother to deny as he delivers his truth.

He takes three steps toward me, leans forward and spews more truth, "Sorry doesn't resurrect what could have been. *Sorry does fuck all to right your wrongs.*"

The tears continue as I welcome his hellfire.

He retreats a few steps and takes a seat putting needed distance between us again. His hostile glare is frightening, not because I fear him, but because I know I created this fury inside this gentle man. "How many affairs were there aside from Loren? While I was sitting at home blindly loving and trusting my wife, how many men were sticking their dick in her?"

274

Shame, it hits me like a wrecking ball. "Dozens," I answer honestly. The time for hiding is over. The admission is humiliating.

His eyes widen, and his mouth drops open. "Dozens?" he questions.

My head weighs five hundred pounds when I nod. "Dozens," I confirm.

Mouth still agape in shock, his head drops back and his eyes go to the ceiling, probably to avoid having to look at me. "Jesus fucking Christ. Dozens," he repeats to himself. "I'm so fucking stupid."

"You're not stupid, Seamus. You were a good husband. I was a shit wife. That's not your fault; it's mine. You deserved better. From the start, you deserved better. I'm just not equipped for better." I wipe my running nose with the back of my hand, the tears still flowing freely.

He runs his hands through his hair before his chin drops to his chest. "Did you feel remorse? When you were fucking them did guilt ever cross your mind?"

More honesty. I shake my head and feel my face scrunch up as a fresh round of regret and emotion batter me. "No, not at the time."

He huffs like the wind's been knocked out of him.

"But now? I'd give anything to go back to the first day we met. I'd give anything to be a different person then. I'd give anything to have been able to love you the way you loved me." My words are shaky and tear stained.

His watery eyes fill quickly and spill onto his cheeks in a silent display, and I know that he knows my secret. "Were you ever going to tell me about Kira?"

I'm not even shocked that he knows. I'm relieved I didn't have to drop the bombshell on him. "No." It's a single syllable delivered on an exhalation of air, all emotion, lacking enunciation.

Hate and hurt are uncorked. Again. His face pinches in with heartache. "You bitch. Kira isn't a pawn in

275

your fucked up games. *She's a child. She's my child.*" His hissing whispers assault me.

It makes my throat tighten. I swallow hard against it. "I know."

"You know?" he says loudly, it sounds strangled, like the words are lodged in his windpipe.

I wait until his wild eyes find mine, and I lay it all out. "I made a lot of mistakes in our relationship over the years. A lot." I take a deep, shuddering breath before I continue, "I'm so sorry. But when I see you with Kira, I know that my getting pregnant with her wasn't one of them. No matter who fathered her, you're her daddy…and she's your little girl, Seamus. That's no mistake."

The sobs wrack his body silently before they find volume, and when they do it's excruciating to witness. His face drops into his hands and his shoulders rise and fall in the stuttering attack of emotion. When he catches his breath, his eyes find Kira sleeping in the chair near me. "She's mine. In my heart she's always been, no question. But she's legally mine too, I signed adoption papers a few weeks back. Loren took care of all of it."

If it's possible for my shattered heart to feel relief, it does. "He never wanted children. I'm glad." I also know that any chance of reconciliation with Seamus is impossible. His heart and mine just aren't puzzle pieces that will ever fit together.

Seamus

They say the truth will set you free.
That's bullshit.
I feel like I've been trampled on.
And Miranda looks like a ghost. Pale. Translucent. Void of life.

I've never felt exhaustion like this. I'm emotionally drained. A vessel of bone and tissue, hollow to its core. I let silence grant us both respite for a few minutes before I wipe my wet face off on the front of my shirt. There's no point in discussing any of this further. It's all been said. Insults have been hurled. Shit's been slung. I'm done. "Do you want some coffee?"

She nods. "Please."

I get us coffee and we drink it in silence.

The kids wake to use the bathroom and go back to sleep.

We get periodic updates on Kai. No change. They assure us that's a good thing. It doesn't feel like a good thing when you're a parent.

Somewhere around five in the morning, Miranda excuses herself to make a phone call.

An hour later she excuses herself again, to the bathroom this time, and I'm left alone with my thoughts. They're grim.

"Excuse me?"

There's a middle-aged man with salt and pepper hair standing in front of me. Drowning in my grim thoughts, I didn't see him walk in.

He speaks again when I don't. "I'm sorry, excuse me. I'm looking for Kai McIntyre's mother, Miranda. You wouldn't happen to know her?"

I nod. "She ran to the restroom. She'll be back any minute." And then I remember my manners because the shock of the past several hours has stifled everything except basic survival skills, pleasantries have been forgotten, and I offer my hand. "I'm Seamus McIntyre. Kai is my son."

He pats the side of my forearm with one hand while he shakes with the other. "I'm so sorry to hear about Kai. Miranda said he was out of surgery, but in ICU, when I talked to her on the phone."

I nod as our hands part.

"I'm Benito Aragon. I work with Miranda at Good Samaritan House." He points with his thumb down the hall. "Is the restroom this direction?"

I nod again.

"I'll just go and look for her. It was nice to meet you, Seamus. My prayers are with Kai."

"Thank you." I watch him walk away, not because I'm interested but because it's something to do to keep my mind off what's happening with Kai. When he's out of sight, my face drops into my hands. I'm bent over thinking. Thinking that the darkness behind my hands is preferable to the overhead florescent lighting. Thinking about the pain in my head, it feels like my skull is being squeezed in a vise. Thinking about—a hand on my shoulder interrupts the thought. I know that touch. "Please tell me you're real?" I beg from behind my hands. I'm talking in a voice that I usually reserve for internal dialogue, it's questioning, but pessimistic. "I need you to be real. *Please.*"

"I'm real," she whispers in my ear.

When I raise my head and remove my hands, she's kneeling on the dingy tan linoleum in front of me with tears glistening in her eyes. I never thought I would see her again. She's even more beautiful than I remember. She doesn't say anything and neither do I. I pull her in for a hug without asking. It's a hug that dissolves everything for a few minutes. "I've missed you, Faith. I've missed you so much."

"I've missed you, too, Seamus." Her voice cracks on my name. "How's Kai?"

"He's in ICU. They won't let me in to see him." I sniff. "How did you know?"

When I pull back from the hug, she swipes her hands under her eyes. "Miranda asked Benito to find me. He drove me here."

I try to smile. "I knew I liked Benito."

She laughs through her tears. "Yeah, he's a good guy. We picked up Hope from Miranda's house too. She wanted to see you all and check on Kai."

Hope is peeking around the corner, keeping her distance, trying to give us privacy. I wave her in. "Come on in and sit down, Hope."

She walks in and sets a grocery sack on the chair next to me. "I brought some food from Miranda's. Figured you hadn't eaten nothing."

"Thanks, Hope. That was very thoughtful of you. The kids will love it when they wake up."

She nods to acknowledge me and takes a seat in the corner.

I look back at the angel in front of me. "How do you know Benito?" I ask.

"Our introduction is a story for another time, but now I rent a room from his brother and work in their bakery."

I don't know if the smile registers on my lips, but I feel it. I'm happy Faith made a change. "That's great. I'm proud of you."

She blushes and changes the subject when the kids stir. "Let's eat."

Rory and Kira are groggy and disoriented when they wake, but after they use the bathroom they're both hungry. Hope made monkey bread. She's officially their hero.

The room fills up quickly when Miranda and Benito join us with several cups of coffee and juice. The monkey bread disappears, and all that remains are sticky fingers and full bellies.

It's then that we receive the news that Kai is improving. If he continues, he'll be moved out of ICU by late afternoon. There was a moment immediately following the birth of each of my children that I felt intensely and overwhelmingly grateful to be given the gift of fatherhood. This news is the trigger that makes it swell within me again. *Thank you*. I repeat it over and over in my mind.

Relief floods the room. I see it in every face. We're a mismatched tribe with a common link—we're Kai supporters. Miranda is weeping into Benito's shoulder. The kids are both hugging me. And Faith and Hope are holding hands in the chairs in the corner. Relief.

"Were your kids all born here? In this hospital?" Faith's looking at me with her inquisitive, blue eyes.

I glance at Miranda before looking at Rory and Kira sitting on either side of me. "They were," I answer with a smile.

"My God, I bet it was breathtaking," she looks at Miranda before tracing her gaze back to me, "watching your babies come into the world." Tears begin trickling down her cheeks, but she's smiling. She wipes them away with her free hand. She's still holding Hope's with the other.

"It was. Each time. Witnessing their first breath. Hearing their first cry. Looking at their sweet face. Counting their fingers and toes. From the very first moment they imprinted on my soul, an unbreakable connection. It was breathtaking."

Hope sniffles next to Faith. Her eyes are a glassy with happiness. "It felt like hope." I've never seen this kind of emotion exhibited by her. She's usually indifferent or detached.

I don't know if that was a statement or a question, but I agree because she's right. "It did feel like hope."

She nods in return.

Faith is staring at me, and she's still smiling. "Do you think my mom felt that way when I was born?" She looks content. The way she asked the question makes me wonder if she's put the search for her birth mother behind her or if she's approaching it with a new perspective and less desperation.

I answer, "I'm sure she did," and I mean it. Faith has this incredible energy about her. I'm sure it was evident the moment she was born, that she was special.

Faith

Hope hops to her feet with an urgency I've never seen her display. She tugs on my hand that she's still holding. "Come with me. I wanna show you something."

"Okay." I stand and follow her out of the waiting room.

When we're in the elevator, she pushes the button for the fourth floor. The doors open to a reception desk where a friendly looking woman greets us with a toothy smile and crinkled eyes. "Good morning. Do you need help with a room number?"

I'm at a loss, so I look to Hope.

She tries to smile at the woman, but the happy tears from earlier have been replaced with sadness she's trying ward off. "Room four hundred."

The woman slides a clipboard in front of us. "Sign in and I'll need to see ID please."

I write down my name and start to write down hers, but she stops me when I write Hope and sets her State of California ID card on the counter in front of me. It reads Jane Marie Martin. I scratch out Hope and write Jane Martin instead. The woman verifies our IDs and buzzes us through a secure door.

"Your name's Jane?" I ask.

She stops walking and faces me. Sometimes Hope's stories are random. She tells them like I'm privy to every detail of her life. I follow along the best I can. This is one of those stories. "When I was eighteen, Mama married Jonas. Jonas moved into Mama's house and told me I couldn't live there no more. Mama knew a lady, Mrs. Lipokowski,

281

who had an apartment. Mrs. Lipokowski was real nice and gave me a job. I wasn't no good at it though, working with customers and money, so she filled out a bunch of papers for me and I got money in the mail every month instead. She says it's called public assistance. She takes a little bit for my rent, and I buy food with the rest. Mrs. Lipokowski's always been real nice to me. Like I wish my mama would've been. When I turned twenty years old, I told her that I didn't like my name, that I liked Hope better. She said I could be called whatever I want. Ever since that day I called myself Hope 'cause I feel better with that name. It's special."

"Where are we going, Hope?" I'm nervous now. I have no idea why, but the tears running down her cheeks are puzzling.

She takes my hand and walks silently to room four hundred. She slows as we approach the open door. We take a few steps inside. There's a woman sleeping in the bed.

When I start to retreat, retracing my steps backward so we don't disturb the patient, Hope stops me with a firm, but gentle hand. "Do you know her?" I whisper.

She shakes her head without turning around to look at me. "No," she whispers.

"Why are we here?" When I ask the question, I know the answer. I feel it in her touch.

Hope.

It felt like hope.

Good at keeping secrets

Jane
past

"You're pretty."

Pretty.

I hear that a lot.

Sometimes it's said nice, and makes me feel good. "Well, isn't she a pretty, little thing," or "Pretty girl, she looks just like her mama."

Or sometimes, when my mama says it, even though she's smiling real big, it makes me feel bad. "Being smart is only important if you're not pretty, Jane," or "Just smile pretty and don't talk, Jane."

My mama's real pretty. Men tell her so all the time.

But when Dan says, "You're pretty," it makes me feel different. Like bees are buzzing in my chest, loud and tickley. And it makes my cheeks feel hot like I been outside on a summer day running around chasing dragonflies. I wanna tell him about the bees in my chest or chasing dragonflies, but I don't. I smile instead, 'cause that's what Mama always tells me to do. And I add, "Thank you," 'cause Mama always says when someone says something nice that I should always say thank you. Just like on my birthday when I get a present, she says compliments are presents, too. I don't really understand what that means, but I do like she says.

Dan smiles big. It makes the bees buzz again. I can see all his teeth. And I start counting 'em in my head. One. Two. Three. Four. Five.

But I stop when he starts talking 'cause I can't see number six, "When does your mom get home from work, Jane?"

"My mama works at the bank. She counts people's money. She comes home at five o'clock."

283

Dan smiles real big again, and I'm counting his teeth starting with six. Seven. Eight. "Wanna watch TV?"

We sit on the sofa. I sit on one end, and he sits on the other end.

We watch a movie that's on. I seen it before. It's funny.

Dan laughs a lot. I like watching him laugh. His eyes squeeze shut and his face looks like someone I wanna be friends with. I ain't never had a friend, Mama said I couldn't. But I want one. "Want a popsicle?"

He does.

I get a popsicle out of the freezer, a red one, 'cause they're my favorite. It has two sticks. Usually, I break it in two and eat 'em both. But this time, when I break it, I give one to him.

We eat our popsicles, and he moves over and sits right next to me.

He holds my hand while we finish watching the movie.

I seen the way my mama smiles when men hold her hand. She looks extra happy and extra pretty when she smiles that way. I think I know why now. 'Cause the bees aren't just buzzing in my chest, they're buzzing in my head, too, and I feel all funny and floaty. My cheeks hurt from smiling, but I can't stop.

At four forty-five he says, "I better go."

"Okay," I say. The bees in my chest turned into a gorilla squeezing tight. It feels like when Grandma Tressa would leave every night when Mama came home from work, and I didn't want her to. It makes me sad.

"I'll see you tomorrow at school, Jane."

"Okay." This time when I say it, the gorilla ain't squeezing tight no more. And I'm not sad 'cause I'll see him in the halls at school tomorrow.

*****

Wednesday is my favorite day of the week 'cause Dan walks me home.

He asks me questions while we walk. "Did you just move here, Jane?"

"No. I lived here my whole life," I tell him. "I just never went to real school before." Grandma Tressa used to home school me, 'cause Mama says the devil's got his hand in the public school system and the lies and filth they teach, whatever that means. But Grandma died this summer, so now I go to real school, 'cause Mama has to work at the bank during the day.

"Well, since you've only been going to real school for a few weeks now, do you like it?" he asks and the way he's smiling at me makes me wanna say yes, even though I don't like it.

"Yeah," I say to his smile. But the kids are mean. They call me names like *dummy*. It makes me sad in my tummy when they say those things. But looking at Dan makes me happy, so I say, "I like you. You're real nice to me."

He smiles his big smile where I can count all his teeth.

When we get to my house, we sit on the sofa right next to each other again. But before I can turn the TV on, he kisses me. I don't know what to do back, but when he says, "Just relax, Jane," I do. And when he says, "Do what I do," I do that, too. And the longer we kiss, the bees stop buzzing in my chest, and my head and my tummy starts twisting, but not like when I'm sick. It's down by my privates, and it feels good like something flipping over inside my belly that makes me tingle.

We don't have time for popsicles.

When he leaves, my lips feel puffy, and my tummy is still rumbling in a good way. I want him to kiss me again.

*****

285

I couldn't wait for Wednesday to come.

Dan walks me home.

He asks if he can see my room.

I don't wanna go to my room. I wanna sit on the sofa and kiss him.

But I show him my room, 'cause mama always says, "Men like it when you don't argue with 'em."

He wants to lay on my bed. It feels weird at first, but as soon as he starts kissing me I decide I like kissing on my bed just as much as I like kissing on the sofa.

He touches me under my shirt while he kisses me.

He touches me under my bra while he kisses me.

He touches me under my skirt while he kisses me.

And the good twisting in my tummy starts.

But when he touches me under my panties while he kisses me, it makes me squirm. I want him to touch me but it feels weird. A good weird, but weird. When his hand stops and ain't touching me no more, I want the weird feeling again and I push my privates into his hand. He keeps kissing me and touching me and the more he does the harder it is for me to do nothing but lie there. The feeling low in my belly keeps tightening, it feels like putting one end of a rubber band around the tip of your finger and pinching the other end between your fingers and thumb and pulling it back and just when you think you can't possibly pull it back any more 'cause it's stretched too tight, it slips through your fingers in a flash and shoots up in the air like a rocket. That's how I feel. Like a rocket. I cry out, "Oh my God," even though Mama says I shouldn't take the Lord's name in vain. I keep saying it over and over again. And when the rocket comes back down I feel like someone's pouring maple syrup into a hole on the top of my head and it's going down slow and coating my insides all the way to my toes.

Dan kisses me on the nose and tells me, "You're so pretty," before he leaves.

286

We didn't have popsicles.
I forgot all about the popsicles.

*****

It's Wednesday again.

The bees are buzzing in my chest and head before Dan even walks me home.

He walks straight to my room, and I follow him 'cause I want kissing and touching on my bed again.

We kiss for a while and then he tells me I'd look prettier with all my clothes off. I don't wanna take my clothes off, but I want him to think I'm pretty, so I do. And when I'm all the way naked he says, "You're beautiful." And my face gets hot like the sun's glowing behind my cheeks, and its rays are shooting out through the rest of me. Beautiful is better than pretty. Mama says when I'm a grown up I'll be beautiful and men won't mind that I'm not smart like other girls.

We kiss some more, and he takes his shirt off. His chest has hair on it, but I like touching it. It feels soft and scratchy at the same time like the rug in the bathroom that I wipe my feet on when I get outta the shower.

We kiss some more, and he takes his pants and underwear off. He asks me to touch his privates. I don't wanna look at it, but I touch it. And when I do he makes this sound like when you take your first bite of chocolate crème pie, and it's the best chocolate crème pie you've ever tasted in your life. That's what it sounds like, and I like hearing it. And now I wanna look. I've seen a penis before. One night Mama had a man friend over, only I didn't know it, and I walked in her bedroom without knocking. I saw her friend's penis. I always knock now.

Dan's penis is bigger than Mama's friend's was. It's real big, and it looks angry. I tell him so, and he smiles and says it's not angry, it's happy 'cause of me.

Then we kiss some more, and he touches me a lot. And when he touches me between my legs I can't help but wiggle against him. My tummy is turning in that good way again, and my privates are all tingly.

And then he lays on top of me and tells me to relax, but I don't know why 'cause I'm already relaxed.

But then there's pain and burning and tearing between my legs, in my privates, and I scream out, "It hurts! It hurts! Make it stop!"

He talks real quiet in my ear. His voice still sounds like he's eating the best chocolate crème pie he's ever had. "Shh. It's okay, Jane. Sex only hurts the first time for a few minutes and then it will feel really, really good. I promise."

I try not to think about the pain. Like that one time when Mama drank too much beer and held her hot curling iron against my arm. It burned for a real long time, but I tried not to think about it 'cause I know she didn't mean to hurt me. She told me so afterward.

And after a while, it doesn't hurt as bad, just like Dan said. And then his hips start moving faster, and he keeps telling me that I'm beautiful in his chocolate crème pie voice. And then he's grunting like an animal and his hips are pressing hard against mine, and my privates hurt way up inside my belly like it's too much. And then he says, "Fuck," and instead of feeling like too much, it feels kinda warm.

And then he pushes up off me, and I feel his penis pull out 'cause it feels like my privates just shriveled back up to normal. "You should go to the bathroom. And clean yourself up."

I don't know why he said that until I stand up, and two things happen. I see spots of blood on my sheets, and when I start walking toward the bathroom in the hall, I feel something wet running down the inside of my thighs. They both scare me.

After I use the bathroom and get dressed Dan leaves. He says not to tell no one what we been doing. He says he could get in a lot of trouble 'cause people wouldn't understand how special I am to him.

I like it that he called me special.

I won't tell.

I don't talk to no one except Mama anyhow.

*****

Every Wednesday Dan walks me home.

Every Wednesday we kiss and have sex on my bed. It don't hurt no more.

Sometimes he puts this covering on his penis, he calls it a rubber. Sometimes he don't, 'cause he says it feels better without it.

He calls me his girlfriend.

It's a secret.

Just like our special time together.

*****

I been real sick all week, throwing up a lot. Mama don't make me go to school. She lets me stay home while she goes to work. I sleep on the bathroom floor, so I don't have to keep coming in to get sick. I don't feel like eating nothing.

Dan comes to my house Wednesday afternoon. He leaves when he sees I'm sick.

*****

Mama brought me to the doctor 'cause I been so sick. They stick a needle in my arm and fill up a glass tube with my blood. I don't like it. It hurts. They also make me pee in a plastic cup. I don't like that either, too messy.

The nurse takes my temperature and asks me some questions, and then she leaves.

289

Mama and me wait for a long time for the doctor to come in. When he does, he don't look nice, and I don't like him.

He looks in my ears and throat and listens to my heartbeat and asks me the same questions the nurse asked me.

And then someone knocks on the door, and a lady hands him some papers. She looks nice, and I want her to stay and him to go. He looks at the papers, and there's a lot of writing on 'em, but he reads 'em real fast.

That's when he looks at my mama and says, "She's pregnant." And I wonder who he's talking about. Only grownups get pregnant, Mama told me so when I asked where babies came from. She said, "When you grow up you'll get married and have babies." But I'm not a grown up yet. Or married.

Mama's looking at me, and I see a lightning storm flashing in her eyes. It scares me. "You been having sex, Jane?" It's loud and embarrassing. Sex is supposed to be my secret with Dan. She ain't supposed to know, and now she's telling the doctor about it too.

I shake my head real fast. I know I'm not supposed to lie. *Lying is a sin*, Mama always says so.

"Lying is a sin, Jane. Don't lie, the Lord will strike you down."

I just sit here quiet and don't move. I'm waiting for the wrath of God or Mama, I don't want either one.

The doctor says, "I'll need to perform a vaginal exam. Would you prefer to stay or go?" He's talking to Mama again.

"I'll stay," she says, but it don't sound like she wants to. It sounds like she wants to hit me with the belt she keeps hanging on a nail in her closet.

The doctor tells me to take my underwear off from under my cloth gown and lie down on my back while he fiddles with some rods at the end of the table that look like they have a big ice cream scoop on the end. I do like he

290

says, and he puts on gloves and gets some packages out of a drawer and tears 'em open. I never saw what was inside, but I hear some clinking sounds when he puts 'em on a little metal table next to him. I don't like the sound they make. It's too loud.

He lifts up each of my feet and puts my heels in the ice cream scoops. They fit perfect, and it makes me smile to think that my heels are like balls of ice cream.

I stop smiling and thinking about ice cream when he tells me to scoot my hips toward him and bend my legs. "No," I say. He'll be able to see under my gown, and I don't want him looking.

I hear him and Mama both sigh. Hers sounds angry, like when she does it right before she punishes me and quotes the Bible, "I will punish the world for its evil, the wicked for their sins." His sounds annoyed, like my least favorite teacher when I tell her I don't understand her questions.

"I can't examine you unless you bend your legs and move closer to me."

I didn't want him to examine me. But when I look at Mama she's telling me with her eyes how mad she is, I know I better just do like he says.

I try not to think about what's happening and bend my knees and scoot down toward the doctor. When he pulls my knees apart, they're shaking, and I can't make 'em stop.

"Stop shaking and just let him look," Mama snaps at me. She says it like she does when she tells me to go to my room when she has a man friend come over.

That's when I start crying. I hold my breath 'cause when I do that the sound don't come out, only tears do.

The doctor's gloves are cold and wet on my privates. I don't like it at all, and it makes the tears feel hot in my eyes. So hot that I squeeze my eyes shut. And when I close my eyes it don't hold in the tears, and more come.

"You may feel a pinch," he says.

I don't understand until there's something sliding inside me. It feels like a spoon. The spoon's cold, but it don't pinch like he said. And then he does something, and it don't pinch, it hurts. The doctor is a big, fat liar. It feels like he's prying me open from the inside out.

I hold my breath through the pain that ain't a pinch.

When he takes the spoon out, the pain stops. But then he sticks his fingers inside me. It makes me feel like throwing up. Only Dan's supposed to touch me there. I keep swallowing, trying not to throw up.

"Everything seems normal. Does she have an OBGYN?" He says this to Mama like I ain't in the room with 'em.

"I'll make her an appointment with mine," Mama says.

And he leaves.

"Put your clothes on and meet me at the front desk. You have a lot of explaining to do." My eyes are still closed, but I can see her anger. It's bright red, like fire.

It's hard to get dressed 'cause I'm still crying hard and shaking harder.

Mama don't talk to me the whole way home. I know she's saving all her mean and mad for when we get home. Inside our house is the only place she lets mean and mad loose on me. And it always hurts when she does. She makes sure of it.

I don't tell Mama I had sex with Dan. I promised him I would never tell no one, and I'm good at keeping secrets.

*****

The next Wednesday, when Dan walks me home, I tell him I'm pregnant. He looks surprised, and his face gets real pale, like Mama's face last year when I told her I'd eaten four of her *special* brownies. We go in my room and

292

we kiss for a few minutes, and then he stands up and tells me to get on my knees in front of him. I do. Then he tells me to open my mouth. I do. Then he puts his penis in my mouth. It makes me choke, but he just keeps saying, "Relax, Jane. This makes me feel good. You want me to feel good, don't you?" I nod 'cause I do. He tells me to suck and pretend he's one of the popsicles I like so much. I do, but he don't taste like a popsicle. He starts moving in and out of my mouth while I suck. Then he grabs my hair by my ears in his hands and moves faster. "That's it, Jane. That's perfect. Keep doing that." I like that he's using his chocolate crème pie voice. Until I feel something hot fill the back of my throat. It makes me cough and gag and when I do I feel something warm and wet on my chin and neck. I swallow back against what's in my mouth, it tastes sticky and salty, and I don't like it. Dan has his hand wrapped around his penis, and he's jerkin' it back and forth. It looks rough like it hurts, but stuff's squirting out of it on my chest, and the look on his face makes me feel good. It's the same look he wears when he does this inside my privates. "Good girl," he says. "Very good. I want to try something else new before I go today."

I don't know what that means, but most things Dan does to me make me feel good, so I nod. "Okay."

"Does your mama have any oil for cooking with?" he asks.

I nod.

"Get it, beautiful."

I like it when he calls me beautiful.

When I come back with the vegetable oil, he takes it and sets it on the floor. Then he tells me to get down on my hands and knees.

I do. I don't like to have sex this way, 'cause he can't kiss me. I like kissing him.

He touches me from behind, and it feels good. Then I hear him tear open the rubber package, and he puts his penis inside me. It feels good, but he's holding my hips

293

and crashing into me with his, a lot faster than he usually does.

"I'm gonna miss this," he says. I don't know what it means. He talks a lot when he's inside me, and it usually don't make a lot of sense. Mostly curse words, which I know is a sin, but when he says 'em with his chocolate crème pie voice, they don't sound like sinning.

I feel him pull out, and he picks up the vegetable oil bottle and takes off the cap. I don't look back to see what he's doing with it. And then I feel the hair on his chest sticky with sweat on my back, and he whispers in my ear, "Just relax, or this will hurt. I don't want to hurt you, Jane. Okay?"

"Okay," I say.

"Deep breaths if it hurts. Deep breaths until I'm done. You want me to feel good, right?"

"Yes," I say without thinking.

And then he spreads my butt cheeks with his hands, and I feel something slick and warm against my behind. And then he starts pushing his way in, but it ain't my privates. It don't feel right. "Relax," he reminds me.

But I can't relax. I don't understand what's happening.

He stops moving. "Breathe." The way he says it makes me wanna please him. So, even though I can't relax, I take a few deep breaths.

"That's it," he says it like my favorite teacher does when I answer a question right.

But then he starts pushing again, and all I wanna do is push him back out. He's going slow, but it don't stop the bad feelings. I feel yucky and like I need to go potty. "I don't like it," I blurt. I shouldn't have said nothing, but I can't keep it in.

"You're doing just fine. You'll be fine. Just keep breathing." He pulls back a little bit, and it feels better, but then he pushes back in real fast. "I'm sorry, this feels too good. It will be over quick. Don't think about it."

294

And then it hurts. It hurts *real* bad. He's holding my hips tight. I can't get away. I can hear his skin slapping against mine, and he's talking, but I don't hear most of it 'cause the pain's making it hard for me to hear. It's like I'm wrapped up in a blanket, only it ain't my favorite blanket Grandma Tressa made me, this blanket's made of hurt and pain.

I'm crying out, "Please stop, it hurts! It hurts! Please stop!"

But he don't, not until I hear him yell, "Fuck me, your ass is so tight."

When he pulls out, the pain's still there. I don't wanna look at him, 'cause he hurt me.

He goes to the bathroom and cleans himself up, and when he comes back to me, I'm lying on the floor crying.

He pulls me into his lap and holds me. It's real gentle, just like when I held a puppy from the neighbor's dog's litter when I was little. "Listen to me, Jane. You're my special girlfriend. I'm sorry that hurt, but you made me feel so good, beautiful. And I needed our last time together to be special. When I leave today, you'll never see me again."

I look up at him. "What about school?"

He shakes his head. "I won't be there. But we'll always keep our secret. We won't tell anyone about our special time together."

"I'll never tell no one," I promise.

He smiles the smile where I can count all his teeth. "Good."

And then he sets me on the floor, and he gets up and leaves.

And I wonder if he meant what he said and if he won't be at school tomorrow.

*****

Dan wasn't at school the next day.

I didn't see him at lunch or in the hallways between classes.

It makes me sad that he's gone, 'cause he's my only friend.

Just to be sure I stop by the office after school and ask Mrs. Peacock, the school secretary, 'cause the first day of school she told me if I ever had questions I could always ask her. "Is Dan gone? Did he leave for good?"

She looks confused. "Dan? Dan who, sweetie? Do you know his last name?"

I don't know his last name, so I shake my head and tell her what I do know. "Dan. He sweeps the cafeteria after we make it dirty at lunchtime."

Her eyes change like she knows the Dan I'm talking about. "Oh, Dan Crestmoor, the custodian. I'm sorry, sweetie, he no longer works here. He called this morning and said he had a family emergency and his family needs him out of state. His elderly mother is sick. He was moving today." She's smiling when she says it, like she don't know her words are making me sad.

Poor Dan. I'm sad his mama's sick. I hope he can make it better when he gets there.

*****

Going to school is hard when you're pregnant. The other kids tease me more than usual. They call me a *slut* and a *whore*. I try to ignore 'em, but it hurts my feelings. I already hear those words enough at home from Mama.

*****

My belly's getting real big. Mama says my baby girl's gonna be born soon. Mama also says I'm too young and can't handle a baby, especially since I ain't married, so she found a family to be my baby's new family when she's born. Adoption she calls it. That makes me sad, but Mama says that's how it's gotta be. I haven't met the new family, but they must be real nice, 'cause they bought Mama a new car. She says it's a Toyota Corolla. It's light blue, her favorite color, and the air conditioning blows real cold. She smiles real big when she drives it. Only it's the kind of smile that don't make me happy, and I don't know why.

You were my hope

present

And then Hope begins the story that I've been waiting twenty-two years to hear. "You were born on a hot July day in this room. July thirtieth."

I clamp my hand over my mouth to muffle my sob. That's my birthday. The tears blur my vision instantly making Hope only a fuzzy outline in front of me. I tug her hand and urge her into the hallway and back out into the maternity ward reception area before I ask her to continue and tell me everything she remembers. And not to leave anything out.

She takes a seat calmly.

I sit next to her dazed, but alert.

She takes my hand in hers and stares at them in my lap.

And then she tells me about the day I was born. "My tummy had been hurting real bad all afternoon. When Mama came home from work and saw the sheets on my bed underneath me all wet, she took me to the hospital.

"Mama stayed in the room with me while you were born. She sat in a chair across the room. She didn't look at me the whole time, but I saw her crying." Hope's eyes look distant with concentration like she's lost in the memory, reliving it, recalling every detail.

"The second you were born, the doctor said, 'It's a girl,' and you cried. Your cry was quiet but loud at the same time like you were a tiny kitty on the outside and a lion on the inside. It made me smile, 'cause I knew you

298

were strong. And I didn't say it out loud, but I named you Hope 'cause that's what I felt. I felt hope.

"You were so tiny, just like a doll, when the nurse laid you on my chest. She smiled at me like she was happy and sad all at once, and she whispered, 'We're not supposed to let you hold her, but I think she deserves to know you, if only for a minute.'

"The tears started running down my cheeks, and I couldn't stop 'em. They weren't sad tears. You were so beautiful. I stroked your head real soft like and talked to you even softer. 'I love you, Hope.' That's what I told you. I'd never told no one I loved 'em before. I never felt like I loved no one until I looked at you, and my heart felt so full I didn't know how else to say it. And then I told you, 'Your new mama and daddy are gonna take real good care of you. You're gonna be smart, and nice, and good, and so pretty. I'm glad I got to be the mama who got to meet you first, I'll never forget you.'" She looks at me. "I was right, you're all those things.

"The nurse came back, and I kissed you on the forehead, and she took you away. To your new mama and daddy that my mama found for you. I don't remember their first names, but their last name was—"

"Groves," we say together. And my heart clenches for Hope and for me.

She nods. "They lived far away and couldn't have a baby of their own, so they wanted you. And since Mama said I was too young and wasn't ready to be a mama, I was glad you were gonna live with 'em, 'cause they promised to take real good care of you." She looks at me thoughtfully, and there's pride in her next words. "You were so special. Special like something that only happens once in a lifetime. When I looked at you, I only saw good things and it made me forget about every bad thing that anyone had ever said or done to me. You took it all away. You were my hope."

"Did you ever think about me after I was gone?" All my life I've wondered. Dreamed that my mom was out there somewhere thinking about me like I was thinking about her.

"I knew better than to ask Mama, 'cause she said you weren't mine no more after that day and 'cause you belonged to another family she said I wasn't allowed to talk about you to no one. She told me to forget you, but I never stopped thinking about you. Every night since, before I go to bed I say a prayer for you, 'Please keep Hope safe and happy.' I don't pray for nothing else. Just for you. And every year on your birthday I sing you 'Happy Birthday.'"

"How old were you when I was born?" I ask.

"Seventeen," she answers matter-of-factly.

I nod. She was young and obviously incapable of caring for a child. No wonder her mother intervened and I was given up for adoption. "What about my father? Who is he?"

Her eyes go dead for a few seconds before she stares off into space. I don't think she's going to answer. And then she does. "His name was Dan. I met him at school. He called me pretty. He was my boyfriend."

"Where is he now? Do you know?" I have a feeling asking this question is a long shot, and to be honest I don't care, hearing Hope's story is enough.

She shrugs. "Don't know. He had to move away after I told him I was pregnant. His mama needed him." She doesn't seem sad, more nostalgic. Like she's thinking of someone she hasn't thought about in a very long time.

"How did you know, Hope? That I was your baby? You only saw me for a few minutes, and that was twenty-two years ago."

She squeezes my hand. "Remember what Seamus said this morning about meeting his babies for the first time and them imprinting on his soul?" She shrugs. "It's true. I knew when you knocked on my door that first time and gave me a pineapple, who you were."

I'm stunned and in awe, searching Hope's face in a whole new light. "Why didn't you tell me?"

"You have a family. You're theirs. I didn't think it was allowed like Mama said." She truly believes it.

I hug her. "It's allowed. And they're not my family anymore."

She pulls back from the hug and looks surprised. "They're not?"

I shake my head. "No. You are."

I'm gifted with one of Hope's rare smiles and for the first time in twenty-two years, I feel complete. Satisfied. I know many would be skeptical, question it, dig deeper. But in my heart, the search is over and this part of my research is done. I found my mom. Or she found me.

When we return to the waiting room, it's empty. The nurse tells us Kai has been moved to a room on the telemetry floor.

I peer in from the hall, with Hope by my side, and see everyone clustered around Kai's bed. Seamus sees me and waves both of us in.

I apologize quietly for disturbing their family time. Kai is sleeping. He's hooked up to various machines and monitors, and an IV drip is administering painkillers. My entire being aches for this little boy.

Seamus is rubbing my back as he takes in my expression. "He'll make a full recovery. He just needs some time," he whispers in my ear. I hear the lack of worry in his voice, and I know it's true.

Still, I can't take my eyes off him lying in the bed, so helpless. "Thank God," I whisper back.

"Everything okay with Hope? You were gone a long time." It's still his soothing whisper in my ear.

I turn my head, look him in the eye, and the overwhelming realization that I just got my miracle hits me. It hits me so hard it fills my eyes and takes away my words. I nod instead.

He puts his arm around me and kisses the side of my head. "Good."

I look back at Kai. "We'd better get going, Seamus, so you can take care of Kai." And then back to Seamus. "I'm glad they moved him to this room, that's a good sign."

Seamus walks out of the room with Hope and me. Hope keeps walking toward the elevator where she stops and waits for me.

When I look up at Seamus, his eyes are fixed on mine. He's looking at me like there are a thousand and one things he wants to say. He starts with, "Can I hug you?"

I wrap my arms around him and for a solid minute, our bodies talk. There are apologies. And questions. And answers. And promises.

When we release each other, he smiles. It's tired, but it's mine. "Please tell me you felt that?"

I nod. I did.

He inhales deeply and lets it all out, smile still in place. "Good. Because, holy shit, I've missed you."

I want to kiss him so badly, but it's so inappropriate given the time and place.

"Would you want to...I don't know...maybe after Kai is released and things get back to normal, we could..." He stops talking, covers his eyes with his hand, and laughs. "Jesus Christ, I suck at this. It's been a long time since I tried to ask someone out."

That giddy feeling rises in me, the one I've only ever felt when I'm around Seamus, and it makes my smile impossible to hide. "Yes. Please."

He bookends my cheeks with his hands and kisses me softly, just a peck, but I feel it all the way down to my toes. And then he rests his forehead against mine. "Thank you."

"I'll have to give you my home phone number, I don't have a cell."

"Good idea."

We walk to the information desk and trade phone numbers. "Just leave a message on the answering machine. It's kind of a community phone set up where I live, but it works. I'll get the message."

He nods. "Sounds good. I'll talk to you soon. Thanks for coming to check on Kai. And me."

I nod.

And I leave the hospital with my mom.

And a grateful heart that's bursting with love.

Sometimes, it isn't that hard

Faith

present

There's a knock on my bedroom door. It's Benito with a cup of coffee.

"Hi." He hands it over with a smile. His other hand that usually holds his cup is empty. "I'm headed to work, but I thought you could use this."

"Headed to work? It's late." He never works on Sunday nights, he usually goes to mass at the Catholic Church down the street.

He shrugs. "Miranda will be out for a while with Kai, there are things that need to be tended to in her absence. We're all a team and family always comes first. It's no trouble at all."

Of course it's not. It's Benito. He helps everyone. I nod to the coffee in my hand. "Thanks for this."

"You're welcome, my dear. Well, I just wanted to say hello and make sure you're doing well."

I smile. "I'm good. Really good. Thanks."

He nods his fatherly nod. "Excellent. I'd better get going." He walks to the stairs and stops like he so often does. "Faith?"

I take a sip of my coffee. "Yeah?"

"He knows," he says wisely.

I tilt my head and wait for him to continue.

"He knows what an unbelievably beautiful circumstance he could be in with you," he adds with a smile.

I smile remembering our discussion from weeks ago and quote him in return, "Sometimes, it isn't that hard."

304

He winks and disappears up the stairs.

Life blooms in second chances

$Seamus$

Kai was released from the hospital last week. He's confined to a wheelchair for the next two weeks due to the cast on his leg, after which he can use crutches. He's not happy about that, but it doesn't stop him from getting outside with his basketball and shooting some hoops every afternoon. I thought the stairs at the apartment would be an obstacle, since I can't carry him, but he navigates up and down them from a sitting position on his butt faster than I can on my feet. The kid is unstoppable. And other than some wicked scarring on his abdomen and legs, and special dietary concerns, he's back to normal. It's amazing how resilient kids are.

Miranda was cleared of any wrongdoing in the accident, and though I was urged by outsiders to take back full custody, I couldn't do it. Because not only was it an accident, it was also a wake-up call for her. Miranda has been a loving parent lately, I won't take that from my kids because of an accident. She's finally trying. My kids need that. They deserve it. We signed the revised custody arrangement this week, it was a long time officially coming — the kids spend the school week with me and weekends with Miranda as planned. Everyone's happy.

The kids are with Miranda this weekend. It's the first time they've been out of my sight, and I've been alone, for a few weeks. Which means I made good on my promise and invited Faith out on a date.

The sand is warm under my palms and coarse between my fingers. I'm sitting on the beach, resting back on my hands, watching Faith walk out into the water and thinking about all the different ways there are to be attracted to someone. She's wearing a simple, ivory, cotton sundress, holding the bottom in her hands mid-thigh to keep it from getting wet. The bright colors have been erased from her dreadlocks, and though I loved it because it was bold like her, the white blond that remains is transcendent. She glows like she's illuminated from within, her personality shining through like rays of sunshine and fire.

When she returns to me, she reaches down and spreads my legs at the ankles. Then she sits down between my legs facing me, her legs bent, inner calves brushing my sides, dress pooled around us providing cover.

"I know I told you this before, but my heart really likes your heart, Seamus." The way she says it pinches and twists, heartfelt tainted by heartache, and she drops her chin.

"Hey." I tip her eyes up to meet mine, and I ask softly, "What's going on?"

"Every day when I wake up, I remind myself that the present is possibility, and the past is a lesson." It sounds like a fragile confession that I want to hold in my hands and protect from the world.

I run my fingertip across the writing on her collarbone peeking out from beneath her dress and pull the strap down her shoulder to read it, *Life blooms in second chances.* "Is that what this is about? Possibility and lessons?"

She nods.

"It's good advice," I whisper before I kiss the script.

She's nodding when I pull back and look at her. I watch her eyes scan my face, pausing on my mouth, before locking her gaze with mine again. "I love the way you look at me, Seamus. No one's ever looked at me like you do. Your eyes speak to me. When I say something funny, your eyes laugh before your mouth does. When I need

307

encouragement, your eyes tell me I'm good enough. When I'm scared, your eyes hold me. And when you're about to kiss me, your eyes undress my thoughts." She pauses and looks away before her eyes dance back to mine. "I don't want any of that to change."

"It won't," I promise her with words while I hold her in a stare.

She's not convinced. There's a look resonating in her eyes, but every few seconds it changes slightly or mixes with another emotion. There's lust and pain and fear and shame.

"Faith." I never knew one word could hold so much hope, but her name does. I can't explain it, but I feel like my future depends on it. My sanity depends on it. My heart depends on it. "Please talk to me. You can tell me anything."

She pinches her lips together painfully until their rosy shade blanches the color away and she shakes her head. "Not this, Seamus. My past is hideous. I made bad choices and bad things happened."

"Everyone makes bad choices. You don't think I've made bad choices? Jesus, I was married to a bad choice for twelve years. Enough said. I hold an advanced degree in bad choices and oversight." I'm calmly pleading with her. "Close your eyes," I say as I close mine.

"Why?" she questions.

"I'm turning off my judgment and your filter," I'm whispering. "Are they closed?" I ask from behind closed lids.

"Yes." Her voice. *That voice.* So close. So trusting. So soft in the darkness.

"Tell me anything. Tell me everything. I want all of you." I do. So much.

I'm met with drawn out silence, but it's not threatening. I can feel her resolve building and apprehension fading in front of me.

"How about we both share?" I coax. "You tell me about your past, and I'll tell you how I feel about you."

"Do I want to hear it?" I feel her warm words on my face, there's a faint glimmer of a smile in them.

I'm nodding, even though she can't see me. "Probably not as much as I need to say it."

She begins and if it's possible her voice is even softer and raises goosebumps on my arms. "I was raised in foster care. You already knew that. The last family took me in at sixteen. I left when I was almost eighteen." She pauses. "Your turn."

I don't know if my heart can take the story she's about to unfold in the air around us, but I wait because that's all that my life is at this moment, words suspended in darkness. Words I'm determined to make count. "My life is easier when you're in it," I offer, "and harder when you're not. Your presence eases a tension inside me that I've carried all my life. You make me hurt less, physically everything's more tolerable when you're near."

"I'm a placebo effect." She sounds doubtful.

"No. You, your goodness is very, *very* real. And very healing. Believe me. You made me realize that, though I have MS, I am *not* my disease. You see me, despite it, and you accept me. That makes everything easier. I don't feel broken."

"You were never broken," she whispers, "You were always Seamus." I can hear her breathing, deep, measured breaths and when she's ready, she continues with her story. "The couple was odd. The woman stayed at home and didn't work. She prided herself being a foster parent, wore the title like sainthood. She wasn't a saint. She was selfish and vindictive. She ran her house like a dictator. He was a drug dealer. She pretended not to know. He pretended not to watch her mistreat us."

I know I should keep quiet, but I have to ask, "You told me before your foster homes weren't bad?"

309

"Most of them weren't. I lied about the last one. The truth is ugly." It's an apology. "Your turn."

My turn to take deep breaths. A deep, anxious ache is settling in my chest and creeping up my throat, but I push it away to share. Faith, the present here and now Faith, is what matters and she needs to know. "When you laugh, I feel your joy. It's a presence that I pretend is all for me. Your eyes sparkle and the smile that takes over your lips is the definition of happiness, radiantly reckless in its bold and heartfelt intent to spread pure joy. You never hide behind laughter, it's always transparent and true. I love that about you."

"Can I hold your hands? I need to hold on to you, Seamus." Words are processed within my mind. But those words bypassed and proceeded straight to my heart. I heard that plea in my heart.

"Yes. *Please*."

Her fingertips find my arms, skimming down, and she twines hers with mine. Her grip is tight. She's preparing herself for what she's about to share. "He was also an addict. And after nine months in their home...so was I." The shame in her voice is unbearable.

I lean forward and kiss her forehead. And then I inch down and kiss each eyelid, they're wet with tears like I knew they would be. It breaks my heart. "When you cry, I want to erase from existence whatever brought you sadness."

"I don't remember much of my last night with them. She was gone, and he and I got high while the other kids slept. Cocaine. It was my drug of choice. He wanted to go to the park a few blocks away, even though it was past midnight. Normally, I would've said no, we didn't hang out. But he insisted, and I was antsy, so I agreed. I drank an orange soda he gave me while we walked. The last thing I remember was sitting on the rusty, old merry go round listening to it squeak in protest with each revolution." Her grip on my hands is tight, so tight, by squeezing it's releasing the hate and hurt that's building inside her.

I tell her something she told me months ago, "Give me your hate, Faith."

She's crying. "I can't, Seamus."

"Give me your hate, Faith," I repeat. My voice is rising, begging her to purge this admission. "Please. You need to get it out. I can take it. Yell at me if you need to. Give me your hate."

It's several seconds before her hate shatters the silence in ragged, hurried, whispers, "I hated him, Seamus. I hated her. I hated myself. I hated my addiction. I hated my life." She pauses before she blasts the next sentence in angry sobs, "I just hated; it's what I did to survive."

The words tear me apart. She's not hate. She's not her past. Damn them for tainting her. I release her hands and hug her. She responds immediately. The hug is a mutated version, strength driven by rage from both of us.

Just when I think the adrenaline coursing through her is going to grant her the strength to split me in two, her grip lessens to her normal loving squeeze, and she sniffs. "We. You and me. We should be standing on your doormat, Seamus."

I smile through the anger, eyes still closed, and kiss her on the forehead. "We should. Later," I add because all I want to do is take her home with me and never let her go.

She hugs me tighter and sniffs again. "Promise?"

"Always," I promise.

"It's your turn, please. I need something good before I finish this. The end isn't pretty."

"Your hugs have the power to change people. I've seen it. I've felt it. You have a genuine kindness about you that's so rare and pure, it brings me to my knees. I could live in your arms forever." I rub her back and hold her, willing her to relax. Her story is housed within her muscles creating tension. She needs to relax to let it out.

311

It's quiet for a long time before she begins. Her voice sounds tired like she's already exhausted from the secret she's about to share. That's the thing about secrets, they're heavy. Getting out from under them requires strength and work. It's not easy. "The doctors and detective filled me in when I woke up in the hospital. It explained the pain and fear I felt. Along with the drugs I'd willingly ingested, they also discovered Rohypnol in my system." Her voice is calm, too calm for the knots in my stomach. "He knocked me out...and then he stripped me and raped me. We were found under a tree like discarded trash by a man walking his dog at dawn. I was naked, and he was dead from a self-inflicted gunshot wound to the head."

I wait for her tears to come. They don't. But mine do. I hold her tighter because I don't know what else to do. I'm trained to receive bad news and make it better, more manageable. This isn't bad news. This is horrific. The things human beings are capable of are incomprehensible. "I'm sorry, Faith. I'm so sorry." I know it doesn't change anything. It doesn't help. But I can't sit here and not say anything.

"Do I disgust you now?" It's the most timid whisper I've ever heard. It's a question that only fears the worst and has already accepted a negative response.

"No. Never. Thank you for trusting me enough to share your past with me. Him, on the other hand? He absolutely disgusts me. Only the vilest type of person is capable of something like that." It boggles my mind that people can willingly inflict harm on others. "When did you get clean?"

"That night. No drugs since. Though, I almost stumbled when I came back to California. It's what led me to the shelter and meeting Benito."

My eyes pop open at her mention of the shelter, and I release the hug. Hers are still closed over tear stained cheeks. It's dark now, and the beach is empty around us. "Faith, open your eyes."

Wet eyelashes cling together, but separate slowly to reveal glistening, deep blue eyes.

"You were living at the homeless shelter?" My heart just broke for her. Again.

She nods. "My lease was almost up. I didn't have a job. I didn't have much money. I didn't have a choice."

She didn't have a choice? Why wasn't I a choice? "You could've come to me. You should've come to me."

She shakes her head, and her eyes soften. "Miranda was there. Hope said you were a family, which I realize now was a misunderstanding, but at the time, I didn't want to interfere and cause any trouble for you and your kids."

I swallow back bad choices and their domino effect. "Miranda. She's like a bad penny. She needed a place to stay when she moved back and took it upon herself to claim my couch. I was desperate. I wanted my kids back, so I let her stay for a few weeks."

She nods, understanding shining in her glassy eyes. "I get it, Seamus. You don't need to explain. You did the right thing. Everything worked out, you have your kids again." She blows out a breath and wipes her cheeks with her fingers. "And Miranda isn't as bad as I first thought. Benito likes her. Hope likes her." Even though I've known about Hope being Faith's mother for a few weeks now, it's still shocking to reconcile their relationship in my mind. "Miranda was the one who convinced her to take a job cooking in the kitchen at the shelter. It doesn't pay much, but it's the first real job Hope's ever had. She loves it."

"I'm glad you found your mom and got some answers."

"Me too." She smiles slightly. "Life blooms in second chances."

I can't help touching more of her, stroking the outside of her calves just to reinforce that this is happening. That she's real. "It certainly does. You're here with me."

Her eyes are thoughtful when she opens her mouth to say something. Hesitation steals it away momentarily before she asks, "Do we get a second chance, Seamus? Knowing about my past, does that change the way you feel about me?"

I stand with the aid of my cane, brush the sand off my jeans, and offer her my hand. "Come with me. I can't answer that question here."

She takes it, and I pull her to stand in front of me. "Why not?" she asks as she brushes the sand off her dress and legs.

"Because you're wearing clothes. And I'm wearing clothes. And my body is begging me to answer that question...in great detail...and at great length...with touch instead of words, behind closed doors in the privacy of my bedroom."

Her lips part in response, and I watch the rise and fall of the swell of her breasts increase as arousal floods her being. "Seamus, do you have any idea how sexy you are?"

Those were the last words spoken that night, with the exception of Faith panting out, "We," between kisses on the W...E mat.

As promised, I led her to my bedroom, closed the door, and removed every stitch of clothing between us. And for the next several hours I laid bare my soul in every touch...every kiss...every connection. I took away her doubts, quieted her fears, and promised a never-ending second chance.

All without a word.

And as we lay tangled up in the darkness, exhausted, but sated in all ways, Faith breaks the silence. "Seamus?"

"Yeah?"

"I love you, too."

314

I smile because she heard every touch loud and clear.

Magic sounds delicious

Miranda

I'm armpit deep in horrendous, yellow, rubber gloves, scrubbing the inside of the oven. I attempted a soufflé for the first time without Hope. It threw up over the sides of the dish before burning to a crisp. The bottom of the oven paid the price, and brunch is in the trashcan. I hope this isn't an indication of how this day is headed.

The doorbell rings.

I pop my head out of the oven and check the clock on the stove. They're fifteen minutes early. Damn, I was trying to hide the evidence. I strip off the gloves and throw them in the oven, I won't be using it at this point anyway.

When I open the door, Rory hands me a bouquet of flowers, an assortment of different varieties. He's surrounded by Kai, Kira, and Benito.

"Thank you," I tell him. And I mean it. It's the first time I've ever received flowers and genuinely thanked the other person for them. That makes me feel a little shitty, because with Seamus I just expected them. The thank you was obligatory, if given at all. It should've been heartfelt like the one I just delivered. But, on the other hand, this one was heartfelt. That's a huge step for me. The past six months since Kai's accident, I've been going through an awakening while he's healed. The evolution was already in progress before that, but everything changed that day. I'm a different person. Not completely different, I mean, I'm still pushy, and impatient, and driven. But I finally figured out what's important in life. My kids, my friends, the people I serve at work. People are what make life worth living. Sacrifice. Love. Compassion. It's pretty goddamn beautiful. Who knew?

316

"Don't get mushy on me, Miranda." My name sounds like Mom, endearing and no longer an insult. He points at Benito. "It was his idea." The fact that Rory was the one who wanted to hand them to me reinforces the growth I've felt in our relationship. We've come a long way in a short time. We're both trying.

The kids walk in, greeting me with hugs, and Benito trails them smirking at Rory dodging responsibility for the kind act. "I suggested flowers. Kai and Kira agreed. Rory insisted they be periwinkle," he whispers in my ear. My heart squeezes when I look at the bouquet in my hand and notice the hydrangea blossoms.

The kids all disappear to drop their overnight bags in their bedrooms and Benito follows me to the kitchen. He sniffs at the air while I arrange the flowers in a vase.

Before he can say anything, I admit defeat. "The soufflé kicked my ass. I can make toast with a fairly high success rate or we can go out." I invited him to join the kids and me for brunch today. He picked up them up from Seamus's apartment on his way over.

He laughs and his easy, laid-back nature shines. "I know a bakery not far from here. I hear the almond croissants are to die for."

"Oh yeah? To die for? You wouldn't be biased, would you?"

He shakes his head innocently, but grins through it and winks. "My brother works magic with dough."

"Mmm, magic sounds fucking delicious," I tease. "I want that."

Magic *was* fucking delicious. I'm glad the soufflé massacre took place after all.

The rest of weekend was spent with my kids. We went to the beach and played in the water. We stayed up too late, watched movies, and ate junk food. We talked, some of it was important stuff and most of it wasn't, but that was the best part. That we could talk about everything

317

and it felt natural. I laughed with my kids. I hugged my kids. I snuggled with my kids.

I felt like a mom, because while it was all happening I was in love with my kids. Real, deep down, love free of plot, or ploy, or misguided intention. It was pure. I didn't think I was capable of pure, but I am. I really am.

It's Sunday evening now. Seamus just picked up the kids. Which leaves me here, sitting in my living room, with a glass of wine, thinking about my life. So many regrets. So many lies. So much pain I caused. I feel like I don't know that person anymore. *Thank God*. And how lucky I am that despite all that's happened over the years, I finally have a respectful friendship with my ex-husband — which was a long time coming and hard earned, not that I blame him at all — a loving relationship with my kids, a few good friends, and some newfound self-love and dignity. I'm my own get out of hell free card. It's of my own volition that good things happen. Effort and intent, that's what it boils down to. You try or you don't. It's good or it's bad.

I'm trying my ass off.

And I prefer good.

I know that sounds like a sack of self-help, Mary Poppins bullshit, but it's true.

Do good or die trying.

That's my new proud-to-be-a-do-gooder rebel motto.

What an unbelievably beautiful circumstance
to be in

Faith

future

Seamus looks so handsome in black pinstripe pants
and a white dress shirt, casually untucked with cuffs rolled
up to his elbows. His feet are bare, as are mine. We're
standing on the W...E mat in the sand surrounded by Kai,
Rory, Kira, Hope, and a few friends. Benito is standing
before us, bible in his hands, proudly doing his ordained —
at least for the day — duties.

And when it's my turn to make my promise, I gaze
into Seamus's dark chocolate eyes that lead straight to his
soul, smile through my happy tears and I say, "We. What
an unbelievably beautiful circumstance to be in. I do."

To which he promises, "So much more than I do."

Epilogue
Love explained

Ask one hundred people to explain love.
And you'll get one hundred different answers.
Because love is like art, it's subjective.
Fluid.
Ever-changing.
Evolving.

Case in point...

Miranda

Love is real.
It's not make believe, like Santa Claus or Vegas. It's substance and heart, full of wish-granting potential.
It's my children.
And my choices.
It's effort.
And compassion.
It's so damn real.
And if only fools believe in love...call me a fool.

Seamus

Love is strange when you think about it. It comes out of nowhere. There's no logic to it. It's not methodical. It's not scientific. It's pure emotion and passion. And emotion and passion can be beautiful, because they fuel love.

I'm an enthusiastic connoisseur of love—an expert through immersion. I know it intimately.

When I fell in love with Faith it was slow and cautious. I was bitter and jaded by divorce.

But she turned into my dreams.

And my dreams turned into reality.

And love.

So much more than love.

Faith

Love is instinct driven, heart over mind. It can be defined. I knew it when I felt it, because it was so bone-jarringly beautiful.

So much more than bone-jarringly beautiful.

And its name is We.

Seamus and me.

Acknowledgments

I love this part, because my heart loves thank you's.

My first thank you is for *you*. So much more than thank you for reading this book. I'm hugging you, I hope you can feel it because I'm squeezing super tight. It's my Faith hug to you.

So much more than thank you to my mom for being brave. She was diagnosed with Multiple Sclerosis when I was seven. I don't really remember her without it. MS was always part of her. A part of our family. But here's the thing, it was never something to be feared or worried on. Why? Because my mom is a warrior and has never let it get the better of her. She's kicked its ass every day for thirty-six years. Does she live in constant pain? Yes. Has she gone through periods of weeks or months of it amping up the fight and really attacking her? Yes. But when that happens you know what she does? *She fights harder.* Because my mom is fierce and the bravest person I know. Thank you for always fighting. For you. And for your family. I love you, Mom.

So much more than thank you to my beta readers: Lindsey Burdick, Amy Donnelly, Allison Dunnings, CM Foss, Gemma Hitchen, BN Toler, and Janet Wallace, for taking time out of your busy lives to help me make something of this story and the characters in my head. But more than that, thank you for your friendship. I love you, you badasses.

So much more than thank you to Amy Donnelly at Alchemy of Words for being a jack of all trades. From editing, to interior design, to teasers, to the trailer, to daily therapy sessions—you do it all. I cannot thank you enough, my coffee drinking, taco eating soul sister.

322

So much more than thank you to Monica Stockbridge for editing yet another book for me. This makes four. I love having you on my side to make sense of my stories, even when I can't. You're the best.

So much more than thank you to Brandon Hando for another beautiful cover. This one was hard. Thank you for putting up with me randomly throwing ideas at you every ten minutes...and then changing my mind five minutes later. Your patience is legendary. Like you. And a big hug to Andi Hando for taking approximately five hundred photos for the cover before we got the awkward hug just right. Two point two seconds of sunlight is hard to capture and make magic out of—I still owe you a classy Waffle House dinner for pulling it off. Love you both.

So much more than thank you to my agent Jane Dystel at Dystel & Goderich Literary Agency for your ongoing support of not only my work, but of me. And a shout out to Lauren Abramo, as well, for all that you do. I appreciate you both so very much.

So much more than thank you to my mom and dad for cheering my on for forty-three years. I love you.

So much more than thank you to B. and P. for being the best husband and son in the history of husbands and sons. I count my lucky stars every day that we are a family—what an unbelievably beautiful circumstance to be in. So much more than I love you.

So much more than thank you to the musicians on this book's playlist for inspiring me and driving the direction of this story. I can't write without you.

And last, but definitely not least, so much more than thank you to every reader, every blogger, every fellow author, and every member of the Bright Side family who has supported me and my crazy dream of writing. The love in the book community is intense and so very real; I feel it in my bones. Your friendship means the world to me. It's my mission in life to hug each and every one of you in person. Until then I'm gathering you all up into one gigantic hug in my mind and squeezing you tight. Love you all.

So Much More
Playlist

"Caroline" Kill It Kid
"Slow Dancing in a Burning Room" John Mayer
"Heartless" The Fray
"Lies" Sunset Sons
"Do I Wanna Know?" Arctic Monkeys
"Unsteady" X Ambassadors
"The Sickness" Future Husbands
"Leave It Alone" Manchester Orchestra
"Low Life" (featuring Jamie N. Commons) X Ambassadors
"Win Some, Lose Some" You Me At Six
"Never Ending Circles" Chvrches
"A Home Without a Heart" Future Husbands
"Trip Switch" Nothing But Thieves
"Incomplete" James Bay
"Brave the Day" Like Thieves
"Down to the Cellar" Dredg
"Let It Go" James Bay
"From Above" The Beach
"Out of the Blue" Prides
"Love, Love, Love" As Tall As Lions

Miranda's Motherfucking Monkey Bread

Ingredients:
¾ cup sugar
1 ½ tsp cinnamon
4 cans refrigerated buttermilk biscuits
1 cup sugar
¼ cup packed brown sugar
¾ cup butter (Don't forget the fucking butter!)
1/3 cup evaporated milk
1 ½ tsp cinnamon
¼ tsp nutmeg (Optional.)
1/3 cup raisins or 1 cup diced green apple (Take them or leave them—it's your call.)

Directions:

1. Put on your apron because you're about to create magic.
2. Throw up a prayer to the Pinterest gods for luck.
3. Heat oven to 350 degrees F. Grease 12-cup glorious Bundt pan.
4. Mix ¾ cup sugar and 1 ½ tsp cinnamon in 1-gallon bag.
5. Separate dough into individual biscuits and cut each biscuit into quarters.
6. Shake biscuit pieces like hell in bag to thoroughly coat.

7. Place biscuit pieces (and raisins or apples, if you choose) in Bundt pan.
8. Combine 1 cup sugar, ¼ cup brown sugar, ¾ cup butter, 1/3 cup evaporated milk, and 1 ½ tsp cinnamon (and nutmeg, if you choose) in saucepan and bring to boil. Pour over biscuits in pan to ensure maximum gooeyness.
9. Bake 30-35 minutes or until golden brown.
10. Cool 5 minutes. Turn upside down and serve.
11. Devour because magic tastes fucking delicious.

About the Author

I love reading, writing, traveling, music, coffee, tacos, nice people, my big dude (husband), and my little dude (son). And lots of other stuff, too.

I also love to make new friends.
Come and find me in one of these spots.
We'll hang out.
It will be fun.

https://www.facebook.com/kimholdenauthor

https://twitter.com/KimHoldenAuthor

www.kimholdenbooks.com

Other books by Kim Holden

Bright Side
Gus
All of It